BEACH THRILLERS

BEACH PARTY
BEACH HOUSE

W9-CBH-565

R.L. STINE

SCHOLASTIC INC.
New York Toronto London Auckland Sydney
Mexico City New Delhi Hong Kong Buenos Aires

Beach Party, ISBN 0-590-43278-8, Copyright © 1990 by Robert L. Stine.

Beach House, ISBN 0-590-45386-6, Copyright © 1992 by Robert L. Stine.

12 11 10 9 8 7 6 5 4 3 2 1   5 6 7 8 9 10/ 0

Printed in the U.S.A.   01

This edition created exclusively for Barnes & Noble, Inc.

2005 Barnes & Noble Books

ISBN 0-7607-5880-8

First compilation printing, May 2005

BEACH PARTY

Chapter 1

Karen Mandell drove the way she did everything
else in life — foot down hard on the gas, full speed
ahead, never look behind. The gray morning haze
was lifting, and a hot, white sun came burning
through as Karen squealed around the curve, roared
past a line of slow-moving cars and vans, and slipped
her navy-blue Mustang convertible into a narrow
space in Lot C at LAX.

Before climbing out of the car, she stopped to
examine herself in the rearview mirror and
straighten the blue, sleeveless T-shirt she wore
over white tennis shorts.

I look okay, she thought. Not as pretty as Ann
Marie, but okay.

Karen's oval face was framed by straight, black
hair that rested comfortably on her shoulders. She
had dark skin that always looked tan, and shocking
blue eyes, shocking because they were so wide, so
blue, and so unexpected. They were eyes that be-
longed on a fair-skinned blonde. On Karen's dark
face beneath her black eyebrows, they looked so

dramatic, so mysterious, it was impossible not to stare into them.

She smoothed her hair, jumped out of the car, searching for some way to remember this parking spot, and hurried to meet Ann-Marie.

"Good timing!" Karen cried. Ann-Marie was just coming out of the gate as Karen arrived. Dressed in hip-hugging designer jeans and a heavy brown sweater, she was carrying a large, red canvas bag and a tennis racket. She dropped everything when she saw Karen, and the two friends rushed forward with beaming smiles to hug each other.

"Putting on a little weight, aren't you?" Karen said, stepping back. It was a running joke. Ann-Marie was as thin as ever. She looked like a fashion model with her slight figure, her straight blonde hair cut fashionably short, her emerald eyes, and her high cheekbones and pale, creamy skin.

"Don't mention weight," Ann-Marie groaned, picking up her bag, which appeared to weigh as much as she did. "They served the worst meal on the plane."

"What was it?"

"I'm not sure. It was bright yellow, burning hot on the outside and frozen solid on the inside."

"Must have been lasagna," Karen said. "How did it taste?"

Ann-Marie rolled her eyes. "Fabulous. I had to have seconds." They followed the signs to the baggage pickup. "I can't believe I'm here, Karen." They walked past a large window. "Oh, look. The sky is yellow from all the pollution. I guess I *can* believe I'm here!"

Karen looked at her watch. "You've been here fifteen seconds, and you've already put down L.A."

"That's a record for me," Ann-Marie said, shifting the red bag to her other hand, and dropping the tennis racket. "I must be slowing down."

Karen laughed. "I'm just so glad to see you." She flung an arm around Ann-Marie, forgetting the weight of the canvas bag, and nearly knocked her over. "Oops. Hey — what have you got in there — presents for me, I hope?"

"Nope. I brought Sandy." She shook the bag and called into it, "Hold still in there, Sandy." Then she looked back at Karen. "He insisted on coming. He's madly in love with you, you know."

"How *is* your little brother?" Karen asked, laughing.

"Compared to what?" Ann-Marie joked. "Compared to Freddy Krueger, he's okay, I guess. He's at that sarcastic age. You know. Everything you say to him, he's got a sarcastic remark."

"Aw, he'll grow out of it," Karen assured her.

"He *will*? I never did!"

They went down an escalator and followed the signs down another endless corridor. Suddenly Ann-Marie stopped. "Karen — what's that around your neck?"

"This?" Karen's hand went up to the crystal she wore on a chain.

"Oh, no. I *knew* it," Ann-Marie wailed. "Get me

back on the plane. I can't stand it out here. That's a crystal, right? You do weird things with crystals, right? You think they have magic powers, and you talk to them and — "

"Stop! Come on, stop!" Karen protested. "I just wear it because it's pretty," Karen said, not meaning to sound quite so defensive.

"For sure," Ann-Marie said. "Like gag me with a spoon."

"Ann-Marie, nobody says that anymore. Not even valley girls," Karen said, making a face. "Actually, Mike gave me this crystal, before I broke up with him."

"I know. I know. The astrology counselor at school told you to break up with Mike, right?"

"Hey — you really *haven't* outgrown your sarcastic phase," Karen said. "Breaking up with Mike was really a bummer, you know."

Ann-Marie apologized quickly, her cheeks coloring. "Sorry. It always takes me a while to lose my New York edge. Really. I'm sorry. I — I just feel like such an alien out here. Like I'm from Mars or something."

"No problem." Karen gave her a warm smile. "I think you'll feel right at home in a little while. Wait till you see where we're staying."

They stopped in front of the baggage conveyor belt. Ann-Marie dropped her bag to the floor and placed the tennis racket on top of it. Two small yellow cases were going round and around, looking very lonesome on the long, winding belt.

"You mean we're not staying at your house?" Ann-Marie asked.

"In Westwood Village? No way."

"Then where?"

"It's a surprise." Karen gave her a mysterious smile.

"Say — how's your mom doing?" Ann-Marie asked.

"Pretty good. It took her a while, after the divorce. I mean, I think she took it a lot more personally than Daddy."

"Divorce is pretty personal," Ann-Marie cracked.

"You know what I mean. Anyway, it took her a while to get going again. I mean, she was like a zombie for months. She'd sit around playing her old Beatles records and cry."

"That's too bad. But she's better now?"

"Yeah. A little. I think she went out on a date last week. Some guy who sells real estate in the valley."

"And your dad?"

Karen shrugged. "He's definitely weirded out."

"Huh?"

"He's driving a red Corvette, for one thing. And he's blow-drying his hair."

"Weird."

"Actually, I don't see him that much. Of course, I never did. He bought me a car. A Mustang convertible. Do you believe it?"

"Is that good?" Ann-Marie asked, not being sarcastic.

"Yeah. It's what you might call an awesome car."

"You might. I wouldn't. I don't drive."

"You don't drive? You're seventeen, and you don't drive?" Karen looked positively shocked.

"No. I take the subway, usually. It's a lot faster."

"The subway? Don't you get mugged and killed if you take the subway?"

"Not everyone," Ann-Marie said, staring past Karen as more suitcases began to magically appear on the conveyor belt.

About fifteen minutes later, they were out in the hazy sunshine looking for where Karen had parked the car. "This *is* an awesome car," Ann-Marie said when they finally found it. "I love the white leather seats. How do you keep them clean?" Karen helped her load her suitcase and bag into the trunk.

"Daddy got me a new wet suit and new skis, too," Karen said, sliding behind the wheel. The seat was hot against the back of her legs.

"He buys you a lot of presents, huh?"

"Yeah. He's definitely trying to buy my love. And you know what? It's working!"

Both girls laughed as Karen backed out. It took a while — even for Karen — to get out of the vast airport. Then Karen headed the car northwest along Lincoln Boulevard. The bright sun had burned away most of the haze, and the air was getting warmer.

"Where are we going?" Ann-Marie asked.

Karen shook her head mysteriously. "You'll see." They squealed to a stop because of some construction up ahead. "Hey — I've been doing all the talking. What's new with you? Did you have a good year?"

Ann-Marie looked away. "Not really."

Karen was more than a little surprised. Ann-Marie was flip and sarcastic, but she always had a lot of enthusiasm. "How come?"

"I don't know. It was sort of a wasted year, I guess. It's hard to explain. My high school is so big, and — well, everyone's so immature. I — "

"And how's Clay?"

"I meant to write — I broke up with Clay. Or maybe he broke up with me. I'm not sure." Her normally pale face was bright crimson.

"Gee, I'm sorry."

"Me, too," Ann-Marie said in a near-whisper. Then she added wistfully, "Maybe it isn't all over. Everything was sort of up in the air when I left."

Karen could see that Ann-Marie was really upset. She and Clay had been going together for two years. Karen wondered what had happened. She probably would never find out. Ann-Marie seldom liked talking about herself.

The girls had been friends since about the age of nine, growing up as neighbors in Westwood Village. When they had started high school, the friendship had seen some hard times. In fact, Ann-Marie didn't speak to Karen for six months after Karen started to date a boy Ann-Marie was interested in.

"You're always making me jealous of you," Ann-Marie had said one day during an angry exchange. And Karen had never forgotten it. It seemed such a sad, revealing thing to say.

But then, Ann-Marie had moved with her family to New York, and the friendship was revived through letters. The anger, the jealousy, the hurt feelings seemed to dissolve over the miles.

Now Ann-Marie was back in L.A. for the first time since she'd moved, and Karen was so happy to see her, she thought she might burst.

The traffic started moving again. "Good old Highway 1," Ann-Marie said, forcing a smile. "Yeah, it's great to be back."

It was nearly an hour later when they pulled up to the low, three-story gray shingled apartment building. "Here we are," Karen said, squeezing the Mustang into a narrow parking space. "What do you think?"

"Speedway?" Ann-Marie asked, reading the street sign. "Where are we?"

"Venice." Karen started to roll the top up.

"Venice? You mean the place with all the weirdos and the roller skaters?"

Karen grinned. "Wait till you see the apartment."

"Whose apartment?"

"Ours. Well, actually, my dad's." Karen locked up the car and walked around to open the trunk.

"Your dad has an apartment in Venice?"

"I told you he's weirded out. He's even rented this apartment right across from the beach. He's having a second adolescence, I guess. I think he wants to bring back the sixties. I mean, he's got psychedelic posters on the walls — and you should see his girlfriend."

"Girlfriend?" Ann-Marie looked positively appalled.

"Yeah. She looks almost old enough to be my younger sister."

"Wow."

Karen laughed. "You're not from California anymore, Ann-Marie. You're not allowed to say wow."

"Wow. Is your dad's girlfriend staying with us, too?"

"No. They're both gone. They went to some spa in the Springs. The apartment is all ours until the weekend. Daddy won't be back until late on Saturday. Isn't this great? Our own apartment right across from the beach!"

Karen helped Ann-Marie lug her suitcase out of the trunk. Ann-Marie looked up uncertainly at the low, gray building, which looked more like a motel than an apartment house.

"Your mom was always so strict," Ann-Marie said, carrying her bag and following Karen up the steps. "I can't believe she's letting us stay here on our own — even for a few days."

"She doesn't know," Karen said, her blue eyes glowing.

"Huh?"

"She thinks Daddy is here with us. I didn't tell her he was going away. It's our little secret."

"But, Karen — " Ann-Marie hung back. "Do you really think this is such a good idea?"

Karen unlocked the door and pushed it open. She tossed Ann-Marie's bag in, then stood back to let her friend inside the apartment first. "Of course it is," Karen said, with a mischievous smile. "What could happen?"

Chapter 2

"The beach is so beautiful at night," Karen said, kicking off her sandals and stepping into the cool sand.

"It — it's not very crowded," Ann-Marie said, looking around warily.

"People don't know what they're missing," Karen said, ignoring her friend's reluctance. "Come on. What's there to be afraid of? When's the last time you smelled the Pacific?"

"Two years, I guess," Ann-Marie said, stepping off the boardwalk and following her friend onto the beach. "Hey — wait up. Do you always have to walk so fast?"

"You're the New Yorker," Karen called back, not slowing her stride. "You're supposed to be used to a fast pace."

"No one could get used to you," Ann-Marie said, jogging to catch up. She heard a noise behind her and turned to see two boys in T-shirts and black spandex bicycle shorts roller-skating at full speed down the boardwalk. "Aren't they cold?" she asked

Karen, shivering. The air grew cooler as they approached the water. The wet sand felt clammy under her bare feet.

"It's a little chilly," Karen admitted. "But who cares? Here we are, Ann-Marie. It's summer, and you're back, and we're on the beach, and we're going to have nonstop fun for the next month!"

"When does the nonstop fun begin?" Ann-Marie grumbled.

"Come on. Just look around," Karen enthused, refusing to acknowledge her friend's sarcasm.

Ann-Marie had to admit that it was a beautiful night. The sun had just fallen, and the sky was pale evening purple, with tiny white dots of stars beginning to pop out and sparkle. The steady, rhythmic rush of the low waves, splashing lightly on the smooth shore, drowned out all other sounds. Against the darkening sky, the water was as blue as an afternoon sky. It sparkled and shone, as if holding the sunlight, refusing to allow the light to slip away.

"Pretty," Ann-Marie said, smiling at Karen. They walked silently along the shore. The water seemed to grow darker with every step they took.

Ann-Marie shivered and wrapped her arms around herself. She was wearing cutoffs and a light wool poncho, but the cold ocean air made her wish she'd worn something heavier. She couldn't believe Karen, who was wearing short shorts and a T-shirt and didn't seem the least bit cold. "Wow. I feel a long way from home," she said quietly.

"Ann-Marie, you lived here in L.A. most of your

life," Karen reminded her, bending down to pick up a shell, then quickly tossing it into the water.

"But I guess two years is a long time. It all seems so different." She turned and looked back at the boardwalk, also known as Ocean Front Walk, which was dark and nearly deserted. The shops had all closed before sunset. The summer season, with its influx of tourists and young people and crazies from all over, hadn't really begun. The Venice Pavilion across from Market Street stood dark and deserted, a low concrete bunker covered with graffiti.

Karen dug her feet deep into the wet sand. "Oh, that feels so good! I love it!" she shouted happily. She lifted her face toward the water to better feel the cold spray. "It's really good for your skin," she told Ann-Marie.

"Too salty," her friend grumbled. "Listen, I'm freezing to death. Could we go back and get changed?"

"Yeah. I guess." Karen couldn't hide her disappointment that Ann-Marie wasn't being more adventurous, more enthusiastic.

"Where is everyone, anyway?" Ann-Marie asked, pulling her light poncho tighter around her shoulders.

"Main Street mostly. That's where everyone in Venice goes at night."

"Aren't there parties on the beach or anything?"

"No. Most people are kind of afraid," Karen admitted reluctantly.

"Afraid? Of what? Afraid of the dark?"

"Oh, you know. Gangs, I guess."

"Oh."

Karen began jogging toward the boardwalk, her bare feet slapping the wet sand. Ann-Marie followed close behind. "Hey — where did we leave our shoes?"

"Up this way, I think," Karen called back to her. "Just past the Pavilion."

It was very dark now. The purples and grays of the night sky had darkened to black, broken only by tiny pinpoints of white starlight. The ocean behind them was even darker than the sky.

They located their sandals and were slipping them onto their wet, sandy feet when the five boys appeared, five tall shadows that seemed to materialize like dark, grinning ghosts.

They wore denim and leather, angry-looking T-shirts with the names of heavy metal groups emblazoned across the fronts, visible even in the dim light. Their hair was short and spiked, or scraggly, down to their shoulders. A couple of them had diamond studs in one ear. They all wore the same amused expression.

They're trying so hard to look dangerous, Karen thought.

The five of them shuffled closer, sneakers scraping against the asphalt of the boardwalk, their hands in their jeans pockets or jammed into the pockets of their open jackets.

Karen was the first to speak. "Hey — how's it goin'?"

This seemed to strike some of them funny. They laughed, short, high-pitched laughter.

"Real fine," one of them said. He was tall and lanky with short, blond hair, spiked straight up. His smile revealed two deep dimples on his narrow cheeks.

He's kind of cute, Karen thought.

He raised his hand to scratch his jaw, and Karen could make out a tattoo of an eight ball on the back of his wrist.

Karen thought she recognized him from school. His name was Vince Something-or-other. He had bumped into her once in the hallway, causing her to drop all her books. When he'd stooped to help her pick them up, he'd seemed very embarrassed. She remembered he hadn't said a word.

"How are *you* doing?" one of Vince's friends, a tall, dark-haired boy with a serious skin problem, asked, leering at the two girls. He took a deep drag from the cigarette between his lips, then tossed it onto the asphalt and stamped it out beneath the toe of his black boot.

"We were just leaving," Ann-Marie said, pulling Karen's arm.

"Hey, it's early," one of the boys said, moving to block their way.

"Yeah. We just got here," the dark-haired one said, staring hard at Ann-Marie.

Karen glanced at Vince, who hadn't said anything. He was standing back, a few feet from his buddies, his face expressionless.

"You guys better not go for a swim," Karen said. "You forgot your rubber ducky inner tubes."

They all laughed sarcastic, phony laughs, everyone except Vince, who stood frozen, watching silently.

"We heard there was going to be a party," the dark-haired one said, looking Ann-Marie up and down. "Isn't that right, Vince?"

Vince shrugged in reply.

"Yeah. A beach party," one of the others said, nervously fiddling with the zipper of his denim jacket.

"Have fun, guys," Karen said, starting to walk past them.

"Hey, wait. You're invited."

"Yeah. In fact, you're the party," the tall one said, his voice filled with menace.

Karen caught Vince's eye. He quickly looked away. He swept a large hand back through his close-cropped hair, his face twisted in a frown.

He looks a little like Sting, Karen thought.

"Isn't it past your bedtime, boys?" Karen asked. "You don't want your mommies to worry about you, do you?"

"You can tuck me in anytime," one of them said.

They all laughed and slapped each other high fives. This time, Vince got into the act, too.

"Come on — let's go," Ann-Marie whispered to Karen.

Karen nodded and tried to step past two of them who looked enough alike to be twin brothers, but they moved to block her path. "Which one do you want, Vince?" one of the twins called.

"He wants *you*," Karen cracked to the twin who had asked the question.

"I like the one with the mouth," Vince said softly.

"Which one do *you* like?" Karen asked Ann-Marie loudly, ignoring Vince.

"I — just want to go," Ann-Marie said, looking very scared.

"I like the one with the brain," Karen said. "Which one of you is using the brain tonight?"

This time, no one laughed.

"Hey, we're not bad guys," Vince said, staring into Karen's eyes. He took a couple of steps toward her, his hands in his jacket pockets.

"Not bad compared to *what*?" Karen snapped.

He didn't smile. His dark eyes burned into hers.

The five boys formed a loose circle around Karen and Ann-Marie.

"Are you going to let us go?" Karen demanded.

No one replied.

Ann-Marie gripped Karen's arm. Her hand was freezing cold.

The circle tightened as the silent boys moved in on them.

Chapter 3

"Hey — what's going on?"

"Whoa!"

The circle opened wide as Vince and his buddies turned to see who was calling out to them.

Two boys stood on the boardwalk, one carrying a skateboard. The other one, tall and powerfully built, wearing jeans and a dark-hooded sweatshirt, stepped forward, taking long, confident strides.

"Hey, you girls — I've been looking all over for you," he said, ignoring the five startled-looking boys.

"Huh?" Karen stared at the boy as he approached. I've never seen him before in my life, she thought.

"Yeah. We thought you were going to wait with the others," the other boy said in a hoarse, scratchy voice. He was wearing a white windbreaker, which flapped noisily in the wind.

"Sorry," Karen said, catching on quickly. "We were looking for you." She glanced at Ann-Marie to make sure her friend understood what was happening.

Ann-Marie looked frightened and totally confused. The wind off the ocean had blown her short, blonde hair straight back. She looked like a little girl, a frightened little girl.

"Well, come on. We're late," the tall boy said impatiently. He grabbed Karen's hand and began to pull her away. "You coming or not?"

Vince and his friends had watched this scene in startled silence. But now Vince moved quickly to block their way. "Hold it right there, buddy," he said in a low, menacing growl.

"My name's Jerry, not Buddy."

Vince smiled for some reason, a thin, slow smile that revealed the deep dimples in his cheeks. "Well, Jerry," he said slowly, "where you going with our girlfriends?"

Vince's buddies all laughed at this and closed ranks behind the two girls.

We're caught in the middle, Karen thought. This could get pretty ugly.

"Girlfriends?" Jerry looked Vince up and down. His friend moved quickly to his side. "Hold on a minute, man," Jerry said. "You're talking about my sister." He motioned to Karen.

Vince sneered. "She's your sister?"

We *do* look a little alike, Karen thought, looking closely at Jerry. He had straight, dark hair like hers, and light eyes, and a perfect, straight nose.

Vince took a step back.

Karen took that as a good sign.

Jerry is bigger than Vince, she realized. Jerry probably works out. He has such powerful-looking arms, such a broad chest. His friend looked as if he was in pretty good shape, too.

"If she's *your* sister, I don't want her," Vince cracked, holding up his hands as if surrendering, and stepping back onto the sand.

"Yeah, she's contaminated!" one of Vince's buddies shouted.

"Don't touch her, Vince. You don't know where she's been!"

They all laughed, except for Vince, who seemed to be thinking hard.

He's backing down, Karen thought. He's going to let us go.

To her surprise, she felt a little disappointed. Not disappointed that a fight had been avoided, but disappointed that she had to leave Vince. She realized that she was attracted to him, the way she was always attracted to danger, to excitement, the way she often was driven to pursue things she knew might not be good for her.

Vince was staring into Karen's eyes. "We didn't mean any harm," he said to her quietly. "Just messing around."

He gave Jerry a threatening look, then turned quickly and motioned for his friends to follow him. They walked off down the boardwalk quickly, laughing about something, slapping each other on the shoulders.

"That was close," Ann-Marie said, sighing. She looked pale in the dim light, but very relieved.

"Where'd you come from, anyway?" Karen asked Jerry.

"Marty left his skateboard over by the rec center this afternoon. We went back to look for it and saw you and your friends."

"They weren't exactly friendly," Ann-Marie said, looking down the dark boardwalk as if expecting Vince and his friends to return.

"No. They were *too* friendly," Karen corrected her. She turned to Jerry. "Listen, it was really nice of you to rescue us."

"Yeah, it was, wasn't it!" Marty said. "I sort of couldn't believe it myself. It was Jerry's idea, really. He's into being macho."

"And what are you into?" Jerry asked Marty.

"I'm into running away!" Marty replied. His windbreaker flapped in the strong breeze. He grabbed at it, trying to pull it tighter, but it flapped out of his grasp. He had curly, brown hair over a round face, small, black eyes and round puffs of cheeks.

He looks like a squirrel, Karen thought. A fat little squirrel storing up nuts for winter. Jerry, on the other hand, was a great-looking guy. A little too straight, too preppy for her taste, maybe. But she might be able to make an exception this time — especially since he had rescued her from those toughs.

"It's kind of cold, don't you think?" Ann-Marie said, looking toward the houses across from the beach.

"Yeah. Let's get warmed up," Jerry said, rubbing his hands together. He looked at Karen. "You two have plans?"

"No," Karen answered quickly. "We were just going for a walk and — "

"Well, do you know RayJay's on Main Street? A bunch of us sort of hang out there. It's not a bad place — "

"We've got to get changed first," Ann-Marie said.

"Yeah. Right," Karen agreed. "We'll meet you there. RayJay's. I think I know where it is. On Main Street near Park?"

"Don't meet us. We'll walk you home and wait for you," Jerry said, giving her a warm smile.

"Okay. Sounds good," Karen said, returning his smile. "And it'll be our treat — since you were so brave."

"Well, you're pretty brave to be seen with *us*," Marty said in his hoarse, scratchy voice, and then laughed as if he'd made a truly hilarious joke.

RayJay's was a small, bustling coffee shop and pizza restaurant in the basement of a two-story house on Main Street between Park and Brooks. Karen found a parking place a few doors past the restaurant, parked the Mustang, and cut the engine.

"It's only a few blocks from the apartment," Ann-Marie protested. "We could've walked."

Marty looked at her curiously from his position beside her in the backseat. "Walk? What's *that*? You're not from around here, are you!"

"Some people out here don't walk to the bath-room," Karen joked.

They climbed out of the car and looked up and down Main Street, which was crowded with people window-shopping, on their way to dinner, or to the many clubs and bars that lined the narrow street.

"Looks like Greenwich Village," Ann-Marie said. "Only everyone looks a lot healthier."

"Don't let looks fool you," Karen said. She hopped down the concrete stairs to the open entrance of RayJay's, the others following behind.

The restaurant was a long, low rectangle with two rows of red vinyl booths going straight back to a mirrored back wall. A rainbow-colored jukebox beside the bar against the near wall was playing a Willie Nelson record. Two waitresses scurried back and forth down the wide aisle. They wore long, red aprons over black T-shirts and red short shorts, and little red plastic baseball caps with *RayJay's* in black on the front.

The restaurant was smoky and hot, filled, for the most part, with loud, laughing young people. Karen spotted an empty booth about halfway to the back. She started to lead Ann-Marie and the two boys to it when they were stopped by an angry-looking girl in tight-fitting black slacks and a pale green Esprit sweater.

"Where've you been?" she asked Jerry, pushing past Karen.

"Oh, hi, Renee." Jerry looked at Karen, embarrassed.

Renee was about a foot shorter than Jerry. She

had a pretty, oval face with big, dark brown eyes, and piles of frizzy brown hair that she swept straight back and kept in place with a long, pearl-white hairband.

"Where were you?" she repeated. She had a high-pitched voice. Karen thought she sounded like a little mouse. "Stephanie and I have been waiting forever."

"Well . . ." Jerry's face grew bright crimson. He gestured to Karen and Ann-Marie.

Renee looked at them suspiciously. "Hi," she said, and quickly turned back to Jerry.

"We met Karen and Ann-Marie," Jerry said. "They were having trouble and — "

"They rescued us," Karen interrupted, jumping right in to help Jerry, who seemed to be very flustered.

"Rescued you from what? From boredom?" Renee snapped.

I don't think I like her, Karen thought.

"These boys were giving us a hard time on the beach." Ann-Marie stepped in. "Jerry and Marty got rid of them for us."

A girl with long blonde hair was waving frantically at them from the first booth near the bar. "Hi, Stephanie," Marty waved back.

"Come on," Jerry said, putting an arm around Renee's shoulders. "We can all squeeze into the booth. Then we'll tell you the whole story."

"It sounds fascinating," Renee said drily. But she allowed Jerry to guide her to the booth. Marty quickly squeezed in next to Stephanie, and Renee and Jerry slid in on the other side. Karen and Ann-Marie were left to sit uncomfortably on the outside edge.

"Don't they have any bigger booths?" Karen complained.

"No. Guys usually only bring *one* date," Renee said pointedly, glaring at Jerry.

"This isn't a date," Karen said quickly. "Jerry said a whole bunch of kids hang out here and — "

"Oh, is *that* what Jerry said?" Renee snapped, her little mouse voice rising.

Karen glanced at Ann-Marie. She wondered if her friend felt as uncomfortable as she did. Jerry could have at least told us that he and Marty already had dates, she thought. From the looks of things, Jerry and Renee and Marty and Stephanie had been couples for quite a while.

"This is my treat," Karen announced, trying to remove some of the tension from around the table. "I promised I'd treat since Jerry and Marty were so brave."

"Them??" Both Renee and Stephanie cried in unison.

Everyone laughed.

Karen realized that Jerry was staring at her. He had the nicest smile on his face.

He looks a little like Tom Cruise, Karen decided. She returned his smile, but cut it short when she saw that Renee was watching.

"We already had dinner," Renee said.

"Me, too. But I'm still hungry," Marty said, his arm carelessly around Stephanie's shoulder.

"I'm starving," Karen said, ignoring the dirty looks she was getting from Renee. "How's the pizza here?"

"It's round," Renee said helpfully.

"Sounds good," Karen said. "Let's get a pizza."

"I just want an iced coffee or something," Renee said unhappily.

Jerry continued to smile at Karen. She began to worry that his face was frozen in that position. When he and Marty got up and went to the back of the restaurant to talk to some guys they knew, Karen actually felt a little relieved.

The four girls talked, awkwardly at first, but then more comfortably. Stephanie had a cousin who lived in New Jersey but worked in Manhattan, so she and Ann-Marie found something to talk about. Renee and Karen talked about what a weird place Venice was. Then Renee bragged about her parents' house in Bel Air and about all of the celebrities she'd met because her dad was "in the business."

Karen was grateful when the pizza finally arrived. It meant she could concentrate on eating instead of talking.

The boys returned when they saw the pizza. Karen drifted in and out of the conversation. Her mind wandered back a few hours, back to the deserted boardwalk. She found herself thinking about Vince, about how he tried to look so tough but how those deep dimples of his betrayed him. She tried to recreate the scared feeling she had had back on the dark beach, the creeping feeling of terror when the boys circled them and started to move in, like

25

vultures to their prey. It was scary but thrilling at the same time.

How far would those boys have gone? she wondered.

What would have happened if Jerry and Marty hadn't happened by?

". . . the best beach parties at Malibu," Jerry was saying when Karen's attention drifted back to the table. She looked up and realized that he was talking to her. "You'll have to come sometime," he said. "You, too," he added quickly, looking across the booth at Ann-Marie.

"Sounds like fun," Ann-Marie said, wiping pizza sauce off her chin with a napkin. "Where is this party beach?"

"It's a secret," Jerry told her. "We slide down these cliffs and onto the beach. It's really great. Especially at night."

"Malibu is so beautiful," Ann-Marie said.

"It's pretentious," Renee said, sighing. She didn't bother to amplify her opinion.

"Maybe we'll all go Friday night," Jerry said, doubling his enthusiasm in an attempt to cover for Renee's definite lack of it.

"Maybe," Karen said, grabbing another slice of pizza off the tray.

The rest of the evening went by quickly and pleasantly. Even Renee seemed to pick up and get into a better mood.

It was nearly midnight when they decided to call it a night. "I can drive everyone," Karen offered, stifling a yawn.

"No. I have my car," Renee said, waving a set of BMW keys under Karen's nose.

As they slid out of the booth, Jerry leaned forward and whispered into Karen's ear, "You have great eyes."

She smiled and started to thank him for the compliment, but stopped when she saw Renee watching them from the restaurant doorway. "So does Renee," Karen said pointedly.

Jerry blushed and hurried back to Renee.

As they stepped out of the restaurant into a surprisingly cool evening for June, the street was still filled with people. On the corner an old man wearing a Dodgers cap over sunglasses was seated on an overturned trash can, playing a funky blues tune on a harmonica. Several couples were clustered outside an after-hours club across the street. Car horns honked. The street was still filled with traffic.

Karen had to pay the cashier, so she was the last one out of the restaurant. As she stepped up onto the sidewalk, she was surprised to find Renee waiting for her, the others having gone ahead.

"It's busier now than it was at eight," Karen said, looking down the street.

"Listen, Karen." Renee grabbed Karen's arm. Her hand was cold. Her fingers tightened around Karen's wrist until Karen felt like crying out. "Stay away from Jerry," Renee said in a flat, low tone, pressing her face close to Karen's, so close Karen could feel Renee's breath on the side of her face.

"I really mean it. Stay away from Jerry."

Then Renee let go, and hurried to join the others.

Chapter 4

"Just watch it, man."

"You watch it, man."

The two boys faced each other, their faces alive with anger. Suddenly they both groaned in recognition.

"Not *you* again!"

"You!"

"You following me or something?"

Vince kicked at the sand with a bony foot. Jerry moved his surfboard in front of him like a shield.

They tried to stare each other down, then Vince spoke first without changing his expression. "Hey — you bumped me, man."

"You're a hard guy. You can take it." The slight tremble in Jerry's voice indicated that his heart wasn't entirely in this fight.

"Maybe you should stick to a boogie board," Vince said, staring with distaste at Jerry's green Day-Glo baggies. Vince scratched his neck. Jerry could see the tattoo on the back of his wrist, a small, black eight ball. "Maybe you should go play with your *sister*," Vince said, sneering, balling his big hands into fists.

Vince kicked his own surfboard angrily. "There's a whole ocean out there, man. Why'd you have to bump me?"

"There's no surf anyway," Jerry muttered, feeling a little calmer. Vince obviously didn't want to fight, either. Jerry had never seen Vince without the other members of his gang around. Vince probably felt insecure on his own, Jerry figured. "The undertow is real strong, but there's no surf."

"You gonna give me a weather report, too?" Vince snapped. He kicked at the sand a little harder, sending a wet clump onto Jerry's surfboard.

Jerry took a step back. He stared past Vince, watching the low waves splash onto the shore. Out in the ocean, two white sailboats glided slowly by. He heard laughing voices behind him and turned to see two guys bombing down the boardwalk on unicycles, their arms waving above their heads.

"Just watch it, man. You've got two strikes against you now." Vince ran a hand back through his short, blond hair and shook his head, as if dismissing Jerry from his thoughts. He walked past Jerry, dragging his board behind him, heading to where his gang buddies were waiting on the edge of the beach near the boardwalk.

Two girls in tight, pink bicycle shorts and white midriff tops skateboarded along the blacktop, looking self-consciously sexy. Vince called out something to them as they passed. They laughed but didn't slow down.

Jerry watched them disappear around the curve of the boardwalk, then started back to the blanket. "Hey — what was that all about?" Renee called.

She sat up on the blanket, her skin pink from the sun. She was wearing a small gold bikini. Her frizzy brown hair was tied behind her head with a rubber band.

"So? What's with you and that punk?" she repeated, shielding her eyes with her hand.

"Oh, nothing," Jerry said, sliding beside her on the blanket. "Mmmmm. Coconut." He inhaled deeply. He loved the smell of coconut suntan lotion. "What number are you using, Renee? A hundred and thirty?"

"No. Eight." She didn't laugh at his joke. She never did.

He inhaled again, then licked her arm. "Mmmmmmm. I love coconut!"

She pulled away from him. "Don't get kinky, Jerry." She laughed, finally.

"Yucccch! It tastes terrible!" He pulled up the top of the cooler and pulled out a Coke.

"I didn't know you and Vince were friends," Renee said, lying back down, stretching out until she was comfortable. A large, high cloud rolled over the sun, covering the beach in sudden shadow.

"Vince? Is that his name? We're not friends. He and his gang were the ones who were giving Karen and Ann-Marie a hard time Monday night."

Renee frowned at the sound of Karen's name. "So why were you talking with him?"

"I accidentally bumped him with my board, and he got mad."

"You shouldn't bump him," Renee said, frowning up at the dark cloud. "He's bigger than you."

"Next time I'll bump someone small," Jerry said, sitting up straight, staring out at the water. "Anyway, he decided to let me live this time."

"That's lucky." The cloud rolled on, and the shadow moved down the beach. Renee pulled her sunglasses down from her forehead and over her eyes. "It's lucky the rest of his gang wasn't there. They'd eat you alive."

"Thanks for the vote of confidence."

"They're *bad dudes*," Renee said, laughing for some reason. She had the strangest sense of humor. Jerry never could figure out what she would laugh at and what she wouldn't — or why.

Jerry sat silently for a while, looking around the beach, which was pretty empty considering what a nice day it was. Of course, some schools hadn't let out yet. It was only the second week of June. But still, Jerry thought, the beach and the boardwalk were pretty empty.

"The water's pretty warm for June," he said. "I saw some jellyfish. It's awfully early for jellyfish."

"I'm bored," Renee said, with an exaggerated yawn.

Oh, no. Here we go again, he thought.

This was the way their arguments had been starting lately, with Renee saying she was bored. Bored with what? She usually couldn't say. Jerry began to realize that she most likely was bored with him but was just afraid to come right out and say it.

Was he bored with her? Maybe. He couldn't really decide. He knew he'd been thinking about Karen an awful lot since Monday night. In fact, he'd been thinking about Karen nonstop.

"What do you mean you're bored?" he said, sighing.

"Bored. B-o-r-e-d. Do I have to spell it for you?"

"You just did."

"Being sarcastic doesn't help, Jerry. Being sarcastic is really boring."

"Look, Renee, I really don't want to start with you. Summer has just started. We're here on the beach, and — "

"But it's boring for me to lie here while you're off surfing all afternoon."

"I *wasn't*." He slapped the blanket angrily. She could get him exasperated so quickly these days. "I wasn't surfing. There's no surf. I was just testing the water a bit."

"You were just bouncing into that creep, trying to get yourself killed."

"That's not funny."

"I didn't mean it to be. What am I supposed to do all summer while you're running from Catalina to Malibu with your surfboard? Sit and watch?"

"I thought you were working on your tan, Renee." He knew that was pretty lame the instant he said it. Why did he always say the first thing that popped into his head? It was such a bad habit.

"Oh, that's real stimulating. Working on my tan."

"Well, you brought your wet suit and that new snorkeling gear. Why don't you try it out?"

She sat up and made a face. "I'm too bored."

"You're always bored lately," Jerry said, challenging her to say what was really on her mind, knowing that he was venturing out into dangerous waters, but annoyed enough not to care.

"Yeah. So? I want a little excitement this summer."

"That's why I think you should try surfing."

"That's not the kind of excitement I had in mind." She flashed him a devilish grin, but remembering she was angry, quickly turned it off.

He picked up the suntan lotion, squirted a white blob of it into his palm, reached over, and started to rub it onto her shoulders. Her pink skin felt soft and tender, like a baby's skin. "I wouldn't mind a little excitement, either," he said softly, leaning over to breathe into her ear.

She quickly rolled away from him. "Don't be a pig."

"Hey — " He reached for her, disappointed, insulted. "You didn't think I was a pig the other night in the back of Marty's van."

She angrily picked up the bottle of suntan lotion and heaved it at him. "Don't talk about it like that! You really *are* a pig!"

She started to gather her things together and throw them into her yellow-and-white-striped Giorgio beach bag. "I don't know what your problem is, Jerry. I saw the way you looked at that girl Karen at RayJay's Monday night. And I saw you staring at those two girls on skateboards just now."

"What are you talking about?"

"You were panting, and your tongue was practically down to your knees."

"What do you care?" Jerry snapped. "You just said you were so bored with me."

She grabbed his arm. It wasn't a friendly touch. She was trying to hurt him. "I just said I was bored," she said, pronouncing each word slowly and distinctly. "I didn't say I was bored with *you*." When she let go, his arm was red. "Don't get any funny ideas, Jerry."

He rubbed his arm. "You hurt me."

"I'll do worse than that if I catch you staring at another girl like that."

Her words gave him a sudden chill.

Then she laughed and gave him a playful shove. "Hey — lighten up," she said, shoving him again.

"Renee, listen. Maybe you and I should talk."

"Talk? What about?" She glared at him suspiciously.

"Well, it's just that — "

He was interrupted by a girl's voice calling from several yards down the beach.

"Jerry — hi!"

"Oh, great," Renee muttered sarcastically.

Jerry had quite a different reaction. "Hey!" he called, jumping to his feet and waving.

It was Karen and Ann-Marie.

Chapter 5

"Maybe we shouldn't go over there," Ann-Marie said, trying to hold her friend back.

"Oh, why not?" Karen replied in typical fashion, and strode quickly across the sand, her wet suit under her arm.

Ann-Marie, carrying the heavy beach bag, struggled to catch up. "Maybe they want to be alone," she argued.

But it was too late. Karen was already calling to Jerry, and Jerry had jumped up and was calling back. As Karen and Jerry greeted each other, Ann-Marie caught the look on Renee's face. It was not a happy one.

"Have you been in the water?" Jerry asked them eagerly, as Karen dumped her wet suit on the sand next to Jerry's blanket.

"Just for a little while," Karen told him.

"The water's so warm," Jerry said.

"Warm? I didn't think so!" Ann-Marie cried. "I was frozen."

"That's because you don't have a wet suit," Karen

said. "We've got to get you one today."

"Oh, right. Just what I need," Ann-Marie laughed. "I'll get a lot of wear out of it. It'll look really great on Madison Avenue!"

So far, Renee hadn't said a word. She was lying on her back, her eyes closed under her sunglasses. Karen looked down at her, wondering where she got the gold bathing suit, and remembered the threat Renee had made to her outside the restaurant on Main Street.

Such a strange thing to do. Karen couldn't imagine why Renee would threaten a total stranger. It was almost unreal, like something out of a TV soap. Was she so insecure about hanging onto Jerry?

Maybe Renee *should* be insecure, Karen thought. Karen had been thinking about Jerry ever since Monday night. She couldn't believe her good luck when she spotted him on the beach just now.

Yes, maybe Renee *should* be insecure, Karen thought. Jerry just might be worth fighting for. And Karen was never one to back away from a fight.

"Hey — whose snorkeling gear is that?" Karen asked, seeing the mask and fins on the blanket and hoping they were Jerry's.

"Mine," Renee said, without opening her eyes.

"Do you snorkel? I've always wanted to try," Karen said enthusiastically.

Renee suddenly sat up and looked at her. "Really? You've never tried it?"

"No. Never," Karen told her. "May I?" She walked over and picked up the mask to examine it.

"My parents are taking me to Cozumel in a few

weeks," Renee said. "They scuba, but my ears aren't good for it. So I just snorkel. They brought me this new gear, and I brought it down here to try out, but — "

"You can't see anything in *this* water!" Jerry exclaimed, standing very close to Karen, pretending to examine the mask along with her. "It's so polluted."

"Well, there's a sandbar over by those rocks out there," Renee said pointing. "The water isn't too chopped up there because of the sandbar. You can probably see a little."

"Oh, I'd love to try it!" Karen cried, fitting the mask over her face and fiddling with the snorkel. "Do you think you could teach me sometime?"

"How about right now?" Renee asked, surprising everyone by springing to her feet. "You've got a wet suit, too, right?"

"Yes, but I don't have a mask or fins or a snorkel," Karen said.

Ann-Marie looked at Karen as if she were crazy, as if to say, "Why are you being so friendly with Renee? Isn't it obvious that Renee hates your guts?"

But Karen seldom thought that way. She always plunged right into an activity no matter who or what was involved. If she wanted to try snorkeling, she would try snorkeling.

"Jerry brought some gear — a snorkel and mask," Renee said. She turned to Jerry, who was still standing very close to Karen. "Let her try on your fins."

"I don't think they'll fit," Jerry said, obediently walking around the blanket to get them.

"Karen has really big feet," Renee said. "They'll probably be okay."

That was an obvious dig, but Karen let it pass. She was too excited to be offended by a crack about her feet. Her feet *were* pretty big, anyway, she realized.

She sat down on the blanket and let Jerry help her into the black rubber fins. "Stand up," Renee said. "How do they feel?"

"I think they'll stay on," Karen said, unsteady on the sand in the big flippers, which were heavier than she'd imagined.

"Okay. Let's get into our wet suits and go down to the water," Renee said.

"This is so exciting!" Karen exclaimed, ignoring Ann-Marie's doubtful looks.

"You're going over by the rocks?" Jerry asked Renee, sounding concerned.

"Yeah. It's the only place we might see a fish or two. Don't worry. We'll be careful."

"What do you mean?" Karen asked.

"Well, the current is funny over there," Renee said, pulling on her wet suit. "It's very calm because of the sandbar. But once you get close to the rocks, the current swirls around and gets pretty powerful. If you're not careful, it can push you into the rocks and make it really hard to get back."

Karen looked out at the blue-green water. She found the line of tall, brown rocks Renee was talking about. They jutted out into the ocean like a natural jetty.

"Maybe you shouldn't go out there," Jerry said. Karen finished zipping the wet suit and turned around to look at him. His face was filled with concern. His eyes darted nervously out to the water.

Renee put a hand on his shoulder. "Don't worry. We'll be okay. Really." She was talking to him softly, soothingly. "You and Ann-Marie can watch us from here. It'll be okay."

That's odd, Karen thought. Jerry seems like such an easy-going, relaxed kind of guy. Why did he get so uptight all of a sudden?

"Come on, let's go," Renee said, motioning to Karen to follow her. They walked down toward the water, carrying their masks and fins. The beach was a little more crowded, Karen noticed, sunbathers taking advantage of the really beautiful afternoon. But there was no one in the water.

"Where are all the swimmers?" she asked, catching up to Renee.

"People don't swim here that much," Renee said. "They come for the freak show on the boardwalk or just to chill out and catch some rays."

They sat down at the edge of the water and pulled on their fins. "So the breathing part isn't hard?" Karen asked.

"No. It just takes a little getting used to," Renee said. "I'll show you. Here. Step into the water." She turned around and started to back in. "That's right. Turn around. It's a lot easier to walk backwards in fins when you're stepping in and out of the water."

Karen followed Renee in. She backed up until the lapping waves were a little above her knees. "The waves are breaking in close today," she said.

"Let's swim out past them," Renee suggested. "I think we can still stand out there."

They swam out a few yards to calm, rolling water.

"Now for the mask," Renee said, holding hers in front of her. "Spit into it."

"What?" Karen wasn't sure she'd heard right.

"Spit into it. On the glass. And rub it around with your fingers. It keeps the glass from fogging up."

Karen obediently spit into the mask and rubbed it around as instructed. "You're a good teacher," she told Renee.

Renee ignored the compliment. "Slip the mask on like this." She pulled it carefully over her hair and slid it into place.

Karen watched her adjust the air hose. Then she did the same. Renee showed her how to bite down on the mouthpiece, and how to clear the hose by blowing really hard if water got inside. "Got it?"

"I think so," Karen said, eager to try it out.

"The important thing is to breathe slowly, normally," Renee said. "If you have trouble, if the mask gets water in it or the snorkel slips out or something, just raise your head out of the water and breathe. It's simple."

"Great. Let's go," Karen said.

"And if you have any problem at all, I'll be there," Renee said. "I'll be right with you the whole time." She gave Karen a reassuring smile.

She's not so bad, Karen thought. Maybe she was just nervous Monday night or something. She's actually really nice.

"Ready?" Renee asked, pushing the mouthpiece between her teeth.

"Ready," Karen said.

"Okay. Remember to kick your whole leg," Renee instructed. "Don't bend your knees. And keep your hands down at your sides."

"Got it," Karen said. This might be a little more complicated than she had thought. Oh, well, too late to back down now. Besides, this was exciting. There was nothing Karen liked better than trying something new for the very first time.

The mask was in place. The straps were tight against her head. She adjusted the mouthpiece and blew hard to clear the hose.

Here goes, she thought.

She watched Renee raise her legs, lower her head, and spread out over the water, and she copied her, breathing hard and fast as she first started to float, then remembering to slow down and breathe normally.

The water was dark and cloudy. She could barely see two feet in front of her.

She raised her head out of the water and was surprised to see that Renee had gotten several yards ahead of her. Her head down, Renee was floating quickly over the rolling water, her legs scissoring rhythmically, swimming straight toward the line of tall brown rocks.

Karen lowered her head again, still breathing rapidly and hard, largely from the excitement of this new experience. She kicked faster, the fins pushing her forward, her arms to her sides. She didn't want Renee to get too far ahead.

The water was a little clearer now. To her delight, Karen saw dozens of small, silver-gray fish, minnows probably. Dark tangles of seaweed bobbed and floated just beneath the surface.

Her breathing slowed. She began to get the rhythm, to feel calm and comfortable.

It was so quiet, so peaceful, so hypnotic. She began to see other fish. A large white fish with yellow markings swam right past her mask.

This is amazing, she thought. Why didn't I ever try this before? In clear water, it must be breathtaking, like descending on another world.

She floated along for a while. The water became cloudy again, green like pea soup. Water tickled her face. She realized the mask was leaking.

She pulled her head out of the water and lowered her legs, allowing the current to take her. Pulling down the mask, she emptied it, then looked for Renee.

Where was she?

Karen had a momentary shock of panic until she realized that she was no longer facing the rocks. She was facing the beach. She must have gotten turned around while watching the fish. With her face in the water, it was so hard to keep track of where she was going.

She spun herself around and was relieved to see Renee just a few yards ahead of her, floating slowly now, her head down, her legs moving smoothly, rhythmically.

She's getting awfully close to the rocks, Karen thought. But I guess she knows what she's doing.

Karen looked back to the shore. They had swum out pretty far. The sunbathers were small dots of color on the yellow strip of beach. Beyond the beach, the boardwalk was just a blur. She wondered if Jerry and Ann-Marie were watching.

Eager to see more, she pulled the mask back up, adjusted the mouthpiece, and ducked her face in once again. She moved toward Renee, and the water cleared as she floated, revealing more and more of its colorful, silent inhabitants.

Renee was right, Karen thought. You can see better here. The water isn't thick and churned up.

A bright blue fish swam up to her, seemed to stare into her mask, then sped away. What an amazing color, she thought. You never see that shade of blue out of the water.

The water felt warmer now. She moved forward, the only sound the steady whoosh of her breath through the hose.

Suddenly she felt a jolt, as if she were being pushed.

She ignored it, but another one followed, a little harder, propelling her forward.

She raised her head out of the water. To her shock, a large rock loomed right in front of her. A wall of smooth, brown rocks jutted before her. She spit out the mouthpiece and turned to find Renee.

"Hey!"

The current was surprisingly strong. It was pushing her, forcing her toward the rocks.

I've gone too far, she thought.

I'm too close.

Where's Renee?

She turned and started to swim away from the rocks. But she was lifted high, as if riding on a wave, and thrown crashing back.

Frightened, she tore off the mask, letting it hang around her neck, and tried swimming again.

But again the current pushed her back.

"Hey! Ouch!"

She was slammed into the side of the rock. Her shoulder hit hard. She bounced off, the pain running down her arm.

I've got to get away from here. I've got to swim, got to move!

"Renee!" she shouted.

Another thrust of the powerful current sent her slamming against the rock again.

"Hey!"

A jagged shard of rock tore through her wet suit. Water poured in, so cold, such a shock.

She was really frightened now.

Where was Renee?

There. She saw her. Renee was only a few yards away, back from the rocks, back from the treacherous current. She was floating tranquilly, her face in the water, the snorkel standing straight up.

"Renee! Help!"

Renee kept floating, her legs kicking slowly.

"Ouch!" Karen slammed hard into the rock.

"Renee — please!"

I know Renee can hear me, Karen thought. She's only a dozen yards away. How can she not hear me? How can she not see me?

"Renee! Help me!"

The freezing water filled her suit, weighing her down. Karen struggled to swim. But her shoulder ached. She couldn't make any headway against the powerful, swirling current.

"Renee — can't you hear me?! Renee!"

She watched Renee paddle along, not lifting her head.

She's ignoring me.

"Renee!" Karen screamed as the current battered her, shoved her against the jutting rocks.

Renee didn't react, didn't look up, didn't turn around.

She did this to me. Deliberately.

She led me out here. She led me to the rocks.

She can hear me. She *has* to be hearing me.

She's deliberately ignoring me.

"Ouch!" Karen couldn't help but cry out as she hit hard against solid rock again.

I'm not going to make it. I can't get out of this current.

She looked up at the rock. Maybe she could climb onto it. Maybe she'd be safe up there.

She reached for it just as the current slammed her forward, and her head hit the rock.

"Got to hang on," she told herself, feeling dizzy, forcing herself not to give in to it.

She tried for the rock again. But it was too slippery. She slid right off.

"Renee — hear me! Please! Renee! Don't leave me here!" she cried.

But the gray-suited figure didn't respond, just kept paddling peacefully, slowly along.

"Renee!"

She hears me, Karen thought. Her terror began to fill her body as the cold waters filled her wet suit.

She hears me. She's not going to look up.

She's waiting there. Enjoying this.

Waiting for me to drown.

Chapter 6

"It's Karen!" Ann-Marie cried. "Look — it's Karen! Up against the rocks!"

"Huh?" Jerry leaped to his feet and, shielding his eyes with his hand, peered out at the line of brown rocks.

"No! Karen! Karen! Karen!"

With the sound of Ann-Marie's terrified cries in his ears, Jerry ran toward the water, kicking up a spray of sand behind him. He hit the water without slowing down, ran several steps, and then plunged into an onrushing wave.

The water was cold, much colder than when he'd been in earlier.

He shuddered and forced himself to keep moving, stretching his arms out in rapid strokes. He could still hear Ann-Marie shrieking, calling Karen's name over and over, even though she was far behind him now.

Where is Renee? he asked himself. Why isn't she helping? Is she in trouble, too?

Jerry was a strong, confident swimmer. But the

shock of the cold water and the horror of the situation had thrown him off stride. The current, he found, was tricky, swirling first in one direction, then pulling him hard in the other.

What happened out there anyway? he wondered. How did Renee let Karen get so close to the rocks?

Where is Renee??

He kicked hard and tried to lengthen his strokes. He couldn't see the struggling girl, but he knew she was somewhere on the rocks straight ahead of him.

"Karen! Karen! Karen!"

He heard Ann-Marie's cry, repeating in his mind, repeating with each stroke.

"Karen! Karen! Karen!"

The name carried on the wind, carried over the water.

I'm coming, Karen, he thought, his chest aching, his biceps tightening. I'm coming, Karen. Hold on. Please hold on.

"Renee — where are you?"

He thought he saw a gray figure, a snorkeling tube. Was that Renee?

Jerry's right leg was cramping up. He stopped kicking for a while and let his arms do the work.

There she is!

He could see the red stripe on the hood of her wet suit.

Are you okay?

Are you conscious?

Let me see your face.

The red stripe disappeared in the swirling water.

It reappeared a few seconds later. What was that bright glare?

It took him a while to figure out it was the sunlight reflecting off the snorkeling mask around her neck.

Hold on. Hold on, Karen. I'm almost there.

He felt as if his lungs would burst. His leg was still cramped, but he kicked through the pain.

"Hey — Jerry!"

It was Renee, calling to him.

She pulled down her mask. She looked very surprised.

"Jerry — what are you doing here?"

"Karen!" he sputtered. He was breathing too hard to talk.

Renee looked confused for a second, and then she must've seen Karen, seen her body battering against the dark rock.

"Oh, no!" she cried. Her mouth dropped open. Her face filled with horror. She swallowed some water, started to choke.

"Renee — are you okay?"

"Why didn't she call me?" Renee cried. "Why didn't she signal or something?"

They both swam toward the rock. Jerry reached it a few seconds later. "Hey — can you hear me?"

Karen didn't reply. Her eyes were closed.

Has she just passed out or something?

Remembering his lifesaving class, he turned her onto her back and put his arms around her.

"Hey — " Renee, breathing loudly, arrived. "Is she okay?"

"I can't tell. She's passed out or something," Jerry said, shivering from the cold. "Look — her suit is ripped."

"Let me help," Renee said. "I can't believe it. I thought she was right behind me."

Jerry was grateful for the help. The current was so strong and so strange. "I've got a leg cramp."

"Let's get out of here," Renee said, grabbing onto Karen from the other side.

They started to pull her back toward the shore. Jerry could see a whole crowd of people at the shoreline. "Come on!" It seemed to be taking forever. It *was* taking forever. The current was trying to force them back, back to the rocks.

"Hope she's okay," Jerry said. "Wish she'd move. Wish she'd talk to us."

It seemed like hours later when they dragged Karen onto the sand.

"Is she okay?"

"Is she alive?"

Anxious voices. The crowd rushed around them, curious, frightened, excited. Jerry and Renee quickly got Karen on her back. They pulled off the hood of the wet suit.

"Get back! Get back!" Renee cried angrily, waving people back.

"Is she alive?"

"Is she moving?"

Jerry, still breathing hard, unable to catch his breath, unable to stop shivering, bent over Karen.

"Get back! Everybody, step back!" Renee

shouted, pulling back the hood of her suit, her frizzy hair matted down against her head.

Suddenly Ann-Marie came running through the crowd and flung herself down next to Jerry. She lifted Karen's head. "Karen? Karen?"

"No, don't — " Jerry started.

"She's dead!" Ann-Marie screamed. "I don't believe it! She's dead!"

Chapter 7

"No!" Jerry cried.

He shoved Ann-Marie away. Then he bent over Karen and pushed hard on her rib cage. He pushed again. Then again. Brackish water spurted from Karen's open mouth.

Jerry kept pushing, rhythmically, the way he'd learned in lifesaving class. The crowd, the voices, the beach, the entire world seemed to disappear as he worked.

Come on, Karen. Come on. Open your eyes, Karen. Breathe. Breathe. You can do it.

He pressed again. Again.

She groaned. More water dribbled from her mouth.

And again.

She opened her eyes.

The voices, the people started to come back. She could hear the roar of the ocean again. She could hear someone crying a few feet behind him. She could see Renee looking on anxiously, chewing on her lower lip, still in her wet suit and fins.

"She's alive!"

"She's breathing!"

The voices were happy now, relieved.

"What's going on?" Karen asked, looking dazed. She started to sit up.

Jerry restrained her. "Are you sure you're ready to sit up?"

"Yeah. Of course."

"She's okay!" Renee cried happily.

Ann-Marie was at Karen's side now. She took Karen's hand and squeezed it, staring at Karen as if she were a ghost come back to the living.

Which maybe she was.

"Uh-oh," Karen said, looking around. "This crowd — because of me?"

"Yes. We thought you had drowned," Ann-Marie told her, looking greatly relieved.

"Renee helped me pull you in," Jerry said, his arm around Karen.

"Renee?" Karen looked up at her.

"Why didn't you call me for help?" Renee asked heatedly, before Karen could say anything. "Why didn't you let me know you were in trouble?"

Karen stared at her in disbelief. Was Renee telling the truth? Had she been too far away to hear Karen's desperate cries?

No, Karen thought. She *had* to hear me. She *had* to.

But there were tears in Renee's eyes.

Was she faking them? Was she putting on a show now so no one would suspect what she had tried to do to Karen?

Two Venice policemen, in dark blue shorts and T-shirts, pushed their way through the circle of onlookers. "What's going on here?"

Renee pointed at Karen, who was still sitting beside Jerry on the sand. "A girl almost drowned."

The policemen moved forward to talk to Karen. "What happened?" one of them asked her.

Karen's hair was tangled and wet, the back covered with sand. She looked as pale as cake flour, but her blue eyes were regaining their lively sparkle. She sat up, propping her hands behind her in the sand.

"I got too close to the rocks. The current got me. I couldn't get back," she told the policemen.

One of them picked up her snorkeling mask and examined it. "Why were you snorkeling there?" the policeman asked suspiciously, handing the mask back to Karen.

"You can't see anything there," his partner added.

"I know," Karen explained. "I never snorkeled before. Renee said she'd show me how. I just wanted to try it."

The policeman turned back to Renee. "You Renee?"

Renee nodded.

"You don't give very good lessons," he said drily.

"There's no lifeguard yet," the other policeman said, turning to look up at the empty lifeguard tower.

"I know," Karen said. "Jerry saved me. Jerry and Renee."

Karen started to get up, but her legs felt shaky.

Ann-Marie helped keep her steady, allowing Karen to lean on her arm. "I'm okay. Really," Karen insisted.

"Get going," one of the policemen yelled, shooing the crowd. "Show's over. Come on. Get moving."

"Party time! Who's got beer?" someone yelled.

A few people laughed.

"This isn't the best place to snorkel," one of the policemen said quietly to Karen. "Your friend should've told you that." He eyed Renee suspiciously.

"She didn't call me," Renee said, sounding more angry than upset. "She didn't let me know she was in trouble."

"Glad everything's okay now," the policeman said, and motioned for his partner to follow him back to the boardwalk.

Eventually the crowd dispersed. People returned to their blankets or to the boardwalk, talking excitedly.

"I never swam so fast in my life," Jerry said, catching up to Karen.

"I'm glad you're such a good swimmer," Karen said.

For some reason, his expression changed. His smile faded. A look of horror crossed his face.

"Jerry — are you okay?" Karen asked.

He didn't seem to hear her. He seemed lost in his thoughts, far away. Finally, he snapped out of it. "Sorry. Guess I'm . . . a little in shock."

"You'd better get a towel or something. Aren't you frozen?"

"Yeah. I guess," he said. But he stood beside her, making no move toward his blanket. "You have beautiful eyes," he said.

Karen saw that Renee and Ann-Marie were walking quickly toward them, Renee carrying her fins, looking very unhappy.

"Jerry, really — go get dried off."

But he stood there, staring into her eyes. "Listen, we're . . . uh . . . having a beach party Friday night," he said. He pushed his dark, wet hair back off his forehead. "On that beach in Malibu. A whole bunch of us. Would you like to come?"

"Yeah, I guess," Karen said uncertainly. "You mean Ann-Marie, too?"

"Uh . . . sure. Of course."

"Well, I couldn't say no to anything you asked," Karen said, giving him her widest eyes, turning on the sex appeal. "After all, you saved my life."

Jerry grinned. "Yeah. I did, didn't I. Listen, I can pick you two up. Marty has a van," he said.

"Okay. That'll be great," Karen said. She shivered. "I've got to get out of this wet suit."

"Yeah. Right. Okay. See you tomorrow," Jerry said. "I've got to get dried off, too." He headed back to his blanket.

Karen stood still for a moment, watching him walk over the sand.

Then she turned and saw Renee staring at her, several yards away.

Was that a smile on Renee's face?

The sun was in Karen's eyes. The sand sent up a bright reflection. Karen thought maybe she was imagining it, maybe she was seeing things.

But yes. Renee had the strangest smile on her face. A pleased smile. A triumphant smile.

Karen raised her hand to shield her eyes from the sun.

When she looked back, Renee had turned her back and was heading quickly to the blanket.

"She heard me. I know she did," Karen insisted, later that night. She and Ann-Marie were in pajamas, sitting on the platform bed in her room, eating Heath Bar Crunch ice cream from containers, half-watching a *Cheers* rerun on the TV. A soft breeze off the ocean invaded the room through the open window, cool and salty, making the light curtains billow.

"Karen, I really think you're wrong," Ann-Marie said, biting down on a hard chunk of chocolate. "Renee was underwater, remember. And she had the wet suit hood over her ears. I'm sure she just didn't hear you calling to her."

"I've got to stop thinking about it," Karen said. She stretched back and rested her head on the stack of pillows behind her. The cool breeze felt so refreshing on her skin. "I just can't seem to relax. I mean, she did threaten me, after all. And then she let me get too close to the rocks and — "

"You're starting to sound a little paranoid, if you ask me," Ann-Marie said. "Please — take away this ice cream. I'm going to eat the entire container!"

"Just hold onto it. I'll finish yours after I finish mine," Karen said. They both laughed.

Ann-Marie put the top back on the carton and returned it to the freezer. A few minutes later, she appeared back in the bedroom, fully dressed. "I'm going out for a minute," she called to Karen.

"Huh? What for?"

"To get a carton of milk. I know it's weird, but I always like a glass of milk after ice cream."

"It's weird all right," Karen agreed. But Ann-Marie was already out the door.

She'd only been gone a couple of minutes when the phone rang.

Karen looked at the clock radio on the bedtable. 11:45. Who would be calling this late? Probably anyone. She reached over and picked up the phone.

"Hello?"

Silence.

"Hello?" Karen repeated.

The voice on the other end was a whisper, more like a rush of wind than a voice. "Is this Karen?"

"Yes. I can't hear you very well," Karen said, confused.

"Stay away from Jerry." The words were so soft, as if spoken by a ghost.

"What? What did you say?"

"Stay away from Jerry." This time they were spoken more forcefully in a rasping whisper that hurt Karen's ear.

"Hey — who is this?" she demanded.

Silence.

"Who *is* this?"

And then a click. The dial tone returned.

Karen sat staring at the phone. Finally, she

shrugged and replaced the receiver.

A few minutes later, Ann-Marie returned, carrying a quart of milk in a brown paper bag. She poured herself a tall glass and carried it into the bedroom. "Hey — what's wrong?" she asked, seeing the tense expression on Karen's face.

"I got a call," Karen said. "Someone warning me to stay away from Jerry."

"Huh?"

"That's all they said. I think they were trying to scare me."

"Well, who was it?"

"I don't know. They whispered. You know, disguised their voice."

"Do you think it was Renee?" Ann-Marie tilted the glass back and drank the entire contents.

"Maybe." Karen stared at the window, watching the white curtains blow into the room like ghosts. "I couldn't really tell if it was a boy or a girl. You know who it sounded a little bit like?"

"Who?"

"Mike."

Ann-Marie dropped down into the white leather armchair beside the bed, casually draping her legs over the side. "Mike? Get real! You said you haven't seen Mike in three weeks, not since you broke up with him."

"I thought I saw him yesterday afternoon," Karen said, removing the headband that held her hair in place. She shook her head, and her silky, dark hair tumbled free. "On the boardwalk. I thought I saw him following us. But that's crazy, isn't it? I mean, what would Mike be doing in Venice?"

"Yeah. It's crazy, all right," Ann-Marie agreed. "And why would Mike call you up and whisper for you to stay away from Jerry? He doesn't even *know* Jerry!"

"You're right," Karen said, pulling her hair back, then releasing it, then pulling it back again. "It was Renee. It had to be Renee. She doesn't know me very well, does she?"

Ann-Marie yawned. "What do you mean?"

"I mean, I don't scare easily."

The phone rang again.

Both girls jumped to their feet.

"There she is again," Karen said, frowning. Without hesitating she picked up the phone. "Just leave me alone!" she screamed.

And then her mouth formed a small O of surprise and she nearly dropped the phone.

"Oh. Sorry, Daddy. I thought it was someone else."

Ann-Marie laughed loudly. Karen gestured wildly for her to hush.

"Yes. Fine. Yeah. Okay. Everything's okay. What? Oh. I see." She chatted for a brief while, said good night, and hung up. Then she turned to Ann-Marie. "That was my dad."

"Did he whisper for you to stay away from Jerry?"

"Very funny. No. It turns out that he and his 'friend' " — Karen made two quote marks with her fingers — "have to go on to Tahoe. So he won't be back here for at least another week."

"We're on our own, huh?" Ann-Marie asked, grinning.

"Yeah. We're on our own."

Karen knew she should be as happy about the news as Ann-Marie was. So why did she have this feeling of cold dread in the pit of her stomach?

Chapter 8

On Thursday, Ann-Marie had to visit relatives in Burbank, so Karen decided to spend the morning shopping. Just before lunchtime, she stepped out of a small boutique on Market Street and ran into Mike. He was wearing white tennis shorts and a T-shirt that proclaimed in big green letters: "GUMBY LIVES."

Mike was big with broad shoulders, muscular arms, and a wide neck. He had straight brown hair that he swept straight back off his square forehead, and small, round brown eyes that always seemed to be searching around, looking for something. He reminded Karen of the movie star Jim Belushi, only younger, of course. He even sounded like Jim Belushi.

Karen uttered a little cry of surprise, but Mike didn't seem at all surprised to see her. "Hey, how's it goin'?" he asked, his eyes finding hers, then looking past her.

"Mike — I was just talking about you. What are you doing in Venice?" It didn't come out the way she meant it. It came out sounding slightly suspicious.

"Oh, I got a job," he said, his eyes trailing a blonde wearing a tiny green minidress over dark tights. "On the boardwalk."

"Oh, yeah?" She was still too startled to speak coherently. She had just broken up with him three weeks before. Now here he was following her to Venice.

Oh, get real, Karen, she scolded herself. Mike didn't follow you. This is a total coincidence.

She knew that was the truth, but she only half believed it.

"Yeah. I'm selling T-shirts. Want a Mötley Crüe shirt? Ha ha. I can get you a discount. Ha ha. Pretty boring job. But I get a lot of fresh air, and I'm right on the beach." He grinned at her, the lopsided grin she used to find irresistible. But now she found she could resist it easily.

"Well, that's great, Mike," Karen said, looking both ways for an escape route. "I've got to — "

"What are you doing this summer?" he asked, blocking her path, standing very close to her.

"Well, I'm staying at my dad's place here in Venice. My friend Ann-Marie is visiting from New York."

"Yeah, I know Ann-Marie."

"Oh. Right. Of course you do. Well, she's visiting for a month. Then I'm going away with my mom."

He nodded his head as if agreeing with something she'd said. She realized she also used to find that nod adorable. Now she found it really annoying.

"You've been shopping?" He gestured toward the boutique.

"Just looking around," she said curtly. Why was he dragging this conversation out? Why didn't he just leave?

"You . . . uh . . . seeing anybody?"

"No. Not really."

"So you want to go out or something?" he said, watching a Jaguar pull out of a narrow parking place across the street. "I know this after-hours club on Main Street — "

"Mike, please," Karen groaned. "Give me a break, okay?"

"Huh? What's wrong?" His eyes opened wide and his face filled with innocence.

"You know what's wrong. Everything," she said, desperate to get away. But he was so big, he was blocking the whole sidewalk. "Don't pretend you don't get it. We broke up. In simple English, we broke up." She pronounced the words slowly and distinctly.

"I know, but it's summer now and — "

"And when people break up, that means they don't go out together anymore," Karen continued, talking to him the way she talked to her five-year-old cousin.

He raised his big paw of a hand and rubbed the back of his neck. "Karen, I thought you said you still wanted to be friends. So I took you at your word and — "

"I just said that," Karen said quickly. "I didn't really mean it. That's what you say when you break up with someone. I hope we can stay friends. But no one ever really stays friends. That would be a little awkward, don't you think?"

Why won't he go away? she thought. Just disappear. Poof. Gone. Into thin air. Please. Oh, please. A tiny earthquake. Just big enough for the sidewalk to open under him. No big deal. No tragedy. Just a small, personal earthquake to remove Mike from in front of me.

"I really think we should sit down somewhere and discuss this," Mike said, still rubbing his neck.

"Mike, please — we did all our discussing before school let out. We decided. You weren't having any fun anymore, and I wasn't having any fun anymore."

He reddened. "Don't say that, Karen. We had fun. We had a lot of fun."

"What's the point?" Karen started to lose her temper. "I don't want to go out with you. Can you understand that?" She didn't realize how loudly she was shouting. Across the street, two girls carrying skateboards burst out laughing.

Mike reddened even more, his eyes following the two girls, who turned the corner and disappeared, still giggling.

"Now are you going to get out of my way?" Karen asked, not bothering to hide her annoyance.

"Not until you agree to give me half a chance," Mike insisted, standing his ground.

"Ohh." She felt like slugging him. What was wrong with him, anyway? Didn't he have any pride?

Mike started to say something, but a loud roar

on the street drowned out his words. At first Karen thought the roar was in her ears. She'd been hearing the ocean ever since yesterday afternoon. The roar of the ocean had followed her, even in sleep, as if the waters were calling her back.

But this roar was too loud to be the ocean.

Mike stepped closer to be heard. He was only inches away from her now. She wanted to shove him and run.

But what was that deafening roar?

"Can you hear me?" Mike yelled.

Karen turned to the street, and there was Vince. He was astride a large motorcycle, leaning over the handlebars, grinning at her with those adorable dimples from under his red-and-black helmet, gunning the engine with his black-gloved hands.

"What's going on?" Mike asked, suddenly confused.

"Jump on," Vince yelled, slapping the space on the leather seat behind him.

"Hey — I'm talking to her!" Mike declared angrily.

"Jump on!" Vince repeated, ignoring Mike.

Karen looked at Mike, who was still blocking her path, then at Vince.

Mike reached out for her. She had the feeling he wanted to hold her in place so she couldn't escape.

The motorcycle roared. The sidewalk seemed to shake.

Karen dodged to the side, out of Mike's grasp, pulled herself up onto the back of the big, black-and-chrome motorcycle, and grabbed Vince's leather-jacketed shoulders as he pulled away with an explosion and a powerful jolt.

As they turned right onto Speedway, Karen looked back. Mike hadn't moved. He was staring after them, red-faced, furious.

Vince roared through a stop sign, nearly colliding with two middle-aged women on bikes. The narrow street whirred by in a blur of parked cars and low, white and gray houses.

Where is he taking me? Karen asked herself. What am I doing here? I don't know him. I don't know anyone like him.

The big motorcycle seemed to explode again and with a burst of speed, Vince roared on, heading north toward Santa Monica.

"Hey — stop! Stop!" Karen cried, suddenly regretting her impulsive decision.

But he couldn't — or wouldn't — hear her.

I've made a mistake, Karen thought, gripping his shoulders, leaning against his jacket to get her face out of the onrushing wind.

I've made a terrible mistake.

Chapter 9

He skidded to a stop at the Promenade in Santa Monica, nearly plowing into the back of a Volvo station wagon. A woman dressed in a gray suit, walking a gigantic rottweiler, sneered at Vince and gave him a dirty look. The big, sad-faced dog sniffed at the motorcycle. The woman tugged its leash and pulled it away.

Laughing, Vince slid off the seat and, pulling off his helmet, turned to face Karen. "Ugly dog, huh?"

Karen struggled to arrange her windblown hair, but it was impossible. "You nearly ran it over."

Vince shrugged.

"Why did you stop? What are we doing here?" Karen demanded, still pulling at her hair.

Vince shrugged again. It seemed to be his favorite reply. "Good question."

The day had turned cloudy. A few people were walking along the tree-lined Promenade, but the beach was nearly deserted.

"Well, do you think you could take me back to

Venice?" Karen slid forward on the seat so that she could grip the handlebars.

"I don't know." Vince grinned. He ran a hand back through his short, spiky hair.

"Well, who should we ask?" Karen snapped.

"Hey — " Vince said. She waited for him to continue, but evidently that was his complete statement.

"You know, I really didn't want to come here. I mean . . . ."

"Then why'd you jump on?"

"Mike, that guy back there, he was giving me a hard time, so . . ."

"So here we are in Santa Monica," Vince said, turning away from her to look at the ocean. The waves were high and capped with white foam. The sky grew darker.

"I'd really like to go home," Karen said.

"You're inviting me to your place?" He grinned and leaned forward, bringing his face close to hers.

"Very funny." She pulled back.

He frowned and reached in his jacket pocket for a bent-up pack of cigarettes. He pushed one between his lips and offered the pack to her with a grunt.

"No," she said, pushing them away. "I don't smoke. And neither should you. I mean, what's the point?"

He pulled the cigarette from his mouth. "Yeah. What's the point?" He jammed it back into the pack and shoved the pack back into his pocket. "What's the point?"

"How come you sound so bitter?" Karen said, looking up at the blackening sky.

"How come you sound so nosy?" he asked.

They stared at each other. He was the first to look away. He laughed, a shy, nervous laugh, and kicked at his back tire.

He's really good-looking when he laughs, she thought. "Are you going to take me back?"

"Why don't we keep going?" he suggested, looking out toward the water. "You know. We'll take the Palisades Beach Road."

"It's going to rain," she said.

"You think you're too good for me."

"What?"

"Nothing."

"No. Really. I didn't hear what you said."

"I didn't say anything. Come on. Move back. I'll take you back." He looked really angry. He jumped onto the seat, forcing Karen to slide back. He started the motorcycle with a roar and, without waiting for Karen to get her balance, burst away from the curb, spun around, nearly causing her to topple off, and headed back toward Venice.

"Hey — slow down!" Karen cried, holding onto the shoulders of his leather jacket for dear life.

He immediately sped up, swerved into the left lane to pass a slow-moving van, and nearly collided with an oncoming bus.

"If I want a thrill ride, I'll go to Space Mountain!" Karen shouted.

But he pretended not to hear her and gunned the

motorcycle forward. Karen closed her eyes and held tight.

It started to rain, a drizzle at first and then steady rain. The road became shiny and slick. "Please — slow down!"

He didn't reply. She pressed herself against his leather jacket, wet and fragrant from the rain.

Trees whirred by, a blurred curtain of green and brown, interrupted occasionally by the flashing colors of a billboard. We're not going to make it, Karen thought, as the tires slid noisily around a curve. I'm having a great week — nearly drowned one day, splattered against the highway the next!

Miraculously, a short while later, they were back in Venice, roaring down Speedway, and a short while after that, she was climbing off the seat in front of her apartment building.

The rain had stopped, but her hair and clothes were drenched. Her white sneakers were soaked through and splashed with mud.

"Thanks for the lift, Vince," she said sarcastically.

He didn't look at her, just stared straight ahead. "Say hello to your *brother*," he sneered.

Then he took off without looking back.

Karen stood on the sidewalk and watched him roar around the corner. What was *that* all about? she wondered. Why did he rescue me from Mike? What did he expect me to do with him in Santa Monica? And then why did he get so angry?

He is weird, she decided. He is full-tilt *weird*.

But the wild motorcycle ride, she decided now that she was safely standing on the sidewalk, was kind of exciting. In fact, she wouldn't mind doing it again sometime, sometime when it wasn't raining.

In fact, she decided, she wouldn't mind it if Vince came to rescue her again sometime. All of that shyness, that bitterness, the quiet anger — it was kind of sexy.

Karen, are you losing it totally? she scolded herself. How can you be attracted to a guy like that?

She thought of Jerry and, even though it was foolish, felt somehow unfaithful to him.

Get inside, she ordered herself. That ride has totally scrambled your brain.

Obeying her own command, she hurried into the apartment house to change. The narrow hallway felt hot and damp. She headed to the back where her dad's apartment was — and then stopped.

She took a deep breath.

Someone had painted on the wall.

Black spray paint. The words were scrawled in huge, black letters over the pale green wallpaper.

It started at her door and covered most of the wall to the next apartment.

The paint looked wet. The words appeared to drip down the wall.

They said: *STAY AWAY FROM JERRY*.

Karen reached her hand forward and touched the paint. It felt sticky. She pulled back and saw that her finger was black.

Whoever did this was just here, she thought.

They know where I live.

They were right outside my door.

She had a terrifying thought: Had they been in the apartment, too?

Fumbling with her keys, she unlocked the door and pushed it open an inch. She could see pale gray light pouring through the open window. Cautiously, she pushed the door open wider, took one step into the apartment — and gasped in surprise.

Chapter 10

"Ann-Marie — what are you doing here?"

Ann-Marie hung up the phone, a guilty look on her face. "Oh, hi, Karen. You startled me." She was sitting at the small, glass dining room table, wearing pale blue shorts and a plain white crew-neck top.

"You startled *me*!" Karen said, sinking down across from her on a white vinyl dining room chair. "I didn't expect anyone to be here. I thought you were in Burbank."

"Oh. Well, I changed my mind." Ann-Marie blushed. Her normally pale skin was bright pink. She twisted a strand of her short, blonde hair into a knot. "I wasn't in the mood for my Aunt Freda. Maybe I'll go tomorrow."

"Someone painted on the wall," Karen said, her heart still pounding from the shock of seeing someone in the apartment.

"What?"

"In the hallway. Come look."

Ann-Marie's face filled with confusion. "What do you mean?"

Karen took her hand and pulled her out to the hallway. "Hey — you're all wet," Ann-Marie cried, pulling out of Karen's grasp.

"I was caught in the rain," Karen said.

"It didn't rain here." Ann-Marie gave her a curious look.

"It's a long story. Never mind that. Look." Karen pointed to the words sprayed in black.

"Oh, no." Ann-Marie slumped back against the opposite wall. "Who would do a stupid thing like that?"

"Someone who really wants to frighten me," Karen said, staring hard at the painted words.

"Is it working?" Ann-Marie asked.

That's a strange question, Karen thought, turning her gaze on Ann-Marie.

"Yes. I think it is," Karen said with a shudder.

Chapter 11

"So you left poor Mike standing there on the street and rode off with this gang leader?"

It was Friday night. Ann-Marie had just returned from visiting her relatives in Burbank. Now she was lying on the bed, wearing gray sweatpants and a faded Hard Rock Cafe T-shirt, watching Karen get dressed, very amused by Karen's story.

"He's not a gang leader," Karen said, pulling a purple Esprit sweater over her head. "He just hangs out with some guys."

"Yeah. Some guys who happen to dress alike, just like a gang," Ann-Marie said. "You are unbelievable. You really will do anything."

"I take that as a compliment," Karen said, pulling the sweater down, admiring her figure in the mirror.

"What did you talk about with this guy, anyway?"

"Vince. His name is Vince," Karen said, leaning down to the dressing table mirror to brush her hair. She examined her face as she brushed. The purple sweater made her eyes seem even bluer. "I didn't talk to him about anything."

"Huh?"

"We didn't talk at all. He took me for this wild ride to Santa Monica. Then I told him I wanted to go back, so he turned around and drove back. It was kind of exciting, in a scary sort of way."

"You mean he drives the way he looks?"

"I mean he doesn't stop for anything. And he never slows down, even in the rain."

"Weird. Do you like him?"

"Like him? I don't know. He's terrible. He acts real bitter. He's always sneering, always angry. I think some of it's an act. I can't really tell. Anyway, he's kind of interesting." She grinned at Ann-Marie. "He's certainly different from anyone I know."

Ann-Marie laughed. "That's for sure. What are you going to do if he asks you out?"

Karen's face grew thoughtful, but she didn't say anything. "At least he got me away from Mike," she said finally, sitting down to put on some blusher.

"Mike isn't so bad," Ann-Marie said, stretching.

Karen stared at her friend in the mirror. "Hey — how come you're not getting dressed?"

"I'm not going," Ann-Marie said, lying back on the pillows and stretching.

"What? Why not? It sounds like fun. The beach at Malibu is so pretty at night. You could meet some new kids. Maybe meet a guy."

"I'm too tired," Ann-Marie said, yawning loudly. "Aunt Freda wore me out. She'd wear anyone out with her nonstop talking. Really. She never takes a breath. It was exhausting!"

"Oh, come on," Karen said, disappointed. "You can just chill out on the beach."

"What do you need me for? Jerry will keep you busy enough," Ann-Marie snapped.

She's jealous, Karen thought. I really think she's jealous.

"Jerry already has a girlfriend," Karen said, slipping into blue plastic sandals. "Someone is working very hard not to let me forget that."

"Jerry doesn't seem to remember he has a girlfriend whenever he looks at you," Ann-Marie said.

That's an odd thing to say, Karen thought. What is Ann-Marie's problem, anyway?

"Listen, I just feel too out of it tonight," Ann-Marie said, staring up at the ceiling. "I think I'll just hang around."

"Well, okay," Karen said reluctantly.

A car horn honked down on the street. Karen ran to the window and looked down. A maroon van was parked at the curb. The back door slid open, and Jerry hopped out. He looked up and waved to her. He was wearing tie-dyed jean cutoffs and a black-and-white-striped crew-necked pullover.

He's real cute, Karen thought.

She could see other kids sitting in the van. "Be right down!" she yelled, then realized the window was closed.

"Have a nice time," Ann-Marie said, yawning.

"Yeah. Okay. See you later." Karen took one last glance in the mirror, brushed back a strand of hair from her forehead, and hurried down to the van.

It was a clear, cool evening, more like spring than summer. It'll be cold on the beach, Karen thought.

"How's it goin'?" Jerry asked, helping her into the van. "You know any of these kids?"

Karen peered into the van. "No, I don't," she said, looking around at the smiling faces illuminated by the streetlight.

"You're lucky!" Jerry said, climbing in after her.

"Hey — you know *us*!" Marty called from the driver's seat.

"Hi, Karen," Stephanie called from the passenger seat beside him.

"Oh, hi. I didn't see you up there. Where's Renee?" Karen asked Jerry.

"Yeah. Where's Renee?" a boy in a white sweatshirt shouted in a teasing voice.

"She had to go somewhere with her parents. She's coming later," Jerry said, more than a little uncomfortable. He slid next to her on the seat and pulled the sliding door shut. They were pressed close against each other.

"That's Kenny, Alicia, Normy, and Seth," Jerry said quickly, pointing.

Karen said hi to them, forgetting their names immediately.

"Bring your snorkeling gear?" Jerry joked, as Marty pulled the van away from the curb, turned onto Speedway, and headed north toward Malibu.

"No. I thought I'd leave it home tonight," Karen said, shoving him playfully in the ribs.

Some joke.

"I went snorkeling last week," a boy in the back-seat said.

"Where? In your bathtub?" Stephanie called from the front seat.

"He doesn't take baths," the girl named Alicia cracked in a surprisingly high-pitched, tiny voice.

"How do *you* know?" Marty shouted. Then quickly added, "Don't answer that!" Everyone laughed.

"Hey — are you the girl whose life Jerry saved?" Alicia asked.

"Uh . . . yeah," Karen said, a little surprised by the question. "I was caught on the rocks. Jerry pulled me in."

"Did he give you mouth-to-mouth?" the boy in the backseat asked.

Everyone laughed uproariously.

"Hey, knock it off," Jerry cried angrily. "It was pretty serious, you know."

Everyone obediently stopped laughing.

Then Alicia broke the silence by asking, "Did you have an out-of-body experience?"

"That's kind of personal, isn't it?" Seth joked.

"Shut up, Seth. You're just jealous because no one's interested in your body!" Stephanie joked from the front seat.

Everyone laughed.

"I don't remember anything much at all," Karen answered. "It's all sort of a blank."

"Think you were dead?" Marty asked. "Just for a few seconds, maybe?"

"Only someone who was already brain-dead

would ask that question," Jerry replied angrily. Too angrily, Karen thought. She wondered what was troubling him.

Was he just embarrassed to have been such a hero?

Jerry was pressed tightly against Karen in the seat. He was so warm and solid. She liked being so close to him.

"You're really gross, Marty," Alicia said, shaking her head.

"Thank you, thank you," Marty said, grinning. "What's so terrible? I just asked Karen if she was dead or not. It's not like I asked if she was a virgin or something."

"I don't know," Karen told him.

"You don't know if you're a virgin or not?"

Everyone laughed. Karen felt embarrassed, but she laughed, too. "I mean, I don't know if I was dead or alive. I really don't remember a thing," she said finally.

Suddenly Marty pulled the van off the highway. They began to bump along a narrow dirt road. A short while later, he pulled to the side, stopped, and cut the lights.

"Hey — where are we?" Karen asked Jerry, whispering for some reason.

"We always park here," Jerry explained, pulling open the van door. "It's great. We can slide down the cliffs here. Then we don't have to pay admission to the beach. Or go through anyone's backyard."

Karen hopped down from the van and took a deep breath. The air smelled fresh and salty. She took a few steps and realized they were on the edge of a sloping, dark cliff. The beach spread out below them, illuminated dimly from the highway. Beyond that, she could hear the steady crash of the waves against the shore.

They unpacked the van and tossed blankets and backpacks over the smooth stone cliffside to the sand below. Marty was the first to slide down, wrapping his arms protectively over a big cooler as he slowly dropped. Stephanie followed him, slipping silently down, landing on her knees and getting up quickly to help the next person down.

Karen sat down on the rock edge. It felt cold to the touch. She took a deep breath and pushed herself down. This is great, she thought. Ann-Marie should have come. I wonder why she's been acting so strange, so tense the past couple of days.

Once they were all down on the beach, they spread the blankets in a wide circle on the sand, and then scattered to gather wood for a fire. Surprisingly, it was warmer down on the beach than up on the road. There was no wind at all. Even the spray off the ocean felt unusually warm.

Karen wandered down the shore, looking for firewood. A long, low house, its ocean side built entirely of glass, stood dark and deserted at the edge of the sand, built into the cliffs. Karen picked up a small pine branch, moving closer to the house.

"Hi." The voice right behind her startled her.

"Oh. Hi." It was Jerry. "I didn't see you. It's so dark."

"It's a nice night," he said, his hands stuffed in his pockets.

"Yeah. Look at all the stars," Karen said, tilting her head up. "It's usually so foggy this early in the summer."

"The sand is cold," he said, smiling.

She looked down at his bare feet, wiggling like field mice in the sand. "Your friends are nice," she said.

"Yeah. They're great."

"You know them from school?"

"Mostly."

They had moved into the shadow of the dark house. "I never really got to thank you," Karen said. "You know. For Wednesday."

He leaned his back against the glass wall. Karen moved close to him. Inside the house, she could see toys on the floor, pull toys, some kind of baby rattle. "You don't have to thank me."

"Well, it isn't too often that someone swims out and saves your life. You must be a great swimmer. The current at the rocks was incredible."

"I'm okay. Not great." His expression changed. He looked almost bitter for some reason.

"Well, I think you're great," Karen said, and impulsively, she reached her face up to his and gave him a quick kiss on the cheek.

As she started to back away, she was startled to feel his arms around her waist. He pulled her to him with surprising strength and, holding her so tight she could barely breathe, pushed his lips against hers, pressing harder, harder until the kiss actually hurt.

What's going on? Karen thought. I just meant to give him a peck on the cheek. He seems so . . . desperate. So needy.

She returned his kiss. His hands moved to the back of her head. He pressed her face against his.

This kiss is never going to end, she thought, her heart pounding.

Stay away from Jerry.

The whispered, threatening words on the phone.

Stay away from Jerry.

The spray-painted words scrawled on the wall.

How could she stay away from him? He was so wonderful.

"Stop," she said softly, not wanting to stop, wanting to stop, suddenly terribly confused and conflicted.

He let her go immediately and stepped back, tripping over a small, wooden wheelbarrow.

Karen's lips still throbbed. She could still taste him, still feel him pressing her to him so tightly.

"Hey, sorry," he said quietly, looking toward the camp fire, which blazed orange and red down the beach. He looked very embarrassed. "I'm really sorry. I just — "

"No. Don't," she started. "It was . . . nice." She stepped forward and took his arm. He smiled and seemed very pleased.

"I like you, Karen."

"So I gathered," she teased. She tasted blood on her lips. Such a hard kiss. "I like you, too, Jerry."

They started to walk back to the others, holding hands, not talking.

But Jerry suddenly uttered a low cry and dropped her hand as if it were a bomb.

She saw immediately what had alarmed him.

That figure standing in the shadows of the house.

It was Renee.

She must have seen everything.

Chapter 12

"Hi! Renee!" Jerry tried to be cool, to act as if he were glad to see her there, but his voice was shaky, and he sounded a bit *too* glad.

"Hi, Jerry." She stepped out of the shadows and walked up to them, her hands in the pockets of the cotton windbreaker she was wearing over jeans.

"We were looking for firewood," Karen said. Pretty lame, but at least it was an attempt.

Renee didn't look at Karen, didn't acknowledge her presence in any way. "Nice night," she said, without enthusiasm, and wrapped her arm around Jerry's.

"Yeah. It's great," Jerry said uneasily.

Karen let Jerry and Renee get a little ahead of her. Maybe she didn't see us kissing, she thought. It *was* very dark, after all.

Renee held tightly onto Jerry's arm, leaning against him as they walked over the cold sand to the camp fire. Karen, a few yards behind, couldn't hear what they were saying. But they both seemed to be acting as if nothing had happened, as if Renee hadn't watched them in their long, passionate kiss.

Karen sighed unhappily. She could still taste Jerry's lips on hers. Renee isn't my problem, she told herself, stopping to pick up a large shell that glowed blue in the moonlight. Renee is Jerry's problem.

She watched him walking over the sand, his long legs, his broad shoulders, the way his head dipped when he walked. He was smiling at Renee now. He has such a nice smile, Karen thought. So friendly. It just makes you want to smile, too.

Squeezing the cool shell in her hand, she followed them back to the camp fire. He saved my life, she thought, staring at Jerry. We were meant to be together.

Chill out, she warned herself. One kiss and your brain has turned to oatmeal.

Glowing orange and yellow faces greeted them from around the camp fire. The flickering, bright colors and the twisting shadows made everyone look strange, eerie, like characters in a horror movie.

Karen headed away from Jerry and Renee and settled on a blanket across the camp fire, beside Stephanie and Marty. Someone passed her a basket of sandwiches and a can of Coke. She suddenly realized she was starving. As she ate, she watched Jerry and Renee through the flickering camp fire flames. They seemed to be arguing now, their expressions angry, sitting far apart on the blanket.

Karen tried to join in the conversation with everyone else, but it was hard to concentrate, hard to get Jerry out of her mind, hard not to think about what had happened back at the dark house on the beach.

Suddenly she felt a hand on her shoulder.

"Could I talk to you?" It was Renee, standing above her, her hair orange from the firelight, her face half hidden by shadows.

She looks like a really scary jack-o'-lantern, Karen thought.

Karen peered through the fire at Jerry. He had left the blanket. Where was he? Then she saw him kidding around with two other kids away from the fire.

"Are you coming?" Renee demanded.

"Okay." Karen climbed to her feet quickly.

Renee started walking away from the fire, taking long strides, expecting Karen to follow her. She stopped at the edge of the water and turned around.

As she walked, Karen's mind whirred. What shall I say to her? What is she going to say to me? How shall I play this?

She decided to play it cool.

It's Renee's problem.

It's Jerry's problem.

It's not *my* problem.

It was easy to decide to play it cool. But could she do it?

"I saw you and Jerry," Renee said, without emotion.

At least she doesn't beat around the bush, Karen thought.

Renee waited a few seconds, then when Karen didn't reply, decided to continue. "I tried to warn you Monday night at the restaurant." Her voice was soft. It was hard to hear her over the rush of the waves against the beach. "Remember?"

"Yeah. I remember," Karen said, trying to sound as emotionless as Renee.

What's she going to do? Challenge me to a duel? She was definitely the one who phoned, Karen decided. She was the one who spray-painted the wall. She's that desperate.

Renee's next words startled her. "I tried to warn you because I know you don't understand about Jerry."

"Huh? Understand what?"

Renee waited a while, building the drama. "He needs special care. But you wouldn't know about that, would you?" For the first time, Renee showed a little emotion. Her words were spoken with rising anger.

"I don't know what you mean." Karen bent down and picked up another shell. She rolled it nervously in her hand, staring into Renee's shadowy face, leaning forward to hear her tiny voice over the steady, insistent rush of the ocean.

"You don't know about Jerry's brother Todd? Well, Todd died." Renee watched Karen's face, pleased by Karen's shocked reaction to these words.

"I don't know much about Jerry," Karen said, not sure what she was supposed to say. "We all just met on Monday, remember?"

"Jerry and Todd were very close," Renee continued, ignoring Karen's words. "They were only a year apart. Todd was older. They were swimming.

Last summer. Somewhere off the Palisades. They were both good swimmers, but Jerry was better."

"Yes, he's a great swimmer," Karen interrupted. She knew she didn't want to hear the rest of this story. She thought she knew how it was going to come out. But there was no way to delay it, no way to stop Renee, who continued talking in her tiny voice, as if talking to herself, as if Karen weren't even there.

"There isn't much to tell. They were pretty far out in the ocean. It was the beginning of summer, just like now. There were no lifeguards, few people on the beach. Todd got some sort of leg cramp. He couldn't get back."

"Oh, how awful," Karen muttered. Without realizing it, she was suddenly reliving Wednesday afternoon, was suddenly back in the wet suit, struggling to swim away from the rocks, shouting and signaling desperately for Renee to help her, feeling the panic overwhelm her, feeling the terror freeze every muscle as she crashed into the rocks again, and again, as Renee ignored her pleas, as Renee continued to snorkel.

"Jerry tried to get to Todd in time," Renee continued, looking out at the ocean now. "But he didn't make it."

"You mean — "

"Todd drowned. Jerry watched him go down." Renee was reciting the words in a flat, toneless voice. "Jerry pulled him back to shore, just the way he pulled you yesterday. But he was too late. Too late. Jerry refused to believe it. He kept pushing on Todd's chest, blowing into his mouth. They had to pull Jerry away. He wouldn't let go of his brother. He just refused to accept the fact that his brother was dead."

"Were you . . . were you with him then?" Karen asked, staring out at the black ocean.

"I was with him. It was so terrible," Renee said, her voice catching. She pulled her windbreaker tighter around her. "Jerry felt so guilty. He thought he should have saved Todd. He thought it was his fault. Of course that was crazy. But that's what he thought."

Karen wanted to say something but couldn't think of anything appropriate. It was such a sad, frightening story.

The two girls stood silently staring out into the darkness, listening to the splash of the waves. "Why did you tell me this?" Karen asked finally.

Renee laughed, a strange, inappropriate laugh. Then she turned to Karen and, in a cold, hard voice, said, "I just wanted you to know that Jerry and I have been through some hard times together, and I'm not going to give him up so easily."

The words stung Karen like a spray of salt water. To her surprise, she felt angry. Renee was using the story of Todd's death, using it to threaten Karen, using it to hold onto Jerry.

"That's kind of up to Jerry — isn't it?" she asked, surprised by her own boldness, by the depth of her angry feelings.

Renee didn't say anything. She swept the windbreaker around her shoulders and strode back to the camp fire in a near run.

Karen let herself in silently, carefully clicking the door behind her so as not to wake up Ann-Marie. The hall light was on, the living room dark. The clock by the window said 1:21.

Yawning softly, Karen started to tiptoe past Ann-Marie's room. To her surprise, the door was open and the desk lamp was on.

"Ann-Marie — are you up?" she called, her voice hoarse, probably from the damp ocean air.

No reply.

"Ann-Marie?"

Karen felt weary from head to foot. Every muscle ached as she stepped to the doorway of Ann-Marie's room.

To her surprise, the room was empty. Ann-Marie wasn't there. The bed was still made. Wrinkled shorts and some clean T-shirts and tops were strewn across it.

That's weird, Karen thought. Had Ann-Marie mentioned going out? No. She hadn't.

Earlier, Ann-Marie had said she was tired, too tired to come to the beach party. So where could she be at 1:30 in the morning?

Without thinking about it, Karen picked up Ann-Marie's best silk blouse from the bed. Yawning, she folded it neatly and carried it over to the white dresser.

She shouldn't leave this out, Karen thought.

Ann-Marie had always been so neat. When did she become as sloppy as Karen?

Karen realized maybe she didn't know her old friend as well as she thought she did.

She pulled open the top dresser drawer. It was filled with socks and underwear. She closed it and pulled out the second drawer.

This was the right drawer for blouses and tops. She started to lay the silk blouse into the drawer when something caught her eye.

What's that?

She pushed away some sleeveless T-shirts.

Her hand trembling, she picked up what she had discovered underneath.

It was a can of black spray paint.

Chapter 13

Karen knew it was a dream, but she couldn't get out of it.

She was back in the purple water, in her wet suit and snorkel mask. The water was cold and thick as Jell-O. The air hose seemed to be clogged. She had to push so hard to breathe.

Wake up, she told herself. Wake up out of this nightmare.

She knew that's what it was. But she had to keep swimming, had to keep struggling against the powerful current.

I can't move, she thought. The water is holding me, holding me back.

And suddenly a wave reached up out of the ocean, a wave darker than the waters around it, a wave as tall as a building, and lifted her up. "No!" she cried in the dream. "Put me down! Let me go!"

The jagged, brown rock loomed up like a porpoise leaping from a pool. And the wave sent Karen crashing onto the rock. She hit hard. She could feel the jolt. She could hear her wet suit ripping, a frightening sound, like a lobster being torn apart. She could see the sharp points of the rock shred the suit.

Wake up, wake up!

But the wave lifted her again, and once again heaved her onto the rock, which now had long needles like a cactus, needles that pierced her torn suit and pierced her skin. She cried out as blood began to seep through the holes in the suit, her blood, trickling out through the suit, puddling on the prickly rock.

Frantically she tore at the suit. She had to pull it off. She had to free herself from it.

She struggled free of it at last and tossed it into the churning ocean. She was in her bathing suit now. She looked toward the beach. She could see her beach umbrella sticking up in the sand. The beach umbrella had been cut to shreds. Broken light glinted menacingly off the sunglasses she'd left there.

How did that happen? Who did that?

And then the wave returned, lifted her high, and slammed her onto the rock, which was now much bigger and glowing like a black jewel.

That sound again, that terrifying ripping sound. This time it wasn't her suit being slashed. It was her skin.

She screamed, as she saw her skin tear apart, her side opening up, the bones of her ribs poking out through the gaping hole.

Wake up! Wake up! This dream has got to end!

She tried to stop screaming; she tried to dive into the water. But the wave was too powerful. It heaved her back onto the rock, tearing her skin, splitting it like an envelope being opened, and all her bones were showing now, and the top of her skull, gray as death, poked through her forehead.

And all she could do was scream.

And wake up.

She sat straight up in bed.

Finally. I finally got out of it. I finally woke myself up. It was such a struggle.

Such a struggle just to breathe.

Why am I fighting against the current in my sleep?

She waited for the dream to go away, for the ugly pictures to fade. She waited to forget it, the way she forgot most of her dreams. But it wouldn't go away, not the pictures, nor the sounds, nor the fear.

She could see it all as clearly now as when she was asleep.

And she had the same urge to scream, scream her lungs out at the black sky.

The sheet was hot and soaked with perspiration. She untangled herself from it and kicked it away. She climbed out of bed quickly, hoping to leave the dream behind. But it followed her as she made her way to the closet in the dark and pulled on a light, cotton robe.

The clock said 7:30. Wide awake, still shaky from the vivid nightmare, she walked to the window and pressed her forehead against the cool glass. The sun, still low in the east, was trying to burn through the yellow morning haze.

She stood there for nearly a minute, the dream still replaying in her mind. Then she walked over to the dressing table and saw the can of spray paint. That's where she had left it when she carried it into her room last night.

Ann-Marie. She hadn't heard Ann-Marie come in. Was she there?

Carrying the can of spray paint, Karen stepped out into the dark hallway. Ann-Marie's door was closed. She walked over and silently turned the knob. The door squeaked quietly as she pushed it open. The room was dark. The blinds were closed.

When her eyes adjusted to the darkness, Karen saw that Ann-Marie was sleeping uncovered in the bed, her pajama top tangled at her waist.

How does she sleep without messing her hair up? Karen wondered. That's the advantage of a short hairdo, she decided. She felt her hair with her free hand. It was damp, a tangled mess.

She decided to let Ann-Marie sleep. She didn't really feel like confronting her over the paint can. She wanted to shake the images of the nightmare from her mind before she did anything.

But as Karen turned to leave, Ann-Marie stirred noisily and looked up. "Karen?" Her eyes only half open, her face filled with confusion.

"Sorry," Karen whispered. "Go back to sleep. I didn't mean to wake you."

"What time is it?" Ann-Marie's voice was still choked with sleep.

"It's early. Really. Go back to sleep."

"I got in so late," Ann-Marie said, yawning. She

sat up and rubbed her eyes. Then she stared at Karen. "You okay? You look *terrible*."

"I had a bad dream," Karen said, leaning back against the door. "A really bad dream. Where'd you go last night?"

"Oh. Just out. Main Street."

"I was surprised," Karen said, rolling the paint can between her hands. "You said you were tired and — "

"I don't know. I got bored," Ann-Marie said. "So I went for a walk. I met some kids I knew, and we went to this club on Main Street. It was fun."

"Kids you knew?"

"Yeah. People from school I hadn't seen since I moved east. Did you have a good time with Jerry?"

"Sort of." She *had* until Renee showed up. But she didn't feel like getting into that with Ann-Marie.

"What's that in your hand?" Ann-Marie asked, squinting.

Karen turned on the light. "Don't you recognize it?"

"Huh?"

"I found it in your dresser drawer." Karen moved closer, holding up the can so Ann-Marie could see it better.

Ann-Marie looked very confused. "My dresser drawer? How come you were in my dresser?"

"I was putting something away for you, and I found this."

"A paint can? It isn't mine."

Karen stared hard at her friend, remembering other times, unpleasant times when Ann-Marie's jealousy had made it hard for them to be friends.

"Really," Ann-Marie insisted. "What would I be doing with a can of paint?"

"I think this is the paint that was used on our wall," Karen said, tossing it from hand to hand.

Ann-Marie's mouth dropped open. She held the shocked pose for a short while. "Then how did it get in my dresser? Who put it there? I thought Renee sprayed that message on the wall."

"But Renee hasn't been in this apartment," Karen said, putting the paint can down on Ann-Marie's dresser. "Has she?"

"I don't think so," Ann-Marie said, looking very bewildered. "You don't think that I — "

"No, of course not." Karen decided to deny her suspicions. She realized it was silly to accuse her old friend. Ann-Marie looked genuinely confused, genuinely innocent. Someone had planted that can there. But who? How? "It's such a mystery."

"Really," Ann-Marie said, sliding back onto her pillow, still not totally awake. "What are we going to do today?"

Karen frowned. Was Ann-Marie changing the subject? "I thought we'd hang out at the beach, work on our tans," Karen said, watching her friend.

Ann-Marie groaned. "Another day at the beach? Can't we do something else?"

"I don't get it," Karen said. "If you don't want to spend time on the beach, why'd you come out to L.A.?"

"To see you," Ann-Marie said.

Karen suddenly felt about two inches tall. Ann-

Marie was being a good friend. And what was Karen doing? Suspecting her of doing terrible things, and trying to bully her into spending her time where she didn't want to. With her light hair and fair skin, Ann-Marie had never been a big beach fan. Karen scolded herself for not remembering that.

"I'm sorry," she said. "Maybe we could drive somewhere today. Maybe we could — " But then she remembered. "Oh, no. I forgot."

"What is it?" Ann-Marie asked.

"I made a date with Jerry for this afternoon. To go roller-skating on the boardwalk."

"Oh." Ann-Marie didn't try to hide her disappointment. "I see."

"I'm really sorry — " Karen started. "You could come with us, maybe, and — "

But Ann-Marie interrupted her. "Guess I'll go back to sleep."

She rolled onto her side, her back to Karen. Feeling very guilty, Karen tiptoed out of the room and closed the door.

Karen looked at her watch for about the hundredth time. Jerry was over half an hour late. She was wearing a short pink skirt over black bicycle tights and a white midriff top, and carrying her skates, pacing impatiently back and forth by the spot on the boardwalk where they had agreed to meet.

It was a beautiful, warm Saturday afternoon, the warmest day of the summer so far, and the boardwalk was crowded and noisy. Skaters and skateboarders in skimpy summer outfits rolled by. Boom boxes blared. People crowded the shops. Beyond the T-shirt shop, a woman in a gold sarong with a matching gold bandanna on her head was giving crystal massages, demonstrating the healing power of a large, sparkling crystal. Further down, two lanky high-school boys wearing jeans and matching Def Leppard T-shirts were having their high-tops whitened by a man with a brush and a large bottle of white polish. Kites were flying. A bald-headed dwarf in Day-Glo green baggies was darting back and forth between the shops, offering to let people touch his head for good luck at a dollar a touch.

A typical day on Ocean Front Walk in Venice.

Normally, Karen would have enjoyed the spectacle, the color, the noise, and the sheer nuttiness of it all.

But it was hard to enjoy it when you were wondering if someone was going to show up or not, and worrying about where he could be, and what was taking him so long.

Suddenly someone caught her eye at the T-shirt store. He was standing at a rack of wildly colored shirts, which swayed in the gentle afternoon breeze, and staring back at her.

Mike.

Yes, it was Mike.

As soon as he realized she was looking at him, he turned away, then ducked behind the rack of shirts.

He must be really mad at me, Karen thought.

Well . . . good.

She walked a bit further away from the T-shirt store so she wouldn't have to think about him. Ahead of her, a group of three jugglers were tossing a dozen colored balls into the air. A boy and a girl zoomed past her on unicycles, laughing and holding hands as they zigzagged through the crowd.

Where *is* he?

Karen draped the skates over her shoulder. Is he coming or not? Is he standing me up?

Maybe he's with Renee, she thought, frowning. What am I doing here, anyway?

Then she saw him hurrying toward her, waving to her and smiling, and she immediately forgot her impatience, her doubts. He was wearing white tennis shorts and a shiny blue, sleeveless T-shirt. His dark hair was blown back, as if he'd been running hard. His skates were flung over his broad shoulders.

He looks gorgeous, she thought.

He caught up to her, dodging a couple of skateboarders, and stopped. "Sorry," he said, out of breath. "I got hung up."

"That's okay," she said. But then, realizing he hadn't given much of an excuse, added, "Hung up?"

"Yeah. I had to see someone." He looked uncomfortable. It was obvious to Karen whom he had to see.

"How's she doing?" Karen asked.

"I don't want to talk about Renee," Jerry said quickly, his face reddening.

"Okay," she replied. There was no reason to pursue the matter. "Want to skate?"

He smiled. "Sure. Come on. I'll race you to the pier!"

The skating date stretched on long after they were tired of skating. They amused themselves on the boardwalk, walking hand in hand, pretending they were sightseers from out of town. They had dinner at a greasy taco stand that advertised an "Amazing Two-For-One Sale," which turned out to be Eat Two, Get One Free. Only, as Jerry pointed out, no one in his right mind would eat two of them!

Then, as the flamingo-pink sun began to descend, they sat down in the warm sand, their arms around each other, to watch the sunset. Karen leaned against Jerry, feeling warm and secure, and very happy. They kissed.

She couldn't believe it when she looked at her watch and it said nine o'clock. "Jerry — I've got to get back before Ann-Marie calls the police!"

He laughed and pulled her back onto the sand. "Come on — it's still early."

"No. Really. She's my guest. I'm being so rude."

"Be rude a little longer," he pleaded.

But she finally persuaded him to walk her home. At the door to her building, they threw their arms around each other and kissed, long and hard. As if we might not see each other again, Karen thought.

What a weird thought.

Karen, it's not like you to be insecure, she told herself.

As if reading her thoughts, Jerry said, "Don't worry about Renee. I'll talk to her. She and I have been through a lot together." His throat seemed to catch on these words. "She'll understand. She'll understand that it's over between her and me."

Karen kissed him again and ran inside.

She pushed open the door, prepared to apologize to Ann-Marie, to fall to her knees and beg forgiveness if necessary. But to her surprise, Ann-Marie wasn't home. A note on the refrigerator read, *I went out with some friends. Don't wait up. A.M.*

Karen stared at the note, then crumpled it up and tossed it into the wastebasket. She knew she had no right to be, but she found herself a little annoyed that Ann-Marie was never home. I'll make a point of spending tomorrow with her, she told herself.

She paced around the apartment for a while, unsure of what to do with herself, thinking about Jerry, feeling excited and happy.

He's such a great guy, she thought. Mainly, he's so *nice*. He's just so nice. Staring out the window toward the dark beach, she decided that nice was nice.

She sat down in the living room and read for a bit, trying to calm down. Then she listened to a few CDs, lying on the shaggy, white rug on the floor, staring up at the cathedral ceiling.

Finally, she felt tired enough to go to sleep. Yawning, she wrote Ann-Marie a note, saying, *Tomorrow is our day together*, and put it up on the refrigerator.

How did people ever communicate before refrigerator magnets? she wondered.

She got undressed, tossing her clothes on the armchair beside the bed, and pulled on a short nightgown. It was warm in the room, even with the window open, so she decided she didn't need the nightgown after all.

Tossing it onto the pile of clothes, she stretched, her bones cracking. She had gone from being so peppy that she couldn't sit still straight to being totally exhausted.

She turned out the lamp on the bedtable and slid into bed.

Whatever it was in bed with her was cold, and very wet, and very slimy.

Karen screamed.

And struggled to get out.

But the wet slime stuck to her arms and back and the back of her neck.

She screamed again.

And lurched out of bed, banging her knee on the bedtable.

So slimy. So cold. All down her back.

She nearly knocked over the lamp, struggling to turn it on.

Finally the light clicked on.

And she saw that her bed was filled with jellyfish.

When Ann-Marie walked in a few seconds later, Karen was still screaming.

Chapter 14

The two girls stayed up all night. It took a long time to scoop the disgusting jellyfish into a wastebasket, dump them into the garbage outside, and remove the bed linens.

"Just throw the sheets away!" Karen had cried, still hysterical. "Throw everything away!"

Even after clean linens had been put on, the sour, fishy smell remained in the apartment. "I can't sleep in that bed tonight," Karen said, shuddering.

In the small kitchen, Ann-Marie poured water from the kettle. She was silently making Karen a cup of hot herbal tea. "You can sleep in my bed," she said quietly, dunking her tea bag. "I'll take the couch."

"No, I won't be able to sleep anywhere," Karen replied angrily. "Who would *do* such a thing? It's . . . just so *disgusting!*"

"It had to be Renee, I guess," Ann-Marie said. "Do you take sugar?"

"What are you doing?" Karen asked.

"Making you a cup of tea."

"Tea? What for? I'm not sick!"

"I just thought — "

"Well, forget it." Karen paced to the window and back.

"I know you're upset, but you don't have to take it out on me," Ann-Marie protested, taking a sip of tea. She put the cup down quickly, having burned her tongue.

"How did Renee get in here?" Karen demanded. "The apartment was locked, right?"

"The window was open," Ann-Marie said, pointing to it. "She could've climbed in. You know, I saw her today."

"What?"

"In fact, I had kind of a fight with her. I wasn't going to tell you because I didn't want to upset you."

"Go ahead," Karen said, "tell me. I couldn't be any more upset."

"Well, I ran into her on Main Street, right after lunch. She immediately launched into this attack on you, about how you were trying to steal Jerry from her."

"That's what she said?"

"Yeah," Ann-Marie said. "She said a lot of crazy things. She said you were looking for trouble and didn't have any idea just how much trouble."

"She was making threats?" Karen felt sick.

"Yeah. I'd call them threats," Ann-Marie said, rolling her eyes. "It was unbelievable. She was screaming at me. I couldn't get her to shut up. I mean, people were looking at us."

"So what did you do?"

"Finally I just said, 'Renee, I'm Ann-Marie — not Karen.' And I walked away."

"How awful."

"Yes, it was. I was really upset. I mean, Renee was really losing it."

"But she had no right to scream at you because of me. I'm going over there right now," Karen decided. "I'm going to have it out with her once and for all."

"Karen, sit down. It's nearly three in the morning." Ann-Marie walked over, took Karen by the shoulders, and guided her back to the couch. "You've got to try to calm down."

"Calm down?! Did you see that disgusting pile of slime in my bed? I'll never calm down! Never!"

"Karen — this isn't like you — "

"What is she going to do to me next? That girl is sick, Ann-Marie. She's really sick. Where does she live?"

"She's staying with a friend in Santa Monica, remember? She told us the address that first night at RayJay's."

"Oh, yeah. I remember." Karen jumped up and headed to her bedroom. "Ugh. The smell. Are you sure all the windows are open? I'm going to have nightmares about jellyfish for the rest of the summer!"

"Listen, chill out, okay? Wait till morning. Then we'll go over to Renee's together if you like."

"Well . . . maybe you're right," Karen agreed. She walked over to the counter and picked up the cup of tea. She took a sip and made a face. "Needs sugar. You want a cup?"

"Yeah, I guess," Ann-Marie sighed.

They stayed up talking for another hour. Then Ann-Marie went to bed, and Karen tried to get to sleep on the living room couch. Staring up at the shifting lights and shadows on the ceiling, she saw the pink-and-purple jellyfish again, saw them glistening so wetly on her sheet, felt the cold stickiness on the back of her neck — and sat up with a jolt, about to scream again.

Get a grip on yourself, Karen, she scolded herself. This is exactly the way Renee wants you to react.

She lay back down, struggling to get comfortable, but it was hopeless. When the sky started to lighten, Karen was still wide awake. She went to the window, settled herself on the sill, and watched the sun come up.

At eight she went into her room, pulled on a pair of straight-legged jeans and a maroon sweatshirt, gave her hair a few careless swipes with a brush, and silently sneaked out of the apartment.

I don't need Ann-Marie to come with me, she thought. I've given her enough grief already. This is supposed to be her vacation, after all.

It's supposed to be mine, too, she thought, suddenly feeling very sorry for herself.

She had a sudden impulse to call Jerry, to tell him what Renee had been doing to her — the whispered phone calls, the spray-painted warning on the wall, and now the disgusting pile of jellyfish. And of course it was obvious that Renee had tried to drown her on Wednesday in the ocean. She wanted to tell Jerry everything, to let him know what Renee was really like.

But no. This was between Renee and her.

Jerry had promised that he would tell Renee it was all over between them, that he was interested in Karen now. But Karen knew she could no longer leave it to Jerry.

Renee had gone too far. Karen couldn't sit around and let herself be victimized any longer.

The morning air was chilly and wet as she hopped down the steps, searching her jeans pocket for her car keys. She let the car warm up for a few minutes. To her surprise, she didn't feel the least bit tired despite not having any sleep at all during the night.

Anger can give you real energy, she thought.

If that were true, she figured she had enough energy to keep going for *days*!

Looking in the rearview mirror at the still-deserted street, she put the car in drive, and headed toward Santa Monica. Where is everybody? she wondered, then remembered that it was Sunday morning. Who in her right mind would be out on the street at eight on a Sunday morning?

Only us angry lunatics.

There was no traffic at all, so the drive was short. The house, Karen remembered, was off Ocean Park Boulevard. Renee had spent some time describing it in detail that night, mainly because she had never stayed in a house that was painted pink with powder-blue trim.

The house shouldn't be hard to find, Karen thought, slowing down. She passed a small, triangular green park, then spotted the house between Second and Third Streets.

She pulled over to the curb, cut the engine, and stared up at the narrow, two-story house. This had to be it. It was definitely pink with blue trim.

She took a deep breath and climbed out of the car. This will all be over in a couple of minutes, she told herself.

As she walked up to the powder-blue front door, she was suddenly filled with doubts. What am I doing here? Why am I here? What am I going to say to her?

But the salt smell of the ocean in the morning air brought back the sight and feel of the jellyfish. And the reminder of the horror of the night before pushed her forward with renewed anger.

She started to knock on the door but, to her surprise, saw that it was open a few inches. She peered in through the crack. It was dark inside.

Just then the front door of the next house opened, and a balding, middle-aged man in striped pajamas stepped out onto his front stoop. He bent down to pick up the Sunday *L.A. Times* and, seeing Karen, smiled and nodded. "Nice morning," he said.

"Yeah, I guess." Karen wasn't in the mood to chat.

"They say it's going to be a hot one." Then, groaning over the weight of the enormous paper, he disappeared back into his house.

His appearance unnerved Karen somewhat. It was so unexpected. She started to knock again, then changed her mind and called into the house. "Renee — are you there?"

No reply.

Karen pushed the front door open a bit wider. The door squeaked as she pushed it. "Renee? Renee?"

Silence.

Karen stepped into the small entryway. She peeked into the dark living room. No one there. The room was furnished with chrome-and-white-leather easy chairs and an enormous, circular glass coffee table, all very expensive-looking.

"Renee? Anybody home?"

Silence.

"Renee — I want to talk to you!"

She walked quickly through a short hallway and into the kitchen in the back. This room was brighter since the sun was pouring in through the window.

Karen's eyes lit on the sink, piled high with dirty, white china dishes and bowls. Then she saw a half-eaten sandwich on a plate and an open bottle of Coke on the Formica and butcher-block island in the middle of the room.

Then her eyes wandered down to the floor, and she saw two bare feet, the toes pointing up.

Her breath caught in her throat.

She walked closer.

"Renee?"

She peered around the island and saw a girl lying on her back, her mouth open in a frozen O of horror, her eyes wide, unmoving, staring up at the ceiling.

"Renee?"

She was wearing shorty pajamas.

"Renee?"

Her frizzy hair circled her head, standing straight out at the sides. There was an enormous bump on her forehead.

Karen reached down and touched Renee's arm. It was cold. As cold as death.

Renee was dead.

Karen dropped the limp, cold arm and stood up. She took a deep breath and prayed that she wouldn't start screaming.

Chapter 15

The police station, with its lime-green cinderblock walls and glass brick separators, had a California flair to it. It was brightly lit, carpeted, and had two miniature palm trees guarding the double-doored glass entranceway, not at all the stereotypical police station of movies or TV.

As she sat on the green plastic bench, waiting her turn to be questioned, Karen would have preferred the more traditional dark, dingy station house. She wanted everything to be gray, even black. She wanted to close her eyes and disappear into darkness, disappear from this nightmare.

How could this be happening?

She had called the L.A.P.D. immediately, pushing 911, with fingers that wouldn't stop trembling. She had told the officers who arrived a few minutes later everything — who the girl lying on the floor was, how she had happened to find her, how she happened to know her. The friend Renee had been staying with wasn't there. She was out of the country for the whole summer, and the police had ruled Renee's friend out.

There really wasn't much more Karen could tell. She had no idea who murdered Renee.

They had already questioned Jerry for more than an hour. Now Ann-Marie was in there being grilled. Karen was next. But why? What more could she tell them?

What good would more questions do? All the questions in the world couldn't bring back Renee. All of the questions in the world couldn't remove the picture of Renee's body in the kitchen from Karen's mind, a picture she knew she would be seeing again and again for the rest of her life.

She had been sitting there on the bench, staring at the unlikely palm trees for about twenty minutes, when her mother arrived, frantic as usual, with her lawyer Ross Garland. "Karen — what on earth? This is so horrible," her mother said, dropping down onto the bench beside her. "Are you all right?"

"I guess," Karen said. What could she say? That she saw Renee's pale, white body every time she closed her eyes?

Mr. Garland started to say something, but the door opened, and Ann-Marie came hurrying out, looking as flushed as her pink T-shirt, and very frightened.

"They think I did it! I know they do!" she exclaimed to Karen, ignoring everyone else.

"Ann-Marie — what do you mean? How can they?" Karen's mother demanded.

"Oh. Hi, Mrs. Mandell," Ann-Marie said, barely

looking at her. "Some friend of Renee's saw me fighting on Main Street with Renee yesterday afternoon. When they heard about what happened to Renee on the radio, they phoned the police. I tried to explain to them that I had no reason to kill Renee. I hardly knew her! But they think I did it! I know they do!"

"Calm down," Mr. Garland said, putting a hand gently on Ann-Marie's shoulder. "The police are a little more sophisticated than that."

"Thank you," said a deep voice. Everyone looked up to see a grim-faced police detective. He was young-looking with blond hair and narrow blue eyes set close together. He was wearing dark brown, pleated slacks and a short-sleeved, white shirt with a dark blue necktie pulled down a few inches over an unbuttoned collar.

"I'm Detective Franklin," he said, looking at Karen's mother. He turned to Ann-Marie. "We don't think you did it," he told her. "We're questioning everyone we can. But you're not a suspect."

Ann-Marie didn't seem to believe him. "That's what the police always say before they spring a trap."

"This isn't TV," he said brusquely. "Sometimes I wish it were."

A tall, uniformed lieutenant came walking by. "Have you reached the girl's parents?" Detective Franklin asked.

"Not yet. They're in Europe, somewhere outside Paris. We're still working on it. The victim's cousin is coming up from Anaheim."

Franklin nodded. He looked down at Karen. "You're next."

"This is my mother and our attorney, Mr. Garland," Karen said, climbing to her feet, surprised by how shaky her legs felt.

"Why don't you wait out here and have a cup of coffee?" Franklin told Mrs. Mandell. "The machine has surprisingly good coffee." He motioned for Karen and the attorney to follow him.

His office was small but cheerful. He had a large, psychedelic-style Grateful Dead poster behind his desk and several thriving, hanging vines over his window. He didn't wait for Karen and Garland to sit down before he began firing questions at Karen.

"How long did you know Renee Watson? When did you meet? Why were you at her house this morning? If you just met her last Monday, how did you know where she lived? Had you been there before? How well do you know her boyfriend?"

Karen answered the questions as best as she could, staring hard at the orange-and-green poster behind the detective. As she replied, several of her own questions ran through her mind: Should I tell him about the jellyfish? Should I tell him how I almost drowned because of her? Should I tell him how I feel about Jerry, how Jerry planned to break up with her because of me?

She decided no. What good would it do to tell the police detective about any of that? It would only make it look as if Karen had a real motive for killing Renee. It would only make Karen a serious suspect in the murder. And since Karen knew she wasn't the murderer, she decided it would serve no useful purpose to reveal those things.

"How well do you know Jerry Gaines?"

"Not very well. I met him last Monday, too. I've seen him a few times since."

"On dates?"

"Not really. I knew he was dating Renee."

"But you were attracted to him?"

"A little."

I'm doing okay, Karen thought. This isn't so hard. It would be a lot harder if I really had something to hide.

The questioning went on for nearly twenty minutes. It became hot and stuffy in Detective Franklin's small office, but he made no move to open the window or turn on the air conditioner. He kept asking the same questions again and again, reworking them, then asking them again.

He's trying to trip me up, Karen realized. He's looking for an inconsistency. He's really pretty clever.

When he finally led her back to the front waiting room, she felt exhausted. Ann-Marie and her mother were seated side by side on the green bench, talking quietly.

"I've got to get home. I'm missing my son's birthday party," Garland said, looking anxiously at his watch.

"It was so nice of you to hurry over on a Sunday," Mrs. Mandell said, getting up and taking Garland's hand.

"Don't worry," Garland told Karen, starting toward the double doors. "Try to forget about it. I know that's not easy. But try." And he disappeared out the door.

Before the door could close, two uniformed officers pushed through it. They were grappling with a young man, who was obviously displeased about having to accompany them. "Let go of me!" Karen heard the young man growl, and she recognized the voice before she saw the face.

It was Vince.

"You've got no right," he was shouting. "Why are you bringing me here?" One of the officers gave Vince a hard shove toward Detective Franklin's office. Vince nearly stumbled, but the other policeman caught him by the arm.

"I didn't do anything," Vince protested.

"Then you won't mind answering a few questions," the first policeman said.

For a brief second, Vince turned and his eyes caught Karen's. He didn't seem to recognize her. Maybe he was pretending not to. Maybe he was concentrating so hard on his struggles with the policemen, he didn't see her.

Karen felt a chill run through her body. Vince disappeared into Detective Franklin's office. The door was slammed behind him.

Did Vince kill Renee?

She didn't realize that her mother was tugging on her sleeve. "This is a little too much real life for me," Mrs. Mandell said. "Come home with me now?"

"Hey, do I look *that* bad?" Karen asked, still thinking about Vince.

"You don't look good," Mrs. Mandell said in her usual, maddeningly direct way.

"I . . . uh . . . didn't sleep well last night," Karen told her. She looked at Ann-Marie, who still looked pale and shaken. "But I think we'll go back to Daddy's," Karen said. "He's expecting us."

"Where is your father, anyhow?" Mrs. Mandell asked, suddenly remembering her former husband's existence. "Why isn't he here?"

"I called you instead," Karen said, thinking quickly. "You know how Daddy is in an emergency."

Mrs. Mandell seemed to find that a reasonable excuse for his absence. Karen secretly breathed a sigh of relief. "Ann-Marie and I are going to try to enjoy the rest of our month together," she told her mother.

Mrs. Mandell looked at her doubtfully. "If only you didn't look so terrible. I really wish you'd come home with me. Both of you."

For a brief second, Karen considered it. It would be nice to be safe and cozy back home with her mother to take care of them. But no. She wanted to see Jerry. She *had* to see Jerry, to see how he was taking this, to make sure he was okay. He must be terribly, terribly upset. After all, he and Renee had been going together for years.

She wondered if Jerry had any idea who might have killed her.

She wondered what he had told the police.

"No, thanks, Mom," she said, and draped her arms around her mother in a long hug. "Ann-Marie and I will go back to Venice. But I'll call you tonight. Promise."

The three of them walked quickly out of the police station. The fresh afternoon air felt good on Karen's face. She took a deep breath and stretched. Having no sleep the night before was beginning to catch up with her.

They said good-bye to Mrs. Mandell, who, still looking very worried, headed to her car. Karen had parked the Mustang a few blocks in the other direction.

She and Ann-Marie were only half a block from the police station, walking slowly, silently, just glad to be outdoors, when a tall, red-haired girl in white denim jeans and an orange top that clashed with her hair, stepped in front of them on the sidewalk.

"Are you Karen?" she asked, looking at Karen with a nervous expression on her face, her large, dark eyes darting back and forth between Karen and Ann-Marie.

"Yes," Karen answered uncertainly. "How did you know my name?"

"It doesn't matter," the girl said mysteriously. "I just want to warn you to stay away from Jerry."

"What?" Ann-Marie cried, appearing more startled than Karen.

"Who *are* you?" Karen asked angrily. "Are *you* his girlfriend, too?!"

"I don't want to make a scene," the girl said, ignoring Karen's questions. "Just — please — " and her dark eyes brimmed with tears as she started to plead — "please stay away from Jerry. I'm . . . warning you."

She turned and hurried away, taking long, quick strides across the sidewalk.

But Karen ran after her, caught up, and stepped in front of her. "Who are you? Answer me. Why are you warning me? Who are you?"

The girl shook her head, her red hair quivering about her face. Finally, she said, "I'm Jerry's sister." She ducked past Karen and started to run.

"Well, Jerry's old enough to make his own decisions!" Karen shouted after her. She started to chase her, but Ann-Marie held her back.

"Come on. We've got to get home. Enough," Ann-Marie said softly.

Karen was still breathing hard, her eyes following the girl until she disappeared around the corner. "Why would Jerry's sister be waiting here for me? It doesn't make any sense."

"Nothing makes any sense," Ann-Marie said. "Nothing at all. Do you think she's the one who's been trying to frighten you away from Jerry? Not Renee?"

An even more frightening thought crossed Karen's mind.

"Do you think Jerry's sister killed Renee?"

"Huh?"

Karen hadn't realized she was talking out loud. "Just a thought."

They drove back, both of them chattering without stop about what had happened. It was almost as if they were afraid to be silent, afraid that silence would give them time to think, that if they could keep talking, keep tuned in to each other, they could shut the real horror out.

But Karen knew she couldn't shut it out for long. Every time she closed her eyes, she saw Renee again. Every few seconds, she was back in that kitchen, looking down at the bump on Renee's head, making the horrifying discovery all over again.

"I've never known anyone who died," Ann-Marie said, as Karen parked the Mustang across from the apartment house.

Karen climbed out of the car wearily. The sun was lowering itself behind the houses and apartment buildings on Speedway. The sky was red. All of the buildings looked red, as red as blood.

"I guess we should get some dinner," she said.

"I — I'm not very hungry," Ann-Marie told her, evening shadows darkening her face.

"Hi," a voice called. Jerry stepped away from the apartment house wall and walked toward them slowly, his hands in his jeans pockets.

It took Karen a moment to recognize him. His usually neat hair was windblown and standing on end. As he came close, Karen saw that his eyes were red-rimmed, his cheeks were puffy, as if he had been crying.

"Are you okay?" Karen asked.

He took her hand and squeezed it. His hand was ice-cold.

"Yeah, I'm okay, I guess."

He stood there, leaning toward her, staring at her, still holding her hand.

"I — I'm sorry," Karen stammered.

"I'm sorry you had to be the one to find her," Jerry said, his voice quavering. He let go of her hand and looked away.

"It's really terrible," Ann-Marie said awkwardly.

"I just can't believe it," Jerry said, still looking across the street. "I just talked to her last night, and today — "

"The police will find whoever did it," Ann-Marie said.

Jerry didn't respond for a long while. "What difference does it make?" He turned to Karen. "I just feel so guilty. I was going over there tonight to break up with her. And now — "

Karen raised a finger to his lips. "Shhh. You shouldn't feel guilty. You didn't do anything to feel guilty about." And then she added, "Oh. By the way, your sister stopped us when we came out of the police station."

"Huh?" Jerry's eyes narrowed in surprise.

"Your sister — she stopped me. She — "

He put a hand on her shoulder. "Karen — what are you talking about? I don't have a sister."

Chapter 16

"Do you think Vince killed her?" Karen asked.

She, Ann-Marie, and Jerry were sitting in the back booth at RayJay's. They had the entire row of booths to themselves, the restaurant uncrowded this early on a Sunday night. They had ordered a pizza, but none of them had much of an appetite.

Once or twice Karen had attempted to change the subject of discussion away from Renee. But they quickly realized it was pointless trying to talk about anything else. And again, talking about it, Karen realized, helped them to keep calm, to keep from falling apart and giving in to a strong feeling of terror that lurked just beyond their words.

"I don't know," Jerry said, tapping his long fingers on the Formica tabletop.

"Did Vince know Renee?" Ann-Marie asked, taking a small bite from her slice, then dropping it back on the plate.

"I think he followed her once on the boardwalk," Jerry said. "You know, whistled at her or something. But I don't think he really knew her."

"So he'd have no reason to kill her," Karen said, thinking about her motorcycle ride to Santa Monica with Vince.

Could she have been riding with a killer?

Could she be so attracted to a killer?

"He's a dangerous character," Jerry said, staring down at his pizza slice. "He could have done it — just for a thrill."

"No. He wouldn't do that," Karen said. The words just slipped out of her mouth before she had a chance to think about them.

"Well, the police thought he could have," Jerry replied, angry for some reason.

Karen was startled by the heatedness of his reply. "Sorry. I didn't mean — "

His expression immediately softened. He took her hand over the table. "No. I'm sorry. I don't know *what* I'm saying. I don't know anything. At first, I was so stupid — you know what I thought?"

"What?" Karen asked.

"I thought Renee committed suicide because of me. Because she knew I was going to break up with her. Do you know how awful I felt?" His voice cracked. His face reddened. He closed his eyes. "Pretty stupid, huh?"

"Jerry, please — "

"Well, the police must've thought I was pretty stupid," he continued, nervously picking at his slice of pizza. "When I sat down in that detective's office, I asked if Renee left a note. Can you imagine? Someone clubbed her to death, and I was asking if she left a suicide note!"

He laughed, a mirthless, painful laugh.

"Jerry, stop." Karen removed her hand from under his. "There's no point in torturing yourself. It won't do you any good to make yourself feel guilty over this."

"I guess you're right," he sighed. He leaned back against the red vinyl seat and closed his eyes.

"You've been awfully quiet," Karen said to Ann-Marie.

"I just can't believe I'm a murder suspect," Ann-Marie said softly, tugging at a short tangle of blonde hair. "I — I'd like to go home."

"Back to New York?"

"Yeah. But the detective said I can't leave town. Do you believe it?" She shredded her paper napkin between her hands and let the pieces flutter to the table.

"I'm sorry," Karen told her friend. "Now *I* feel guilty. You're a prisoner here. It was supposed to be a fun vacation, and — "

She stopped because something at the restaurant window caught her eye.

A boy. With straight brown hair.

He was staring at them from outside on the sidewalk, nose pressed against the window glass, shielding his eyes with both hands.

It took Karen a few seconds to recognize him. But she was sure she was right.

Mike!

Why was Mike watching them like that? What was he doing here?

Without saying a word to Ann-Marie or Jerry,

she climbed out of the booth and hurried up the aisle to the front door.

When he saw her coming, Mike's face filled with surprise, and he took off.

By the time Karen got to the sidewalk, he had disappeared.

Chapter 17

"I'm going for a walk. Want to come?"

Ann-Marie climbed to her feet and adjusted her bathing suit.

Karen sat up and looked around. The ocean was calm, the blue-green waves low and nearly as flat as a lake. Above them, two sea gulls swooped and climbed, wings outspread, a billowy white cloud for their background.

It was the next afternoon, and both girls had thought that a few hours of baking in the sun might help them relax. But Ann-Marie couldn't sit still.

"Well, are you coming?" Ann-Marie asked impatiently.

"No. Think I'll stay here." Karen settled back down on the beach blanket and closed her eyes. "Wake me up when you get back, okay?"

"Have you got suntan stuff on?" Ann-Marie asked, slipping a light cotton shirt over her bikini top. "The sun is pretty strong today."

"I don't need it. I want to burn for a while. Have a nice walk."

"Okay. Have a nice roast." Ann-Marie headed off in the direction of the Venice Pavilion, walking close to the shore, the water lapping over her feet.

Karen looked up at the sky through her sunglasses. The sea gulls and the cloud had disappeared. The sun was beginning to feel like a real summer sun.

She closed her eyes and saw Renee lying dead on the floor in the kitchen. Then she saw Vince being dragged into the police station. Then she saw Mike staring into the window at RayJay's.

If only I could close my eyes and just see *nothing*, she thought.

She had been up nearly the whole night. Renee had kept her up — poor, dead Renee.

Renee. Renee. Renee.

Renee probably would enjoy the fact that she was haunting Karen now.

What a wicked thing to think, Karen scolded herself.

Poor Renee.

She drifted into a light, troubled sleep. She was awakened a short time later by a hand on her shoulder. Sitting up with a start, she realized that her arm had fallen asleep.

"Hey."

She looked up, startled to see Vince staring down at her, smiling, the dimples deep in his cheeks. He was wearing faded cutoffs and no shirt. His chest was broad and hairless and tanned.

"Vince."

"Sorry. Did I scare you?"

Something about the smile on his face frightened her. He seemed secretly delighted that he had scared her.

"Vince, I didn't expect — "

"How you doing?" His smile faded. "You okay? I mean — "

"Yeah. I guess. I didn't sleep last night. Every time I close my eyes — "

"Come take a walk with me, okay?" he interrupted, reaching his hands down for her. He took her hands and started to pull her up.

He was stronger than Karen realized. He pulled her to her feet so easily, she felt frightened again.

He's strong enough to kill someone, she thought.

She shook her arm, trying to make it stop tingling.

"Come on. Just a short walk," he said, staring into her eyes. "Or will your *boyfriend* mind?" He sneered as he said the word boyfriend, making it sound like a term of pure disgust.

"Okay," she said hesitantly. "You don't have to pull my arms off."

He looked genuinely embarrassed. "Sorry." He turned and started walking down to the water, expecting her to follow.

She held back for a few seconds. What does he want? she asked herself. What if he really did kill Renee?

He couldn't have, she decided. His toughness, it's mostly an act. I can tell.

She jogged across the sand to catch up with him. "Ouch. The sand is really hot!" she cried, slipping and catching his arm to hold herself up.

"It'll be cooler down by the water," he said, staring out at the gently rippling ocean. A sailboat far out on the horizon seemed to be standing still, its sail a small white triangle against the blue sky.

She held onto him, the water splashing over their feet and legs as they walked. His arm felt solid, hard. He's like a rock, she thought.

I need a rock now. Someone solid. Someone to lean on.

Stop being stupid, Karen, she thought, shaking her head.

The cold spray felt good on her face. She closed her eyes and saw Renee.

"The police let you go?" she asked. A stupid question.

"Yeah, sure." He frowned and kicked at a shell with his bare foot, missing.

"I saw you there."

"I know."

He started walking a little faster. The beach curved to the right, past the line of brown rocks where she had nearly drowned. She looked back at the beach. It was nearly deserted here.

Where is he taking me? she thought, chilled more by her thoughts than by the cold spray off the ocean.

Maybe I don't want to walk too far with him.

"Did they ask you a lot of questions?" she asked, looking back at the lifeguard tower, which was now far in the distance.

"Yeah. A waste of time. My time and theirs."

"Well, why'd they bring you there?" she asked,

feeling stupid again. What she really wanted to ask was: Did you kill Renee?

"Whenever something bad happens, they find an excuse to bring me in. My pals, too."

"They do?"

"Yeah. They do. But the whole thing was a crock. I mean, I didn't even know the girl. And I wasn't anywhere near Santa Monica. I was right here in Venice. My buddies backed me up."

He stopped at a large piece of driftwood, a long log burned black and made smooth by the sea. He grinned at her, but it wasn't his usual relaxed grin. He looked nervous. "I don't look like a killer — do I?"

Karen laughed, a phony laugh. "Of course not." She wondered if she looked as nervous as he did. She could feel the fear begin to tighten her throat. Looking around, she realized they were the only ones in view.

Where was everybody? Why had he brought her here?

"That poor girl," she said, picturing Renee again.

"She and your boyfriend were . . . uh. . . ."

"He's not my boyfriend," Karen said, flustered. She knew she sounded like a ten-year-old. Why did Vince always make her feel so weird?

She was afraid of him. And she was attracted to him at the same time. He was just so different from anyone she'd ever known.

"Maybe we should start back," she said, trying not to reveal that she was frightened, but her voice sounded tight and high-pitched.

"Hey, look at that!" he cried, pointing to a splash of water out several dozen yards in the ocean. "Look — there it goes again."

She followed his gaze and saw a long silver fish leap out of the water.

"How pretty."

Without warning, he pulled her to him and wrapped his arms around her, pressing her against his warm, bare chest. He leaned his head down and kissed her.

Uttering a low, startled cry, she began to pull back. But she was overcome by a rush of feeling.

He was so warm. His chest felt so hard, so rock-solid hard.

He kissed her hungrily. He needed her.

And she needed him.

She kissed him back.

When the kiss was finished, she pushed herself away from him, her hands on his chest. He let her go, dropping his arms to his sides.

"Vince, what are we doing?"

He grinned, the deep dimples making him look so . . . devilish.

Karen felt terribly confused.

She thought about Jerry, so good-looking, so sensitive, and caring . . . so *nice*.

She stared at Vince, his short, spiky hair, the diamond stud in his ear, the bold, black tattoo on his hand.

How could she like two boys who were so totally different?

Vince moved toward her, about to pull her into

his arms again. But Karen raised her hands as if to shield herself from him. "No. I don't think so."

He stopped. He looked surprised.

"I'm feeling a little mixed up," she said, embarrassed.

"You have great eyes," he said.

"I think I just want to go back to my blanket now."

He started to protest, but quickly relented. "Okay." He started to lead the way.

"No." She didn't follow. "By myself. I'd just like to walk by myself for a while, try to figure things out. Or something."

He shrugged. "Tough times, huh?"

She couldn't decide if he was sincere or if he was making fun of her. "Listen, I'll see you, okay?"

"Yeah. Okay." He stood and watched her hurry off.

She started jogging across the sand, her heart pounding. She turned back once and saw that he hadn't moved from the spot near the driftwood. He waved, and she waved back and kept jogging.

It felt good to run, the warm sand so soft under her bare feet, the sun on her face, the air so warm and fresh. If only she could run and run and run — and not stop to think.

She saw her blanket up on the beach. Ann-Marie wasn't back yet. Karen decided to keep going. She jogged for another twenty minutes or so, until she was breathing hard, bathed in perspiration, her legs aching.

Where was Ann-Marie? Karen hoped she would

run into her heading back. Maybe she had gone up to the boardwalk.

Karen took several deep breaths and began walking back to the blanket. The slower speed allowed her thoughts to catch up with her. She relived the kiss with Vince. And that made her think of Friday night in Malibu, kissing Jerry in the shadow of that abandoned beach house.

With Renee looking on.

Was that only three nights before?

It seemed like a lifetime.

It *was* a lifetime, for Renee.

She dropped down on a beach blanket. Where was Ann-Marie? Karen looked up and down the beach but didn't see her.

She reached into her bag and pulled out the plastic bottle of suntan lotion. A folded-up slip of white paper fell onto the blanket. Curious, she put down the suntan lotion and picked up the paper, unfolding it quickly.

The typewritten words jumped out at her and then burned themselves into her eyes.

The same message was typed over and over again, in all capital letters, without any punctuation.

STAY AWAY FROM JERRY STAY AWAY FROM JERRY STAY AWAY FROM JERRY STAY AWAY FROM JERRY

Disgusted, Karen crumpled up the sheet of paper and tossed it down on the beach blanket.

Who could have put that in her beach bag?

She picked up the bottle of suntan lotion,

squeezed a white blob of it onto her shoulder, and started to massage it in.

The sudden stab of pain was so sharp, so overwhelming that at first she didn't recognize it as pain.

Her shoulder — her hand — they were burning, burning.

I'm on fire, she thought.

What were those hideous shrieks she heard?

Grabbing her shoulder in agony, Karen was in so much pain, she didn't realize that it was *she* who was screaming at the top of her lungs.

Chapter 18

Dr. Martinez put a hand gently on Karen's other shoulder and led her out of the examining room. "How does it feel now?" He smiled in that reassuring way that all doctors have, a closed-mouth smile beneath his black mustache.

"It aches a little," Karen said, disappointed that the pain hadn't completely gone away.

"It will continue to ache as it heals," the doctor said, nodding at a passing nurse. Her rubber heels squeaked down the long hospital corridor. "You were very lucky."

"Lucky?" Karen rolled her eyes.

"Well, you were lucky you only spread the cream on the one shoulder. If you had rubbed it over a larger portion of your body, the burn — "

He was interrupted by a young black man in a starched, green lab coat who appeared from around the corner, a clipboard in his hands. "Lab report," he said brusquely, shoving the clipboard into Dr. Martinez's hands.

Martinez frowned in concentration as he glanced

over the top sheet. "This is the analysis of what was in your suntan lotion bottle," he told Karen, still reading.

Karen had a stab of pain in her hand. She wanted to scratch it, but it was heavily bandaged. The palm had been pretty badly burned.

"Any of your friends into chemistry?" Dr. Martinez asked, handing the clipboard back to the lab assistant, who disappeared as quickly and as silently as he had arrived.

"No, I don't think so," Karen replied, confused.

"Well, somebody managed to mix a pretty good solution of hydrochloric acid into your lotion."

"Acid?"

"Yep. Do you know of anyone who might want to play a really cruel trick on you? A deadly trick?"

Deadly? The word made Karen shudder.

Who had done it? Who was there on the beach with her? Only Ann-Marie and Vince.

"Could it have been done in the store, by some crazy person? Or at the factory?" Karen suggested hopefully.

Please, please, don't let it be someone I know. Someone I like.

"Well, that's the first thing I would've said," Dr. Martinez said, walking her slowly down the long, white-walled corridor. "But the bottle is two-thirds empty."

"You mean — "

"I mean you've used it before, right? You've been using the lotion with no problem up to now."

"Yeah, that's right," Karen said, a sinking feeling

in her stomach. "I've been using it all month."

"So someone tampered with it recently," Dr. Martinez suggested. "Someone added the hydrochloric acid very recently."

"But who would do that to me?" Karen blurted out, her bandaged shoulder starting to burn and throb.

"I can't answer that," he said. "I think we have no choice but to call the police."

"The police?"

Karen's mind flashed back to Detective Franklin's office, to the endless questions, repeated over and over. "No, please."

"If we don't inform the police, we at least have to inform your parents. You're still a minor, and — "

"But my parents are away," Karen said. It was only half a lie. "They're . . . out of the country. I'm sort of on my own until they get back."

They were interrupted by a call for Dr. Martinez on the loudspeaker. "I've got to check on that," he said, pulling back the sleeve of his white coat to glance at his watch. "Stay right here, okay? We've got to settle this. Don't move. I'll be right back." He took off in a fast walk around the corner.

As soon as he was out of sight, Karen headed to the front reception area. I'm getting out of here, she told herself. She hated hospitals, the sterile look of them, the disgusting medicinal smells, the sick people walking the halls. She didn't want her mother to know about this. Mrs. Mandell would force Karen to come home. And she would find out that Karen had lied about her dad staying with them in Venice.

No. No way. And she certainly didn't want to see that police detective with his accusing blue eyes again, either.

"Hey, Karen — wait!"

She was past the reception desk, heading to the front doors.

"Karen!"

She kept going. She just wanted to get away.

A hand grabbed her good shoulder. She spun around, expecting a confrontation with Dr. Martinez. "Vince!" she cried. "I didn't know you were still here. I didn't think you'd wait."

He looked embarrassed. "Yeah, well. I wanted to see how you were."

"I'm okay, thanks to you," she said, giving him a warm smile. If he hadn't pulled her off the beach, gotten her onto the back of his motorcycle, and bombed off to the hospital at the speed of light, her burns might have been a lot more serious.

"What was it?"

The way he asked the question made her suspicious. Had he done it? Switched bottles, maybe?

No. Of course not. Don't get totally paranoid, she scolded herself. You can't start suspecting every single person you know. This boy came to your rescue. He wouldn't have done that if he had been the one trying to hurt you — would he?

She thought about the typewritten note with its repeated warning. What had she done with that note? Left it on the sand, probably.

Someone was getting serious about keeping her from Jerry. Was it the same person who had murdered Renee?

"Well?"

"Oh. Sorry." Karen was so lost in her own thoughts, she'd forgotten that Vince had asked her a question. "I don't know. Something wrong with the suntan lotion," she said. She tried to shrug but it sent a stab of pain down from her shoulder. "They're still testing it."

"What did the doctor say?" Vince asked.

"Just that it'll heal. I have to change the bandages every day. Keep it wrapped up. Keep it out of the sun. There goes my perfect tan. I guess you won't be interested in me anymore," she joked, giving him a sly smile.

"Who's interested?" He smiled back, revealing his dimples.

How can I be interested in him? Karen thought. He's not my type at all. My mom would have a fit if she knew I was hanging out with a *gang leader*. Vince's tattoo would probably give her the cold shakes for a month!

"I can go swimming in a few days, if I wear a wet suit," she said. "So I guess it's not too bad."

"Want a lift home?"

She suddenly felt extremely weary. The adrenalin rush from all the pain, all the terror was wearing off. "Yeah. That would be nice."

He drove almost carefully on the way to her apartment, only running a few lights and riding on the wrong side of the road for only a few blocks.

She guessed he was being careful because of her hand and shoulder.

She leaned forward as he drove the motorcycle through the late afternoon traffic, holding onto him with her one good hand, pressing her face against the back of his leather jacket.

He's someone to lean on, she thought. He's so solid. And he smells so good. She closed her eyes, hoping it might make the trip go faster. Or last forever. At this point, she didn't care which.

With her eyes closed, she pictured Renee, dead on the kitchen floor.

Poor, dead Renee.

Go away, Renee. Please — go away.

And then she pictured Ann-Marie.

Ann-Marie, where were you when I was burned? Ann-Marie.

Karen opened her eyes, but Ann-Marie's face stayed in her mind. A cold feeling spread over her body, and she knew it wasn't just from the rush of wind on her as they sped through the narrow Venice streets.

Ann-Marie had said she was going for a walk, but then never returned. Ann-Marie had shared the blanket with her. Never mind that. Ann-Marie had shared the apartment with her. Ann-Marie could have tampered with the suntan lotion at any time.

As Karen approached the apartment, the case against Ann-Marie grew in her mind. Where had Ann-Marie been spending her time, anyway? Karen had seen so little of her since she'd arrived. When Karen got the threatening call, Ann-Marie had been out. And then . . . and then . . . the can of spray paint in Ann-Marie's dresser drawer. The jellyfish in the bed. It would be easier for Ann-Marie to put them there than anyone else. She had a key to the apartment, after all.

Suddenly Karen was remembering back, back before Ann-Marie moved east. She was remembering the jealous rages, always over one boy or another. Ann-Marie had always been jealous of Karen.

But was she jealous enough now to hurt Karen? Was she so desperate to have Jerry for herself?

It didn't make any sense.

Did it?

Vince screeched the motorcycle to a halt, almost sending Karen flying over the handlebars. "Whoa," he said, climbing off quickly. "Sorry."

Karen climbed off, her shoulder aching, and looked up at the apartment house. Home at last.

But who was that running out the front door?

It was Mike.

Mike?

Yes. Without a doubt. It was Mike.

Mike saw her, then immediately turned his face away, leaped over the low hedge, and took off, running at top speed.

That's odd, Karen thought. What on earth was Mike doing here? And why was he leaving in such a hurry?

Confused, she turned back to Vince, who was standing awkwardly with his large hands stuffed in his jeans pockets. "Thanks, Vince. For everything."

"Should I come in?"

144

"No. I'll be okay." She started up the concrete stairs. "Thanks again. You were great."

She turned back at the entranceway to the building. He was still standing there by his motorcycle, watching her, the golden afternoon sun on his face.

She gave him a weary wave and walked inside. The spray-painted wall hadn't been cleaned, even though the landlord had promised to take care of it. She sighed loudly as she passed it.

I just want to get into bed, she thought.

She turned the key, pushed open the door, and stepped into the living room.

What was that behind the armchair?

It was a pair of feet.

Ann-Marie's feet.

Lying on the floor.

"Ann-Marie?"

Why was she lying facedown on the floor?

Chapter 19

Karen's breath caught in her throat. She could feel the blood rushing to her head. Dizzy, she grabbed onto the side of the doorway.

No, no, no, she thought. And the picture of Renee haunted her once again.

"Ann-Marie?"

Ann-Marie stood up quickly. "Oh. Hi."

"Oh, thank goodness!"

"Karen — what's the matter?" Ann-Marie's face filled with concern. Leaning on the chairback, she pulled herself to her feet. "Your shoulder — what happened?"

"Ann-Marie — you just gave me such a scare."

"Huh?"

"I saw you lying on the floor and I thought — "

"Oh! Oh, no. I'm sorry, Karen. I was just — my pendant — the chain broke. It fell behind the chair, and I was picking it up. I didn't hear you come in. I was just — "

Why did she look so embarrassed? Her normally pale skin was nearly scarlet.

"Your shoulder — what's with the bandage? Look at your hand. What did you do to yourself?"

"I got burned," Karen said, her suspicions about her friend coming back to her now that she realized Ann-Marie was okay.

"Sunburned?"

"No. Burned. Where were you, anyway, Ann-Marie?"

"I went for a walk. A long walk. I met some people, and then when I got back, you were gone." She walked over to Karen and took Karen's bag for her. "I never dreamed you were hurt or anything. Where did you go? Come. Sit down. Tell me what happened. Want a Coke or anything?"

Ann-Marie walked into the attached kitchen and pulled open the refrigerator door, burying her head inside it. Like an ostrich trying to escape, Karen thought.

"Ann-Marie, come back. We have to talk. I just saw Mike outside."

"Huh?" She slammed the refrigerator door shut and spun around.

"I saw Mike. Was he here?"

"Okay, okay," Ann-Marie said quietly, coming back into the room and dropping down on the chair across from Karen. Her green eyes burned into Karen's. "You had to find out sooner or later, I suppose."

Karen was totally confused now. "Find out about . . . ?"

"About Mike and me," Ann-Marie said, sighing. "We've been seeing each other."

"You and Mike!?" Karen's voice slid up to where only dogs could hear it.

"I was worried you wouldn't approve. I didn't know if you were still interested in him or not. I felt so guilty sneaking around with him. But I just didn't want to confront you about it. I guess I should've said something right away. I just — "

"You mean that's where you've been all the time? With Mike?"

Ann-Marie nodded her head guiltily, her face still flushed.

Karen felt like laughing out loud. And so she did.

Ann-Marie's mouth dropped open in bewilderment. "What's so funny?"

Karen wanted to tell her, but she was laughing too hard.

Here she was, suspecting her friend of the most hideous things, wondering why Ann-Marie always looked so uncomfortable, so *guilty* — and all she was doing was seeing Mike!

Karen laughed until tears rolled down her cheeks. Finally, gasping for breath, she forced herself to stop.

"Does this mean you don't care if I see Mike?" Ann-Marie asked, which started Karen laughing all over again.

"Stop me. Please. I'm hysterical!" Karen exclaimed, ignoring the pain in her shoulder and lying down on the white shag rug and staring up at the ceiling, tears of laughter running down the sides of her face. "I'm hysterical!"

"I don't get it," Ann-Marie said. She started

laughing, too. "What are we laughing about?"

"I don't know. But it's better than what's been going on here up till now," Karen said.

The phone rang, immediately jarring them out of their laughter. Karen sat up, wiping her cheeks with her hands. The phone continued to ring. She stared at it, considering not picking it up.

But what if it's Daddy? she thought.

Or Jerry.

Or Vince.

Jerry or Vince?

She climbed to her feet, walked over to the table, and picked up the receiver. "Hello?"

"Hello, is this Karen?"

"Yes, it is," she said warily, trying to remember where she had heard the girl's voice before. "Who's this?"

"This is Jerry's sister. I — "

"I don't know who you *really* are," Karen angrily interrupted, "but I know you're not Jerry's sister."

The girl at the other end started to say something, but Karen slammed down the receiver.

When was the horror going to stop? she wondered, feeling her arm throb. When were the threats going to stop?

She slumped back to the floor and closed her eyes. She no longer felt like laughing.

Her shoulder hurt.

Someone had tried to kill her, she realized.

Someone had tried to burn her to death.

No, she didn't feel like laughing. Now she just felt very tired. And very scared.

Chapter 20

"Are you sure you should be going in the water?"

Karen pulled the hood of her new wet suit over her hair and made a face at Jerry. "Yes, I'm sure it's okay, Mom."

He reached over and tenderly helped her tuck a strand of hair under the hood. "Don't make fun of me," he said seriously. "I'm just concerned about you, you know."

She picked up the snorkeling mask and straightened the straps. "Well, I wouldn't have come to this beach party if I couldn't go in the water, would I?"

She looked back at the other kids, who were sunbathing, standing around talking in small groups, playing volleyball, or preparing to go swimming or snorkeling. There was nearly a hundred of them here at the cove on this Friday afternoon. She even saw Vince and his gang huddled together away from the crowd, by the rocks that jutted into the water.

How did all these kids find out about this party? Karen wondered. Somehow word had gotten out, and everyone for fifty miles had shown up at the cove, ready to party.

The cove was such a beautiful place to snorkel. It was protected by rock jetties on two sides so that the water stayed clear and calm.

Karen couldn't wait to put on the mask and fins and try snorkeling again. Her first experience had been horrifying. She knew she had to snorkel again to get it behind her.

If only Jerry wouldn't be such a worried mother hen. He'd been acting that way ever since two days before when she had told him about how her shoulder had been burned and showed him her bandaged hand and shoulder. A look of horror had frozen on his face when she told him. He hadn't said a word, just stared at her in disbelief.

After telling him about the suntan lotion, she decided she might as well tell him everything that had been happening. There was no reason to keep it from him. She probably should have told him sooner.

They were sitting on Venice Beach, shaded by a large yellow beach umbrella. She leaned against him, her back against his side, and told him about how someone was trying to keep her away from him. At first, she admitted, she had suspected Renee. She had even suspected Renee of trying to murder her on the rocks.

But someone else was trying to murder her. It was clear. Most likely, it was the girl pretending to be Jerry's sister.

She couldn't see Jerry's face, but she could tell

by the way his muscles tensed that he was very upset by what she was telling him. Finally she turned and stared into his eyes. "Do you have any idea who is doing it, who is trying to keep me away from you?"

His face went blank. His eyes seemed to die. Karen thought she saw real sadness in his eyes. But the sadness faded, too. "I'm really sorry this is happening," he said finally.

"But who *is* it?" she insisted.

"I don't know. I'm just so . . . shocked. I had no idea this was happening to you. I'm just so . . . sorry."

For a brief moment, she was sorry she had told him. He seemed even more upset about it than she did.

But he had to know.

He had to help her.

"You've got to help me find out who it is," she had said.

"Of course." He had put his arm around her. They hadn't talked about it again.

Now, two days later, her shoulder feeling better, she was about to go snorkeling in the cove with him. "We won't go out too far," he said, as they pulled on their fins at the edge of the shore. "In case your shoulder gets tired."

"Please, Jerry — stop worrying about me," Karen snapped. He really was getting on her nerves. "I'll go out by myself if you don't shut up. I really will."

He looked hurt. She realized she was nervous

about going snorkeling again and was just taking it out on him. She apologized quickly, putting a hand on his shoulder.

He smiled. "Ready?"

She spit into her mask and rubbed the saliva around the glass. "Ready." Before pulling on the mask, she looked back at the crowded beach, searching for Ann-Marie. She shouldn't be hard to find, Karen thought. She was wearing a Day-Glo green bikini.

But Ann-Marie wasn't back on their blanket. Karen couldn't find her anywhere. She's probably sneaked off with Mike, Karen thought.

Every time she thought of Mike and Ann-Marie together, it gave Karen a laugh.

"Come on. Let's go see what's out there," Jerry called, already several steps ahead of her. Karen pulled on her mask, adjusted it, pulled the mouthpiece into her mouth, and followed him into the clear, blue-green water.

The water of the cove was shallow for only a few yards. Then the bottom dipped drastically and the water became deep and even more clear. It's so beautiful here, Karen thought, floating forward, breathing steadily through the snorkel, kicking the fins slowly behind her.

Jerry was floating right ahead of her. She pulled back to avoid bumping into his pedaling fins. She stared down at the secret, blue-green world beneath her. Dozens of silvery fish swam past, ignoring her.

I feel like a visitor to another planet, she thought. When she raised her head above the surface to find Jerry, she saw that they had floated out a lot further than she'd imagined. "The current — it's taking us straight out!" she shouted.

Jerry, several yards ahead of her, raised his head and let some water out of his mask. "What?"

"I said the current is taking us out," Karen repeated.

She wasn't sure if he heard her this time or not. "How's your shoulder?" he called.

"It's okay, I guess." Actually, it ached a little. "What?"

She floated closer so he could hear her. "We shouldn't go out too far," she repeated. "It's the current," she said. "It's deceptive. The water looks perfectly calm, but there's a real pull."

"There's so much to see." He fiddled with his snorkel. "There's a reef right out there," he said, pointing, "with some really amazing formations."

He slipped his mask back on, blew some water out of the air hose, and headed straight out toward the reef. Karen, a little reluctant because of her shoulder, watched him. He's such a strong, confident swimmer, she thought. He really is like a sleek fish in the water.

Impulsively, she flattened out over the water and floated after him. Holding her arms low at her sides kept her shoulder from hurting. But now her burned hand was throbbing with pain.

Maybe this wasn't such a good idea after all, she thought. Maybe I should've waited a few more days.

But it was so beautiful down there; slender, silent fish were slithering through shafts of cloudy yellow light. She floated further, listening to her breathing, alone, alone in this new world of swimming colors.

Where was the reef Jerry had pointed to? She couldn't see it. The ocean floor seemed to drop once again.

Had she gotten turned around?

She raised her head out of the water, pulling down the mask. "Jerry?"

She didn't see him at first. It took a while for her eyes to adjust to the brightness. "Jerry?"

There he was, several yards up ahead.

She looked back at the beach, so far away.

Too far.

Her shoulder ached now. Her hand throbbed with pain. "Jerry?"

She had gone too far out. Normally, she would have been able to swim back. But now she was in too much pain. Jerry would have to help her.

"Jerry?"

Finally he raised his head and spun around, searching for her. "You okay?" he smiled, then pulled down the mask, letting it hang down over his neck.

She had been feeling a little panicky, but his smile reassured her. He swam back to her, with long, sure strokes that cut through the current.

He looked so sweet, so concerned, she impulsively leaped up and kissed him. After a few seconds, he pulled away. His expression had changed. "Why'd you do that?" he asked.

"Uh . . . I was thanking you in advance," Karen said, surprised by the coldness of the question. "I think you have to help me get back."

He frowned. "Your shoulder?"

"And my hand. I guess this was stupid." She put a hand on the shoulder of his wet suit. "Take me back?"

"But we just got here." His anger startled her.

"Really. I'm sorry, but I can't swim back by myself. I need your help."

"I can't help you," he said.

Something about the way he looked at her gave her a chill. His face grew hard, his eyes as clear and cold as the water.

"What did you say?"

"I can't help you."

Why was he staring at her like that, so coldly, as if he didn't know her, as if he didn't like her?

"Jerry, did you hear me?" She couldn't keep the panic from her voice. "I need your help to get back."

"I'm not Jerry," he said, staring hard, not blinking. "I'm Todd."

Chapter 21

"Jerry — stop it!" Was this some kind of a joke?

His cold expression didn't change. "Jerry's gone." Even his voice sounded harder, colder. He still hadn't blinked.

"Jerry, that's enough."

"I told you — I'm Todd."

"Please — help me! My shoulder hurts. I can't stay here. You've got to help me." She suddenly felt sick. The bobbing up and down, the beach so far away, the chill of the water, the throbbing of her shoulder — none of it was as frightening as the look on Jerry's face.

"Jerry hasn't been the same since I died," he said.

"What? What are you talking about?"

It wasn't a joke. There was something seriously wrong with him. What could she do? How could she snap him out of it?

"Ever since I drowned, Jerry hasn't been quite right. Know what I mean?" He didn't wait for an answer. "It was Jerry's fault that I drowned. He knew he could have saved me. I knew it, too. That's why I keep doing this to Jerry."

"Doing what?" Karen asked, not recognizing her trembling voice, staring hard into Jerry's frozen eyes, unable to look away.

"That's why I keep coming back. To warn people."

"To warn people?"

"Yes." He pulled back his lips in an eerie, terrifying smile. "I keep coming back to warn people to stay away from Jerry."

Karen cried out in shock. She choked on a mouthful of water. Finally she sputtered, "It was *you*?!"

"I tried to warn you. It wasn't easy. Jerry doesn't like it when I take over his body like this."

"*You* were warning me against *yourself*?"

"I warned you to stay away from Jerry. I warned Renee, too, but she didn't listen. So I had to do something *bad* to Renee."

"No!" Karen cried. "No! No! No!" She forced herself to look away from those cold, unblinking eyes.

How could this be Jerry? He seemed so sweet, so . . . nice.

She turned and started to swim away from him. The beach was a ribbon of yellow in the distance. She was too far from shore to scream for help. Too far . . . to swim back. The current was pulling her back. Her entire right side throbbed with pain.

I'm not going to make it, she realized.

And then he grabbed her by her bad shoulder,

and turned her around. "Let go of me!" she screamed.

He shoved her hard. She cried out from the pain.

"I warned you, Karen. I warned you about Jerry. Jerry is bad. Jerry let me drown."

"Stop, please — " She struggled to get away from him, but her arm hurt too much. She couldn't swim. She couldn't think straight because of the pain. She couldn't escape.

"Jerry is bad," he said. "Jerry has to be punished."

"Please, please, please!"

"Too late for please, Karen. Too late for you. Too late for me. Too late for Jerry. Jerry is bad."

With startling quickness, he grabbed her snorkeling mask with one hand, pulled it off, and tossed it away. Then he dived beneath the surface. A few seconds later he reappeared, swimming to shore with strong, steady strokes.

He swam nearly halfway back before he turned around. When he looked back, Karen had stopped her struggles to stay afloat.

He watched her go under. She didn't come back up.

I warned her, he thought. I did my best to warn her.

He continued swimming back to shore.

Chapter 22

Her right side throbbing, Karen did a surface dive down into the water.

"I'm not Jerry. I'm Todd." The words repeated and repeated in her ears. *"Jerry is bad."*

She opened her eyes and forced herself down, holding her breath. The salt water stung, but she could see clearly.

There it was. She reached out, kicked hard twice with her fins, and pulled the snorkeling mask in with her good hand.

Holding it tightly, she burst up to the surface, gasping for air.

If I snorkel back, I think I can make it, she thought, straightening the mouthpiece and clearing the air hose of water. It will take a while against the current. But it's my only hope.

If she snorkeled, she realized, she wouldn't have to use her arms. She could keep her throbbing, aching arm down at her side and, breathing with her head under the surface, propel herself by kicking the fins.

That's probably why Jerry tossed away her mask. He didn't want her floating back, able to take her time and breathe as she made her way.

Poor, crazy Jerry.

Bringing back Todd the only way he knew how.

Punishing himself again and again for Todd's death.

Poor, crazy Jerry. Poor, crazy Jerry.

She kept up the refrain, repeating it in rhythm, as she kicked and breathed, kicked and breathed, not seeing anything now but a blur of blues and greens, pushing against the current, forcing her way back to the beach.

It seemed like hours later that she stood up in the shallow water near the shore and stumbled toward the sand, pulling down the hood of the wet suit, breathing so hard, her legs like jelly, her chest feeling about to burst.

"Hey — Karen!"

She shielded her eyes from the lowering yellow sun. Who was it?

"Karen — you okay?"

"Vince — is that you?" She was still too dizzy, too out-of-breath to talk.

He ran up to her in his cutoffs and sleeveless blue T-shirt, and she slumped against him, holding herself up by putting an arm around his shoulder.

"Vince, how did you know . . . ?"

"I saw Jerry come back. But I didn't see you." He put a strong arm around her waist and led her up onto dry sand.

"Jerry? Where is he? We've got to stop him."

"What?"

"He's crazy, Vince. He's very sick. He tried to kill me."

"Okay, okay. Calm down, Karen," he said softly, helping her walk. "First, let's take care of you. Then — "

"NO!" Karen shrieked, seeing the tall, red-haired girl running toward her.

Vince was so startled by her scream, he let go of her.

Karen took a few uncertain steps back. This girl who claimed to be Jerry's sister — she had threatened Karen before. What did she want now? Why was she following her?

"What are *you* doing here?" Karen screamed as the girl came running up, looking flushed, and desperate.

"Where's Jerry? Have you seen him?" she asked.

"He tried to kill me," Karen blurted out. "Who are you? Why are you here? Why are you following me?"

"I've been trying to tell you," the girl said, her eyes searching the crowded beach. "I'm Jerry's sister. I knew Jerry was sick — but I didn't know how sick. You've got to believe me."

"Jerry said he doesn't have a sister," Karen replied skeptically.

"Yes," the girl said sadly, still searching the beach. "Ever since Todd died, Jerry has been so confused, so guilty. He closed the rest of us out. He's pretended I don't exist. It was as if he only had room for Todd. I've been trying to get help for him, but it's been impossible. He just — "

"There he goes!" Karen interrupted, pointing.

Several yards up the beach, beside the now deserted volleyball net, Jerry turned and saw them.

"Get him!" Jerry's sister cried. "Please — before he does something awful!"

Chapter 23

Vince took off, his bare feet kicking up sand as he ran.

"Get him! Please — don't let Jerry run away!" Jerry's sister cried, running after Vince.

Karen stood frozen on the spot.

"I'm not Jerry. I'm Todd."

She heard the hard, cold voice once again. Then, shaking her head hard, as if trying to drive the sounds from her mind, she started running toward Jerry, too.

What will he do if we catch him? Karen wondered. She thought of poor Renee. Renee had trusted Jerry. Renee had been with Jerry through the bad times after Todd's death. Did she have any idea how sick Jerry was?

Did she have any idea that sometimes Jerry thought he was Todd? Had Todd terrorized Renee, too, the way he terrorized Karen?

The morning Jerry killed her, did Renee have any idea why?

To Karen's surprise, Jerry made no attempt to

run from Vince. He stood there on the sand by the volleyball net, watching the three of them approach.

And then he started to run *to* them.

"Hi!" he called, a cheerful smile on his face.

Karen realized he was smiling at *her*.

"Karen — hi! How's the shoulder? Feel okay?"

Jerry started to run right past Vince, but Vince grabbed him around the chest and held on. "Hey — what's going on?" Jerry protested, but without any real anger.

"It's going to be okay, Jerry," his sister said softly.

Jerry looked at her as if he didn't recognize her. "Karen, how was the snorkeling?" he asked.

Karen stared into his eyes. They were alive and warm again.

"It was okay," she said quietly.

"I'll take him," Jerry's sister said to Vince.

Vince let go reluctantly. "You sure?"

Jerry made no attempt to run. "Come with me, Jerry. I'm going to get you help." His sister took his hand and started to lead him away. Jerry allowed her to pull him, having to hurry to stay with her.

After they were halfway to the parking lot, Jerry turned back and called to Karen, "See you later. I'll call you, okay?"

"Okay," Karen said, tears welling up in her eyes.

Poor, crazy Jerry.

He was going off with his sister so willingly.

He *wanted* to be stopped. He *wanted* to be helped.

He had tried to let her know from the night that he had met her.

Stay away from Jerry.

That was his desperate message, his plea to her.

He tried to tell her. She just wouldn't listen.

Without realizing it, she was leaning against Vince again as they made their way to get her belongings, and he had his arm securely around her waist.

"Hey," she said, stopping. "Are you really someone I can lean on?"

He laughed.

"You don't *look* like someone I can lean on," she teased.

"Try me," he said. He scooped her off her feet and carried her across the sand.

BEACH HOUSE

PART ONE

Summer of 1956

1
A Call for Help

"Ooh, turn up the radio," Maria said. "I love this song!"

Lying on her back, Amy reached lazily across the beach blanket and turned the knob on the red plastic radio. "Sh-Boom Sh-Boom," poured out of the speaker.

"Sh-Boom Sh-Boom Sh-Boom."

"I love the words," Amy said, giggling. "Who sings this?"

"The Crewcuts," Maria said, eyes closed under her pink plastic sunglasses. "This was the first record I bought when I got my new 45-player." She opened her eyes and pulled herself up on her elbows. "Can't you make it any louder?"

Amy shook her head, her tight blonde curls catching the golden light of the afternoon sun. "The batteries are almost dead. They only last a few hours."

"Sh-Boom Sh-Boom. Yadadadadadada."

"It's so neat!" Maria gushed. "I've played it over and over. I played it so much, the needle wore out and the record turned white."

Amy squinted up at her friend. "My dad would never let me buy a rock-and-roll record," she said unhappily. She fiddled with the shoulder straps of her bathing suit. Amy was small, very thin, with a boyish figure, and the blue and white flower-patterned, one-piece suit was a bit big on her. "He says it's just noise."

"Sh-Boom Sh-Boom . . ."

They settled back on the beach blanket, soaking up the sun's warmth, listening to the rest of the song. In front of them, the green-blue ocean waves rolled onto the sand, gentle, lapping waves. Children squealed happily, running along the shore. A few swimmers were testing the waters, still winter-cold.

Maria could feel the sun on her shoulders. I should put on more lotion, she thought. But she was feeling lazy today. So lazy . . .

The song ended, and the bright-voiced disc jockey's patter blared from the box-shaped portable radio. "And now the Singing Rage, Miss Patti Page." "Moonlight in Vermont" started. Amy turned the volume down.

"A whole summer of this," Maria said dreamily, closing her eyes contentedly. "Not bad, huh?"

"I think I can take it," Amy replied.

"Just lying on the beach, swimming in the ocean,

messing around in town." Grinning, Maria adjusted
her ponytail, tugging at the rubber band that held
it. She had straight, silky black hair, which she
almost always kept swept back in a ponytail, with
bangs cut straight across her forehead, an inch
above her dramatic brown eyes.

"Don't forget Ronnie," Amy said, reaching for
the bottle of suntan lotion. "Ronnie's here at Dunehampton for the whole summer, too."

"Lucky you," Maria said coyly.

Amy and Ronnie had been going steady for
nearly a year. Maria thought they were a funny
couple. Ronnie was so tall and lanky, he practically
had to stoop over to talk to little Amy. He called
Amy "Mouse," a nickname she hated. But Maria
had to admit that with her tight blonde curls, gray-
blue eyes, and tiny button nose, short, skinny Amy
really *did* resemble a mouse.

A very cute mouse.

Maria tried not to be jealous of Amy, but it was
hard. Maria didn't have a boyfriend. In fact, even
with her dark, dramatic looks and her fun, enthusiastic personality, she had never gone steady with
anyone.

Oh, well, she thought wistfully, gazing past her
friend, watching the wide, yellow beach fill with
sunbathers, maybe things will change this summer.

She and her aunt had arrived in Dunehampton a
week ago, and Maria had already met two boys who
seemed interested in her.

First there was Buddy. She had met Buddy her first day on the beach. He just popped up in the sand beside her, as if out of nowhere. He seemed lost, so Maria had started talking to him.

They had hit it off immediately. Buddy was good-looking in a clean-cut sort of way, but shy and awkward. And sort of clumsy. He was intense, very serious, Maria realized. He didn't like to kid around the way most kids did. As a result, Ronnie and some of the other guys went out of their way to tease him, to try to get his goat.

But Maria found herself drawn to Buddy, despite his earnestness, his awkward shyness. Buddy was . . . different.

And then there was Stuart. Stuart was a friend of Ronnie's, although he didn't go to their school. Ronnie had introduced Stuart to Maria in town.

Stuart was Mr. Rock and Roll. Mr. Real Cool Cat. Stuart was a lot of fun. Always joking, always messing around. Always snapping his fingers to some tune no one else could hear. Always combing his heavily Brylcreemed hair, which came up in a tall wave in front and then was swept into a ducktail over his shirt collar in back.

He thought it made him look tough. Maria guessed he wanted to look like the juvenile delinquents in *Rebel Without a Cause* or something.

But Stuart could never really look tough. He was too cute. Too funny.

Silly sometimes, Maria decided. In many ways, the opposite of Buddy.

She thought of the other evening when a whole group of teenagers, summer people as well as townies, had gathered on the beach back in the low, grassy dunes. She wasn't sure how it had started. Maybe someone had urged Stuart on, put the idea in his head. But all of a sudden, he had jumped up, pretending to play the guitar, and began leaping around like Bill Haley & the Comets, singing "Shake, Rattle & Roll" at the top of his lungs.

Before long, a whole bunch of guys had joined in, all of them shouting out "Shake, Rattle & Roll" and dancing about like wild men. And the girls had formed a big circle, laughing and clapping their hands, and chanting, "Crazy, man, crazy! Crazy, man, crazy!" in time to their singing.

It was so much fun.

But Buddy had just stood there with his hands in the pockets of his shorts. Trying to keep a forced smile on his face, but looking as uncomfortable as ever.

Clapping and chanting, Maria had spotted him at the edge of the circle. He was attempting to clap along, but couldn't get the rhythm.

She felt sorry for him, in a way.

Poor, serious Buddy.

Buddy and Stuart. Stuart and Buddy.

Yes, it might be an interesting summer, Maria decided.

"Hey — look at that girl!" Amy cried, poking Maria in the side excitedly, interrupting her thoughts.

Maria followed Amy's gaze several blankets down and saw a girl with short, red hair standing on the beach in a two-piece bathing suit, carrying a large picnic basket.

"Get a load of that bathing suit!" Amy declared. "It's so tiny."

"It's one of those French ones, I think," Maria replied, staring hard as the girl set the basket down.

"Huh?"

"I think they're called *bikinis*," Maria said. "I saw some pictures of them in *Look* magazine."

"Well, maybe they wear them in France," Amy said, unable to take her eyes off the girl, who knew that she was causing a commotion and that her bathing suit was attracting a lot of staring eyes. "But they'll never catch on here."

Maria laughed.

"Well, you'd never catch *me* in one!" Amy insisted. "Look — her belly button is showing!"

"I think it's kind of neat," Maria said. She started to say something else, but stopped when she saw Ronnie and Stuart running toward them at full speed, dodging blankets and beach unbrellas as they ran.

"Hey — what's happening?" Maria cried.

Surprised, both girls jumped to their feet, adjusting their bathing suits.

"It — it's Buddy!" Ronnie cried.

Both boys pointed to the ocean.

Staring past them, Maria saw him.

Buddy was in the water, pretty far out, the waves rolling him about.

And he was screaming, Maria saw.

Screaming at the top of his lungs.

Screaming for help.

2
Humiliated

"Buddy!" Maria cried in alarm.

She started to run toward the water, but stopped as she realized that Stuart and Ronnie were laughing.

They were both dripping wet, their baggy swim trunks clinging to their legs. Wet sand stuck to their feet as they approached the bewildered girls.

"Ronnie — what's so funny?" Amy demanded.

In the ocean, Buddy rolled with the waves, only his head and shoulders visible in the sparkling blue-green waters, one hand waving frantically at them.

"We've got to help him!" Maria insisted. "Why did you run away and leave him there?"

Stuart's grin grew wider. He held up a pair of navy-blue swim trunks. "We depantsed him."

"Huh?"

Maria saw Buddy gesturing frantically now, waving with both hands, his head tossed back as he shouted, his cries drowned out by the steady wash of the waves.

"We depantsed him," Stuart repeated, waving the trunks in the air like a flag, taunting Buddy with them.

"Look at him! He'll freeze his — " Ronnie started.

Maria interrupted by grabbing the trunks from Stuart's hand and slapping Ronnie with them. "How could you do that? It's not funny!"

Ronnie quickly grabbed the wet trunks back. "Sure, it is!" he declared, and burst out laughing.

The other three burst out laughing, too.

It *was* pretty funny.

Especially watching Buddy bobbing in the waves, calling frantically, waving to them, unable to come out or even come close to shore.

"He'll freeze!" Maria said, glancing at the swim trunks, which Ronnie had wrapped around Stuart's head like a turban, and starting to laugh all over again. "The ocean is still freezing cold!"

"So?" Stuart asked with a shrug.

"Buddy *hates* jokes like that," Maria said. "Why are you two always picking on him?"

"Because he's so weird," Stuart answered quickly.

"Because he's so square," Ronnie added.

"Yeah. He's so square, he's cubed!" Stuart added.

"Poor guy," Amy said quietly, gazing at the water.

"Where's the lifeguard?" Maria asked, searching

the beach, her eyes stopping at the empty lifeguard post to their left. "How can they let Buddy carry on like that without — "

"The lifeguards don't start for another week," Amy said.

"Come on, Stuart — " Maria made a grab for the trunks, but Stuart dodged away, giggling. "Give Buddy back his trunks."

"Come and make me," he said playfully, pulling the trunks off his head and waving them at her like a toreador in a bullfight.

"Come on, guys. We can't leave him in there. Remember — there were sharks spotted real close to the shore yesterday. And there could be *jellyfish* out there!" Amy cried heatedly.

That made the two boys collapse in laughter.

Maria made a diving grab for the trunks, but missed.

That started an enthusiastic keep-away game, with the trunks flying from Stuart to Ronnie, and the girls making valiant but unsuccessful attempts to get them away.

Buddy had stopped calling and waving and was floating quietly now, watching the game.

"Got 'em!" Laughing, Maria grabbed the trunks and began running to the water.

She was at the edge of the shore, water lapping over her ankles, when Stuart, running hard, tackled her from behind. As she toppled forward onto the sand, she flung the trunks toward the ocean with all her strength.

"Ooof." She hit the wet sand hard with Stuart's arms still around her waist. "Get off me!"

He rolled away, laughing. When Maria looked up, Buddy's trunks were floating just beyond where the waves were breaking, and Buddy was desperately making his way to them, half-running, half-swimming, his handsome features tightened in anger.

"Oh, no," Maria groaned as the trunks sank out of sight, disappearing into the green waters before Buddy could get to them.

He made a surface dive as a tall, frothy wave crashed over his head. All four of them watched eagerly, waiting for him to reappear. A few seconds later, he floated up behind the wave, shaking his head, sputtering — without the trunks.

Stuart clapped his hands, laughing gleefully. "I saw his buns!"

They all laughed, even Maria. Buddy did look ridiculous, floundering around out there. Even she had to admit it.

He shook a fist at them and dived under another wave, swimming hard now, searching for the drowned swim trunks.

Again, he came up without them.

"Bring me another pair!" he cried breathlessly, swimming as close to shore as he dared.

"Huh? Can't hear you!" Stuart pretended, cupping a hand over his ear.

"A towel!" Buddy shouted unhappily. "Just bring a towel — okay?"

"Can't hear you!" Stuart repeated.

Buddy shouted his request again.

"I guess he wants us to leave," Stuart said and, taking Maria's hand, started to pull her away from the shore.

"Hey — Stuart — whoa! We can't just leave him like that!" Maria protested.

"Want to bet?" was Stuart's reply.

And before Maria quite realized what was happening, the four of them were walking away, shoving each other playfully, talking and laughing, with Stuart doing a very funny impression of Buddy trying to get off the crowded beach without any swim trunks.

A while later, with blue shadows sliding over the beach as the sun lowered behind the dunes, Maria collected her things, shoving them into her straw beach bag.

Sea gulls patrolled the sand, searching for items left behind by sunbathers. Terns hopped comically in blue puddles near the shoreline. A few swimmers braved the cold of the late afternoon ocean. But the waves were taller now, and the air carried the chill of approaching evening. Most people, including Amy and Ronnie, had packed up and headed home.

What a crazy afternoon, Maria thought, smiling to herself. That Stuart is such a clown.

And as she thought his name, he appeared beside her, an orange and yellow striped beach robe over his bathing suit, a towel slung over his shoulder. "Maria, what are you smiling about?"

She shrugged. "Just smiling."

Grinning, he pulled the towel off his shoulder and snapped it at her, deliberately missing. "Listen . . . uh . . . Ronnie and Amy are going to the Dune-hampton drive-in tonight."

"What's playing?" Maria asked, only half-listening as she struggled to squeeze the folded-up beach blanket into her bag.

"*Creature from the Black Lagoon*," Stuart said. "Want to come, too? I mean, with me?"

"Yes," Maria answered quickly. But then her smiled faded. "Oh, no. I mean, I can't. I sort of made plans to do something with Buddy."

Lugging the heavy straw bag in both hands, she began heading for home, making her way along the low dunes at the back of the beach.

"Buddy?" Stuart laughed, snapping his towel at a clump of tall dune grass. "He's probably still in the ocean!"

They both laughed. Maria stopped first. "That was so mean."

"Yeah. I know," Stuart said, grinning. "Where's he live, anyway? Is he a townie?"

"I don't think so," Maria replied. "He's staying in that new beach house that's at the end of the beach."

She pointed to it. The house, a large, hulking redwood structure, stood at the edge of the shore, jutting out into the ocean on tall, wooden stilts.

"Huh? I heard there's something weird about

that house. I heard it's been empty ever since it was built," Stuart said, stopping beside her to gaze at it.

"Not anymore," Maria told him. "I've seen Buddy there."

"Stand him up tonight," Stuart urged, still staring into the distance at the dark beach house.

"Huh? Why?" Maria started walking again.

"Because he has cooties," Stuart joked.

"Very mature," she scolded.

"No. Really. Stand him up," Stuart pleaded, hurrying to stay up with her, their bare feet padding silently along the soft sand of the dunes. "He's so . . . weird."

"He's very sensitive," Maria said, feeling she had to defend Buddy.

"Sensitive? You mean he has no sense of humor," Stuart replied heatedly. "He's a sourpuss. When he tries to smile, he looks like Howdy Doody. You know. Like his smile is painted on." He did an impression of Buddy's smile.

Maria burst out laughing. It was a really good impression. Buddy *did* look like that TV puppet Howdy Doody when he smiled.

"He's no fun at all," Stuart added, the wooden smile still locked on his face.

"Yeah. Well . . ." Maria had to admit that Stuart was right about that. Buddy wasn't exactly a million laughs.

But laughing wasn't everything, she argued with herself.

There was more to life than practical jokes and acting silly all the time.

"I like him because he's different," she told Stuart. "He's very smart."

Stuart groaned, insulted. "Dump him, Maria. I think I can borrow my dad's Thunderbird tonight. We can go to the drive-in in style!"

"You have a Thunderbird?" Maria set down the heavy basket for a second and turned to him. "What color?"

"Pink."

"Really?"

"With gray leather seats. It's a convertible."

"A Thunderbird convertible? I've never *been* in a Thunderbird convertible!" Maria exclaimed.

"So you'll dump Buddy and come with me tonight?" Stuart asked eagerly.

"Okay," Maria agreed. "I'll just make up some excuse for Buddy tomorrow. He'll get over it."

"All *reet*!" Stuart exclaimed happily, snapping his towel in the air. "Pick you up at seven, Maria." And with a cry of "Later, alligator!" he went running back in the other direction toward his parents' cottage.

Maria hoisted up the straw beach bag and started back on her way. The house her parents rented every summer was along the narrow road that led away from the dunes, just a ten-minute walk from the beach.

As she walked, she stared straight ahead at the dark beach house at the beach's end, now covered in gray-blue shadow as evening descended. Leaning out to the water, perched on its four tall stilts, the house looked as if it could walk away, step right into the water.

Darkened in shadow, it looked like a large, low animal huddled on the shore.

Who had built it in such a strange, dangerous spot? Maria wondered. All by itself. Half in the water.

And why did it stand empty for so long?

A glint of sunlight reflected red off one of the house's windows. The window immediately went dark again.

It's as if the house just winked at me, Maria thought.

Then, shifting the weight of her bag, she turned onto the road and began to follow it home.

As she walked, she didn't see the dark figure crouching low, hidden behind the low dune.

She didn't see Buddy, a beach towel wrapped around his waist, pressed tightly against the dune, peering over the tall grass, watching her. Listening.

Listening.

He had heard everything she and Stuart had said.

And as she disappeared around a curve in the road, he remained there in the puddle of darkness at the back of the dune.

Trembling all over.

Trembling so hard, his teeth chattered.

Trembling not from the cold.

But from anger.

3
Worried About Sharks

"Did you have a good time with Stuart?" Amy asked.

Maria nodded, smiling coyly.

"The movie was really neat," Amy said.

"Our speaker wasn't working too well," Maria said. "We had to move the car to three different spots before we found a good one."

It was the following afternoon, a bright but overcast day, hazy with a fog moving in off the ocean. The two friends had decided to take a long walk along the shore since the sun wasn't cooperating.

"Did Stuart take his dad's Thunderbird?" Amy asked. She had been pumping Maria all afternoon for details about the night before, but with little success. Maria was in one of her quieter, more thoughtful moods.

"Yeah," she replied, staring into the white haze over the water. "It's a real dreamy car. Like something in a magazine."

"I think Stuart really digs you," Amy said, turning her eyes to Maria's.

"Well . . . I guess I dig him, too," Maria replied after a long while. "He's a little immature, but — "

"All boys are immature," Amy interrupted. She bent down to pick up a clamshell.

Maria gazed straight ahead at the mysterious beach house a few hundred yards in front of them. The white, hazy afternoon light made the house seem even darker than usual. The tide was coming in, and waves rushed under the house, frothing white against the stilts, then pulling back with a *whoosh*.

Suddenly, as she stared, the glass door facing the ocean slid open, and a figure came running out, running at full speed toward them. As if he had spotted them from inside the house.

"Buddy!"

Maria's stomach knotted in dread.

She hadn't looked forward to seeing him, to having to explain why she had stood him up the night before.

She knew he'd be angry. About that. And about the swim trunks.

He hated to be teased. And yesterday was much worse than teasing.

"Hey — " he called to them, waving as he ran.

Maybe I should turn and run, Maria thought in a panic. She glanced at Amy and caught a fearful expression on her face as well.

But there was nowhere to run.

Besides, that would be childish.

She had just been talking about how childish and immature boys were. She had to face him like a mature adult.

"Hi, how's it going?" he asked, his bare feet skidding to a stop a few yards in front of them. He smiled, first at Amy, then at Maria, his eyes lingering on Maria.

He was wearing a sleeveless, blue cotton T-shirt and baggy Hawaiian-style swim trunks. He had a white beach towel wrapped around his broad shoulders, which were already tanned, even though summer had just begun.

"Hi." Maria gave him a shy wave. "About last night — "

"The sun should burn through soon," he said, shielding his eyes with one hand and peering up at the bright white sky. "Have you been in the water?"

"No. Brrrrr," Amy replied, wrapping her hands around her shoulders, pretending to shiver.

"No. The water's really warm," Buddy said, gripping the ends of the towel around his neck with both hands. "I guess because the air is cold."

Maria waited for him to return his eyes to her.

Was he avoiding her?

Was he so angry at her that he planned to ignore her?

No.

He reached out and swatted a green fly off her

shoulder. "Look out. The green ones bite."

"They sprayed the beach and the dunes with DDT last week," Amy said.

"But it only kills the mosquitoes. Not the flies," Buddy told her.

"About last night," Maria said, practically bursting to make her phony excuse. "I'm really sorry, Buddy."

His brown eyes narrowed, but his easy, relaxed expression remained. "Hey, I thought we were going to go into town and mess around," he said casually.

"Yeah. I know." Maria glanced at Amy, who turned her eyes to the ocean. "I wanted to. But I wasn't feeling very well. Too much sun."

She studied his face, trying to determine if he was believing her at all. If only I were a better liar, she thought. Maria could hear her voice trembling guiltily, and she knew that she was blushing. "I tried to call you — " she started to add.

"There's no phone in the beach house," he interrupted, gesturing back to the shadowy structure perched over the shore.

"No phone?" Amy asked, feeling it was safe to return to the conversation.

"The phone lines don't go that far. The house is out of the town's limits or something." He turned back to Maria, his face filled with concern. "Are you feeling better?"

She nodded, feeling even more guilty. "Yeah. I'm really sorry about last night."

"Hey. No big deal," he said, shrugging. "I'm just glad you're feeling okay."

Maria stared at him, studying his dark features, surprised by his casual reaction to being stood up.

I guess he believes me, she thought. Maybe I'm not such a bad liar after all.

"Sorry about yesterday," Amy said. "You know. The swim trunks and everything." Her gray-blue eyes twinkled, and she was unable to keep a mischievous grin from spreading across her pale face.

"Amy and I tried to get your trunks away from the boys," Maria said quickly. "How did you get back?"

"I swam," Buddy said, frowning.

Maria thought she detected a flash of anger in his eyes, but it quickly faded.

"I swam to my house," he said, gesturing with his head to the beach house. "Then I just ran inside. No big deal."

"But that was a long swim," Amy insisted. "We were way down there, by the lifeguard station." She pointed.

"Luckily the current was going my way," Buddy explained, tugging the towel behind his neck first one way, then the other. "I sort of floated most of the way, just let it carry me."

"That was a dumb joke," Maria said, shaking her head, then nervously tugging at her black ponytail. "Sometimes Ronnie and Stuart — "

"I was pretty cold when I finally got out," Buddy admitted. "But, hey — I'll pay them back." He laughed. Mirthless laughter. Not as casual as he had intended.

Amy tossed the clamshell into the water.

"How about a swim?" Buddy asked suddenly, tossing the towel to the sand.

"It's awfully cold without the sun," Maria said, glancing up at the white glare of the sky.

"It's pretty foggy out there," Amy said.

"The water's real warm, and the waves are gentle," Buddy replied. "Come on. I'll show you."

"I can't," Amy said, glancing at Maria. "I promised I'd take care of my little sister. I'm late already."

"I'll come with you," Maria said quickly.

"No. Stay. Come on. We'll have last night's date today," Buddy urged, grabbing Maria's arm gently.

"Well . . ."

"Yeah. Stay," Amy urged, starting down the beach. "I'm really gonna catch it if I don't hurry. Call you later, Maria." With a wave to them both, she began running across the beach, the man's shirt that she wore over her bathing suit flapping behind her like Superman's cape.

Maria watched Amy until she appeared to be swallowed up by the encroaching fog. Then she turned to Buddy, who was still holding her arm. "You sure you want to swim?"

He nodded, staring into her eyes. "Yeah. Come on. It'll be great. Just the two of us." His expression remained earnest, but his dark eyes suddenly seemed alive, excited.

"I'm not that good a swimmer," Maria admitted, following him as he jogged to the water's edge.

"Look how calm it is," he said, pointing.

The waves were low, lapping softly against the sand before sliding back with a gentle *whoosh*.

"Amazing!" Maria exclaimed softly. "It almost looks like a lake." She took a few steps into the water, the surf rolling over her ankles, her feet sinking into the sand as she walked. "Ooh — I thought you said it was *warm!*"

Buddy laughed. He was several steps ahead of her, in up to his knees. "You'll get used to it." He came back quickly, taking both her hands and pulling her out deeper.

"Oh!" Maria cried out from the shock of the cold.

She pulled her hands from his and dived under the water. The only way to get used to it is to get in fast, she thought. Surfacing, she looked for him. He had been right ahead of her. Where had he disappeared to?

"Right here!" he called from behind.

She spun around in the water, disoriented.

There was more of an undertow than she had thought.

"I got turned around," she explained, swimming to him.

"Let's go out further and get away from the undertow," he said. He ducked under the water, then surfaced, taking long, steady strokes, gliding easily.

He's a really good swimmer, Maria thought. She found herself to be a little surprised. He had always seemed so awkward, almost clumsy, on shore.

She did pretty well in the water, considering she'd only had a few months of Red Cross lessons at the Y, and had never really gotten to swim except during her family vacations in Dunehampton. She was probably a better swimmer than she'd realized. She just didn't have much confidence.

"Hey — we're getting pretty far from shore!" she called to Buddy.

But he didn't react, didn't seem to hear her. He was several yards ahead of her now, swimming straight and fast despite the roll and sway of the water.

"Hey — Buddy!" Maria called.

He kept swimming, his arms stretching out in those long, regular strokes, his face turned away from her.

"Buddy!"

Her arms ached. She floated for a moment, catching her breath.

"Buddy — too far!"

The fog seemed to swirl about her. She turned back. The shore was a faint outline, buried in haze . . . so far away.

The dark water offered the only color out here. Everything else was gray and white, the white glare of the sky, the gray fog . . . circling her, circling her.

"Buddy!" she screamed.

Where was he?

Was she all alone out here?

All alone in the fog?

The water rolled and tilted, tossing her one way, then another.

I'm dizzy, she thought.

And then she scolded herself: Don't panic.

You're a good swimmer. And you're not really that far from shore.

The fog just makes it seem farther.

The white glare and the fog.

She closed her eyes for a moment, swimming hard.

"Buddy!"

And there he was. At her side.

"What's wrong?" He flashed her a reassuring smile. He wasn't even out of breath.

"I — I didn't see you." She held onto his shoulder, which was surprisingly muscular. He had never seemed very strong on shore.

"Here I am." She had never seen him smile so broadly, so easily. He seemed so *happy* out here.

But she was frightened now. Of the fog. Of how far they'd swum.

"I want to go back, Buddy."

He lowered his lips in a pout, playful but seriously disappointed. "Just a little farther. The water's so great today."

She realized that she was still gripping his shoulder. "I'm cold. And I'm worried."

His eyes widened.

They both bobbed as a current carried them to
the side. It felt cold, colder than the water that
remained behind it.

"We're not that far," he said, gazing back to
shore.

"There were sharks. Remember? Not too far
out," she said.

"Sharks won't bother you," he said, his expression a blank, his dark eyes suddenly dull. "Unless
they smell blood."

Was he trying to scare her? To be funny?

Why did he say that?

"No. Really," she said, and then sputtered as she
swallowed a mouthful of water.

When she stopped choking, trying to spit out the
salty taste, he was swimming again, pulling himself
further out, deeper into the swirling, heavy gray-
ness of the low fog.

"No — Buddy — wait!"

He stopped his stroke, floated, waited for her to
catch up.

"Buddy — really. I want to go back now. I'm not
that good a swimmer."

To her surprise, his expression had completely
changed. It was as if all the warmth had floated
away. He stared at her with cold, narrowed eyes.

He grabbed her shoulder. Hard.

"I'm going to take care of you," he said. Without
warmth or concern.

"What?" Was he trying to reassure her? That
didn't seem to be his intention.

Was he trying to *scare* her? Why would he do that?

"Buddy — I'm going back now."

"No. You're not. I'm going to take care of you, Maria."

Reading his expression, she gasped. "Let go of me!"

4
Hurt Feelings

"Let go!" Maria repeated.

Buddy released his grip and gave her a hard shove.

She felt suddenly heavy, heavy with fear. So heavy, she felt that she might sink, just drop out of sight to the bottom of the ocean and never come up.

Why was he glaring at her like that?

What had she *done*?

"You hurt my feelings," he said, as if answering her question.

A strong current raised them both up toward the graying sky, swirled them around. Thick wisps of fog lowered around them, floating toward the shore.

I'm dreaming, Maria thought. This is a bad dream.

I can't be out in the ocean in the hazy fog, so far from shore, with this boy so filled with anger, with hatred.

"Buddy — it was a joke!" she shouted, pleading, her fear choking the sound of her voice. Again, she swallowed a mouthful of water, salty and thick. She coughed, cleared her throat. "We were just joking!"

"It was no joke!" he screamed, anger tightening his features. *"You hurt my feelings."*

"Well, I'm sorry," she said, turning her eyes to shore. The beach had been swallowed up by the haze. She couldn't tell where the water ended and the land began.

How far out *am* I? she wondered.

Can I make it back by myself?

She realized she was trembling. From the cold? From her fear?

Buddy turned away from her sharply and, with long, steady strokes, swam further out, gliding through the bobbing water.

"No. Buddy — come back!" Maria pleaded. "Please!"

Should she swim after him?

Should she turn toward shore? Try to get back without his help?

She stared through the fog. If only she could see how far from shore she had swum.

If only she weren't so frightened.

He had seemed like such a nice guy. Quiet. Serious.

"Hey!"

He popped up beside her, shouting in her ear.

Startled, she uttered a short cry. "You scared me."

"I know."

"Buddy — stop. You're really scaring me. I want to go back now."

"I know."

"You're not funny," she said, trying to hold herself together, trying to hold back the loud sobs that were welling in her chest, trying to keep the tears from bursting from her eyes.

"I know."

"Stop saying that!" she screamed. "Come on — I'm cold, and I'm frightened."

"I know."

He stared at her, unblinking, silently treading water, his breathing steady, calm.

He's crazy, she thought.

She dived under a sloping wave, turned, and came up facing the shore.

At least she *thought* she was facing the shore. The fog had thickened, had formed a wall between her and the beach.

I don't even know which way to swim, she realized, feeling so heavy now, her arms so heavy, her legs. She had to force herself to keep breathing.

The sky, the gray, hazy sky, seemed low enough to reach up and touch. The wall of fog circled, closed in.

Everything was closing in on her.

Her own heart seemed to close in, to tighten.

"Buddy — what are you going to do? My arms are tired. I can't keep floating like this."

"You hurt my feelings," he repeated, staring

hard into her eyes. For the first time, she noticed a slender scar on his chin, like a tiny, white snake catching the white glare of the sky.

"Buddy — can we go back and dry off and talk about it on the beach?" she begged, her voice high and tight, a voice she'd never heard before.

He ignored her question. "You lied to me, Maria."

"Huh?"

I can't breathe, she thought.

I can't breathe, and I can't move my arms.

"I know you went out with Stuart last night."

"I'm sorry, Buddy. Really. I am. But you have to take me back now. *You have to take me back!*"

"I just hate to be lied to," he said flatly, his face expressionless.

Maria suddenly realized he wasn't staring at her. His gaze was over her shoulder, past her in the rolling waters. She turned to see what had caught his eye.

Dark shapes. Skimming rapidly along the surface of the water.

Like submarines. Dark triangles moving silently toward them.

Buddy returned his eyes to hers.

She saw the smile form on his face. The strangest smile.

"Sharks," he said.

5
Where Is Buddy?

Maria took another glance at the approaching black triangles, gliding so quickly, so easily over the water toward them.

The strange smile hadn't faded from Buddy's face. His eyes glowed, almost gleefully.

Choked with panic, Maria turned and began thrashing toward shore. Her arms ached. Her legs kicked wildly.

I don't want to die.

I don't want to die.

Was she swimming in the right direction?

Was she moving?

She couldn't tell which way the current was pulling her. Surrounded by the thick, wet fog, she couldn't even see which way to swim.

"Buddy — help me!"

She wasn't even sure it was she who was screaming — screaming Buddy's name again and again as the dark triangles swam closer, deadly shadows against the white fog wall.

"Buddy! Buddy!'

Thrashing in panic, kicking out frantically, she held her breath, dived down, tried to stroke normally, then emerged, gasping for breath.

And felt a hand grip her arm.

"Buddy!"

Water poured down her face, so cold, so salty.

And when her burning eyes cleared, his strange smile was close to her face.

She pulled away. Or tried to. But he had her in a powerful, one-handed grip.

And in his other hand?

She struggled to focus.

Her eyes blurred by the saltwater, by her panic.

The fog seemed to be inside her head now, descending, blocking out her thoughts, as thick as the fog that surrounded her in the tossing waters.

And when her eyes finally cleared, she saw the small, red-handled knife in his hand.

Knife?

She thrashed harder. But he wouldn't let go.

Knife?

"Buddy!"

Yes. A knife.

She gasped, swallowing water, choking, spitting.

"Buddy — the knife!"

His voice was so calm, so cold and calm. "The sharks won't attack without blood, Maria."

He slashed her arm, the blade digging deep into

her flesh. The dark liquid poured into the water.

She cried out as the pain ran up her arm, cutting through the fog in her mind.

The pain shot through her entire body, as fast as sharks through water.

And then another stab of pain. And another.

As Buddy stabbed her. And slashed her.

And it was hard to tell where the blood stopped and the ocean began.

"Shark food." She thought she heard him say that.

And she thought she heard him laugh. A high-pitched, crazy giggle.

"Shark food."

Yes. He repeated it.

So calm. So cold.

And then she heard his high-pitched laugh again. And she heard him call: "See you later, alligator." He sounded so . . . happy.

Then, he was gone.

Thrashing, choking, she felt herself sink, pulled down into her own blood, down, down into the cold, swirling darkness.

Buddy made his way easily to shore. Running onto the beach just a few yards from the beach house, a dark, hovering square against the steamy fog, he turned back to the water.

Shielding his eyes from the glare with both hands, he searched for Maria.

No.

No sign of her.

Gone.

"Shark food."

He said it aloud a few more times.

It was funny, actually.

He realized he was shivering.

The thrill of it was wearing off, and now he was just cold.

The excitement wasn't quite what he had expected. Sure, it was thrilling, he thought.

Sure, it was really *neat*.

But the thrill of it had worn off already.

And now he felt . . .

What did he feel?

Nothing. Nothing at all.

Just cold and wet. And eager to get home.

He scanned the dark water one more time. No sign of her.

Then, shivering hard, he picked up the towel he had left on the sand. Draping it over his shoulders, he jogged to the beach house.

He climbed up the four steps to the deck, then walked around to the sliding-glass door, not the slightest bit out of breath. He slid the door open, stepped quickly inside, then carefully slid it closed behind him.

Dunehampton police officers, in their knee-length black shorts and black, short-sleeved uniform shirts, covered the beach like dark seabirds, poking everywhere, eyes darting along the shoreline, their radios crackling. Police from two neighboring towns had been called to join the search.

A dark Coast Guard ship prowled the waters offshore, slicing through the early evening fog. From shore, the ship seemed to drift in and out of the haze, a ghostly shadow on the horizon.

"They won't find her," Amy said miserably, wiping tears from her eyes with both hands. "She can't still be swimming. She has to be dead."

"She wasn't a very good swimmer," Stuart said sadly, hands shoved into the pockets of his tan Bermuda shorts. "She told me so."

"I can't believe we're talking about Maria in the past tense," Ronnie said, his voice breaking with emotion.

Normally, Stuart loved to imitate Ronnie when his voice cracked like that. But now he didn't raise his eyes from the sand.

The three friends continued walking aimlessly along the drab, cold, fog-ridden beach, watching the policemen, hoping against hope that Maria might show up alive.

"It's so gray," Amy said. "Everything is gray — the sand, the sky, the water." She uttered a loud sob and covered her face with her hands. "I can't believe I was standing right here with Maria. Less than a few hours ago we were walking here, kidding around. And we had no idea that in a few hours, Maria would be — "

She sobbed again. She didn't want to finish her sentence.

Ronnie stooped over and put an arm around her shoulder, his yellow windbreaker flapping in the wind off the ocean.

"As long as her body isn't found, there's still hope," Stuart said. But his quavering voice showed that even he didn't believe that.

"You know what I feel bad about?" Ronnie asked, still holding Amy. She pressed her face against the front of his shirt to muffle her sobs, her shoulders bobbing up and down.

"What?" Stuart asked, staring out at the shadowy Coast Guard ship.

"We were so mean to Buddy."

"Yeah." Ronnie kicked at the wet sand. "We weren't too nice to him, were we?" he said regretfully. "He wasn't such a bad guy."

"Yeah," Stuart agreed softly.

Amy pushed herself from Ronnie, rubbing away the tears that streaked down her cheeks, which were red and swollen from crying. "I think I'm all cried out," she said, her chin trembling. "It — it's just so strange. I can still picture Maria and Buddy standing here. They can't be dead. They *can't* be!"

"Buddy was a real good swimmer," Stuart said thoughtfully. "He was a real champ. Something bad must have happened out there. I just don't understand — "

They were interrupted by a solemn-faced, young policeman, who came jogging up to them, his black high-top Keds squishing over the sand. He was boy-

ishly handsome, with a short blond flattop and clear
blue eyes.

He looks like Tab Hunter, Amy thought. And
then scolded herself: How can I be thinking about
movie stars at a time like this?

"Sorry to bother you," the policeman said in a
surprisingly deep voice. "I'm Officer Barrett. I'm
stationed in Westhaven."

"Hi," Stuart said uncomfortably, staring at the
silver badge pinned over the pocket of the young
policeman's short-sleeved shirt. Poking out of the
pocket was a pack of Old Gold cigarettes.

The others nodded silently at the officer. Amy
reached for Ronnie's hand. "Do you have bad
news?" she asked reluctantly.

Barrett shook his head. "No. I just wondered if
you'd repeat a few things. I know you told your
story to someone from the Dunehampton station.
But I'd just like to double-check."

Amy breathed a sigh of relief, but held tightly
to Ronnie's hand. "They haven't found them?" she
asked.

The policeman shook his head again. "It's real
foggy. Can't see very far. No sign of anything on
the beach. The Coast Guard spotted a number of
sharks pretty close in to shore, but — "

"Sharks?" Amy cried, her eyes wide with alarm.

The policeman blushed, realizing he'd made a
mistake. "Nothing to be alarmed about," he said
quickly, shifting his weight uncomfortably, staring
at Amy over the notepad in his hand. "I mean, it's

pretty normal to see sharks this time of year. I mean — " He cleared his throat and turned his eyes to the notepad. "You say you saw her go off this morning with a boy named Buddy?" he asked, lowering his voice, assuming a more businesslike tone.

"Yeah," Amy said, nodding.

"Did you see the two of them go into the water?"

"No," Amy replied. "I left. I had to go take care of Mary Ann. My little sister. But I know Buddy *wanted* to go swimming. He wanted all three of us to — " She shivered, realizing that if she had stayed, she might have drowned with them.

"But you didn't actually see them go swimming?" Barrett demanded, locking his blue eyes on Amy.

"No," Amy said uncertainly. "Not actually. Do you think — ?"

Barrett shrugged his broad shoulders. "Your guess is as good as mine." He glanced back at the pad. "And no one knows this Buddy's last name?"

None of them did.

"His parents haven't called the police to report him missing or anything," Barrett told them. "Do you know Buddy's parents?"

Again, none of them did.

I've never seen his parents, Amy thought.

"Maybe they're away for the day or something," Barrett said, rapidly jotting a note in his pad. "Maybe they don't know he's missing. Now, tell me again where Buddy and his family are staying."

"Right up there," Stuart said, pointing to the dark beach house. All four of them turned their eyes to the house. When the tide was out, the stilts underneath looked even more like legs.

"I'm going to take a look over there," Barrett told them. "Thanks for your help."

"Is it okay if we come, too?" Ronnie asked, squeezing Amy's hand.

"I guess," Barrett replied, starting to jog toward the beach house. "Just keep out of the way. And don't touch a thing."

Four steps led up to a wooden deck that circled the house. A sliding-glass door faced the ocean. Barrett pulled the handle with both hands. The door slid open easily, and they stepped inside.

"Anybody home?" Barrett called.

Silence.

Even with the doors and windows closed, the steady wash of the ocean filled the house. "Like being on a boat," Barrett muttered, his eyes surveying the living room.

Amy and the two boys stood in the doorway. From there they could see the big living room, with its sloping cathedral ceiling, and, beyond it, the bright, pale green kitchen. A hallway at the far wall led to the bedrooms in back.

The living room was sparsely furnished, they saw. The furniture was very modern-looking. A pastel-green and blue vinyl couch with wrought-iron legs stood against one wall behind a low, oval-shaped, glass and wrought-iron coffee table. A very low, canvas chair stood at an angle to the couch beside a chrome floor lamp. Bookshelves made of white two-by-fours and red bricks lined the wall. But the shelves were empty.

The house, Amy saw, was empty.

No magazines or newspapers on the coffee table.

No food, no dirty dishes or glasses on the pale rose-colored Formica kitchen counter.

No bathing suits or beach towels tossed on the floor.

The couch cushions were perfectly smooth, as if no one had ever sat on them.

Nothing out of place. No sign of anyone.

"Stay here," Barrett ordered. "I'll be right back."

He disappeared into the hallway, and they could hear him walking around on the uncarpeted floors. "Big closet," they heard him mutter from the front bedroom.

He reappeared a few seconds later, scratching his short blond hair, shaking his head.

"No clothes," he told them. "No suitcases. No toothbrush in the bathroom." He walked past them into the kitchen and pulled open the refrigerator. "Empty."

"But we saw him — " Amy started.

He pulled open the cabinet door under the sink. No waste basket. No cleaning supplies.

He pulled open the broom closet. Empty. He opened the door on the white enamel oven. Spotless inside.

"No one lives here," Barrett said, giving Amy a suspicious stare. "Look at this place. It's untouched. No one has *ever* lived here."

"But we saw him come out of this house!" Amy protested. "Maria and I. This morning."

"Yeah. Buddy *told* us he was staying here," Ronnie told the policeman.

Barrett narrowed his eyes and scowled at them. "Buddy lied."

PART TWO

This Summer

6
Carried Away

"Wow! Is this beautiful or what?" Ashley declared.

She slid to the bottom of the dune and stared across the crowded beach to the ocean, sparkling under the brilliant afternoon sun as if lit by millions of tiny diamonds.

Dragging his yellow Styrofoam boogie board across the sand, Ross came up beside her. "Ow! The sand is *hot* here. Let's go closer to the water."

Ashley twisted her pretty face into an expression of mock sympathy. "Oooh, the little feet are too hot?" she asked in a sarcastic baby voice.

Ross scowled, furrowing his dark eyebrows. "The sand is *hot*, Ashley. You don't have to make fun of me."

"Yes, I do," she replied, giving him a playful shove that sent him toppling into the side of the dune. "It's my hobby."

"Well, get a new hobby," he said, not smiling.

He used the boogie board to help pull himself up
and brushed sand off his orange Day Glo baggies.
"Why not take up aerobics or something and get off
my case?"

"Hey — " She put a hand tenderly on his tanned
shoulder and pushed her lips into a pout. "You think
I need exercise or something?" She took a step back
and struck a pose for him.

Ashley was thin and beautiful, and knew it. She
had very fine, straight, silvery-blonde hair, high
cheekbones, and striking green eyes over a perfect,
straight nose and delicate, heart-shaped lips.

She looked like a model in *Seventeen* or *Sassy*
and, in fact, she had done some fashion modeling
back home in Ridgefield. She also knew that the
chartreuse bikini she was wearing was a knockout.

"I didn't say you need exercise," Ross insisted,
smiling finally. "I said you needed a different hobby.
Something better than picking on me. Why don't
you go save the rain forests or something?"

"Why don't *you*?" she snapped back. "I think
teasing you is a perfectly good hobby. Keeps you
from getting a swelled head."

Ross didn't reply. Instead, he tugged at the handle of his boogie board and started down toward
the water.

"Hey — wait up!" Ashley had to jog to keep up
with him.

They made their way past a fast and furious volleyball game. A boom box resting on an enormous

Mickey Mouse beach blanket blared rap music.

"Keep going," Ashley instructed, putting a hand on Ross's shoulder. "I think I see Lucy and Kip."

"Don't you think Kip looks like Vanilla Ice?" Ross asked, picking up the boogie board and making his way between two tilting beach umbrellas.

"He's trying," Ashley said dryly.

Ross stopped suddenly. "You're glad you came?"

Ashley smiled at him. "Yeah. Somehow I couldn't get too pumped about spending the day on a smelly fishing boat with Mom and my two brothers."

His dark eyes peered into hers. "Were they crying their eyes out because you decided to come with me?"

"Not exactly," Ashley admitted. "In fact, I think Robin's exact words were, 'Who cares?' "

She expected him to laugh, but his expression turned thoughtful. Ross looks just like Matt Dillon, Ashley thought. The straight black hair and heavy eyebrows, the intense, serious face.

She smiled and gave the lifeguard, a beefy blond with bright red cheeks, a friendly wave as they walked in front of the tall, white, wooden chair.

Ross scowled. "Hey — don't flirt with him. How could you come on to a guy who looks like that?"

Ashley turned angrily. "You *said* you weren't going to be so jealous all the time, Ross."

He shrugged. "You promised you wouldn't come on to every guy on the beach."

"I didn't come on to him. I just smiled. Are you

going to keep your promise or not?"

"Yeah. Okay," he muttered, avoiding her stare. "Sorry."

"Hey — there's Lucy and Kip. On that big MTV blanket. Over there. See?" She waved to Lucy, but Lucy was talking to Kip and didn't see her.

"Look at him," Ross urged, hurrying to keep up with her. "Vanilla Ice. Right?"

"On a bad day," she muttered.

"You don't like Kip, do you?"

Ashley shook her head. "I think he's mean. He's not very nice to Lucy. And he has no sense of humor at all."

Ross started to say something, but they had reached Lucy's blanket. Lucy was lying on her stomach beside Kip, but she jumped up, adjusting her bikini top, to greet the two arrivals. She had curly auburn hair, a face full of freckles, and enormous blue eyes.

"Hey — how's it going?" Kip asked, reaching for a bottle of suntan lotion.

"Isn't this a gorgeous day?" Lucy said excitedly. She had a slight lisp, which made her sound like a little girl. Lucy didn't mind. Most boys thought it was really cute.

Lucy never had any trouble attracting boys, which made Ashley really wonder why she chose to hang out with this tough-looking townie, Kip.

Ross propped the boogie board up in the sand and dropped down next to Kip on the beach towel. "What number is that?" he asked, pointing to the lotion Kip was slathering onto his narrow, white shoulders.

"Two hundred and twelve, I think," Kip replied, squeezing more from the bottle. "I need a lot of protection." The diamondlike stud in his ear glinted in the sun.

"Did you quit your job?" Ashley asked Kip, trying to be friendly for Lucy's sake. Kip's summer job was driving an ice-cream truck from beach to beach.

"No. My day off. The little animals will have to get their ice cream from someone else today." He rolled onto his side, turning his back on the others.

"I'm so jealous of you," Lucy said to Ashley.

"Huh?" Ashley reacted with surprise. "What are you talking about?"

"You get to stay here and party all summer. I have to go back to Ridgefield in two weeks." Lucy slapped at a green fly on her leg.

"Bummer," Kip muttered without turning around.

"Maybe you could stay with us," Ashley said, kicking off her rubber thongs. "There's an extra guestroom at the house we're renting. I could ask my parents."

"No, I can't," Lucy said, shaking her head. "I'm taking the second term of summer school, remember? A little brushup on the French I practically flunked last spring."

"Well, we'll just have to make sure it's a great two weeks," Ashley said enthusiastically. She

turned her gaze down the crowded beach. A few
brave souls had ventured into the water, little children, mostly. But even with the June sun burning
down, the water still was cold enough to make your
ankles ache.

Her eyes came to rest on the old beach house
jutting into the water on stilts at the end of the
beach. Who ever decided to build a house there?
she wondered, as she had been wondering every
summer since her family had started coming to Dunehampton. There were no other houses on the beach,
certainly not right in the water.

And why hadn't the house ever been sold or
rented?

She and Ross had walked over to it a few nights
before. They had found it as dark and empty as in
previous years. The redwood walls had been darkened nearly to black by the moisture and salt in the
air. The floorboards of the deck had started to rot,
and a window pane in one of the bedrooms had shat-
tered, leaving a gaping hole.

The house is kind of sad and creepy, Ashley
thought. She wished someone would tear it down.

"Could you get us some free Fudgsicles from your
truck tomorrow?" Ross asked Kip. "Or maybe some
toasted almond bars?"

To everyone's surprise, Kip spun around and sat
up, glaring at Ross angrily. "Hey, man, are you
putting me down because I have to work this
summer?"

"Whoa — " Ross started, raising both hands as

if to shield himself. He edged away from Kip on the blanket.

But Kip wouldn't let Ross get a word in. "You think it's some kind of a joke because I have to wear a stupid uniform and sell stupid ice cream while you lie on the beach all day?" he raged, his pale face reddening, his hands balled into tight fists.

"Whoa — " Ross jumped to his feet. "I wasn't putting you down," he insisted heatedly. "I've had summer jobs before. I work after school. My dad was laid off for over a year, Kip."

Kip scowled and looked away.

"I was just kidding around," Ross said, glancing at Ashley.

"Well, don't kid around," Kip snapped, but his angry tone had softened. "I don't like kidding around." And then he added, "Unless I'm doing the kidding." A weak joke, but at least he was trying to show Ross that he wasn't still angry.

"You've got to watch out for Kip," Lucy added with a phony laugh, trying to keep things light. "He's a *baad dude.*"

"You summer people come here and think you own the place," Kip grumbled, ignoring Lucy. "Meanwhile, the rest of us are here all winter, just trying to hang on. Just hanging on."

He dropped back down on the big MTV beach blanket, again turning his back on them. "You like the blue Italian ice, comes in a cup?" he asked Ross quietly.

"Yeah. I guess," Ross replied.

"I can probably get you some of those. It's my worst seller."

"Ugh. Blue food," Ashley said, making a face. "What flavor is it?"

"Blue," Kip told her.

Ashley started to protest that blue wasn't a flavor. But her words caught in her throat as a hulking figure spun her around from behind.

She screamed as he picked her up in his powerful arms, his long, black hair wild about his face, his eyes wide with excitement, his mouth fixed in a determined grin.

Lucy leapt back in surprise, covering her mouth with her hands.

Ross and Kip struggled to their feet.

But they were too late.

The enormous intruder was running off with Ashley, carrying her toward the water.

"Help!" Ashley screamed. "Ross — help! *Please!*"

7
Ashley's Fear

"Ross — help me!"

Ashley's pleas for help were drowned out by an openmouthed roar from her captor. She struggled to free herself, pounding his broad chest with her fists, but he held her tightly, running rapidly to the water.

His feet were splashing up water now.

Roaring at the top of his lungs, he carried her straight into a crashing wave.

"Let go!" she shrieked.

And he did.

And Ashley plummeted into the freezing cold water, sputtering and thrashing her arms and legs.

Her feet found the sandy bottom. She stood. Ducked under a wave.

Then leapt at her captor, shoving his shoulders. "Denny — you're an animal!" she screamed, shoving him again.

Denny Drake laughed. "You looked hot, Ashley.

I thought maybe you needed to cool off."

Struggling to stay afloat, she splashed him with one hand. "And you know what *you* need? You need a *keeper*!"

He laughed again, enjoying his triumph.

Denny had grown up a few houses down from Ross back in Ridgefield. He wasn't really a friend. But he always seemed to be around.

A tall, muscular guy with big shoulders and a well-developed chest, Denny could have been a stand-in for the Incredible Hulk. In fact, that was his nickname back at Ridgefield High — Hulkster.

"You and I have *got* to stop meeting like this, Ashley," he joked, giving her a final splash before hauling himself out of the water.

"Shut up, Denny," she shouted. "You got my new bathing suit all wet!"

He laughed again, shaking his long hair like a dog after a bath. "You *love* it. Why don't you lose that wimp and go to the six-plex with me tonight?" He gestured toward Ross, who was still back with the others, all three of them laughing at Ashley's abduction.

Ashley came running out of the water, moving quickly past Denny, heading toward her friends. "You're joking — right?"

"Huh-uh." Denny shook his head.

"Go *out* with you? That's your funniest joke yet."

Denny's expression changed. He looked hurt. "Thanks for the swim." He snarled and clomped away.

Lucy came running with a towel for Ashley. She dried Ashley's hair and shoulders, then draped it around her. "Denny really is a beast," Ashley muttered.

"I think he likes you," Lucy said seriously.

"Thrills and chills," was Ashley's sarcastic reply.

When they got back to the MTV blanket, Ashley was surprised to see that they had been joined by a new boy, someone she had never seen before. He was tall and good-looking, with wavy dark hair and a shy smile. He was wearing blue spandex trunks, very tight, and a red and white Grateful Dead T-shirt, several sizes too big.

"How was the water?" Kip asked, chuckling.

"Just great," Ashley told him. "You should try it."

"You gonna *carry* me in?" Kip teased.

Ashley made a face at him, sticking out her tongue. She searched her bag and pulled out a dry towel. Then she turned to the new boy. "Hi."

"This is Brad," Ross said to Ashley. He shrugged at Brad. "Sorry. I forgot your last name."

"Brad Sayles," the boy replied, keeping his dark eyes on Ashley. "Ross and I took tennis lessons together last summer. Remember — we had that instructor who couldn't serve the ball over the net?"

"Yeah. He was a real winner," Ross said. "He couldn't serve, but he had a great follow-through. All he ever talked about was follow-through."

"Are you a townie?" Ashley asked, embarrassed by the way Brad was staring at her. She wrapped the towel around her waist like a sarong.

"No," Brad said, smiling as if Ashley had made a joke. "We live in Cambridge. But my family has always had a house here. On Ocean Drive."

"Ocean Drive?" Kip exclaimed. He had been drowsing, but the two words snapped him back to life. "You mean where all the big mansions are?"

Standing behind the blanket, Brad shifted his weight uncomfortably. "Our house is pretty big," he said, as if confessing to a major sin. "I guess you could call it a mansion." All the while, he kept staring at Ashley, smiling at her, studying her.

"Does it have an east wing and a west wing?" Lucy asked, dropping down beside Kip. "I've always wanted a house with wings."

Brad chuckled pleasantly. "Well, there's a servants' wing. And then the rest of the house. Oh. And a guest house. And . . . a pool house."

Kip whistled appreciatively.

"Wow," Lucy said.

Brad blushed. "You guys are embarrassing me. I can't help it if my grandfather made a ton of money. I had nothing to do with it."

He's sweet, Ashley thought. She liked the way his cheeks turned pink. He's really very good-looking. And he doesn't seem at all stuck-up like some rich people. Just the opposite.

I think he likes me, she thought. The way he's staring at me, as if trying to give me a message with his eyes.

Well, I got the message, Brad.

And you know what? I'm kind of attracted to you,
too.

She glanced at Ross and caught an angry expression. Ross looked quickly toward the ocean.

How can he be jealous already? Ashley thought,
extremely annoyed. Aren't I even allowed to *talk*
to another boy?

Ross and I have really got to discuss this, she
decided.

He promised me he'd try to control his stupid
jealousy. But look at him — standing there so
tense, so totally bent out of shape, hovering there
like a mother hen, flashing me dirty looks. And for
no reason at all.

The more she thought about it, the angrier Ashley became.

She had a sudden impulse to grab Brad by the
back of the head with both hands, pull his face close,
and plant a long, passionate kiss on his lips.

Give Ross something to *really* be jealous
about.

Instead, she dropped down onto the sand, sitting
cross-legged, and motioned for Brad to sit down
beside her. He obediently sat down, stretching his
long legs out, leaning back on his hands.

"So you have a pool?" she asked him.

He nodded. "Yes, it's really neat. It's Olympic-
sized."

"Heated, of course?"

"Of course," he said, grinning. "Do you play tennis, too, Ashley?"

"Yeah. Ross and I have been playing every morning. Before it gets too hot."

"Well, maybe you'd like to come play a few sets at my house. We have our own clay court."

"That would be excellent," Ashley replied enthusiastically. "Wouldn't it, Ross?" She glanced up. "Ross?"

Where was he?

"Hey — Ross?"

Then she saw him walking away, taking long, angry strides. Ashley jumped to her feet and called to him, cupping her hands around her mouth. "Ross, come back!"

He must have heard her. But he kept walking without turning around.

Oh, wonderful, Ashley thought, sighing. She watched him disappear over the dunes, heading for the road.

Now what have I done?

"Ross, how can you be jealous? I was just *talking* to Brad." Ashley tried to take Ross's arm, but he angrily pulled away from her.

"Ross, come *on.*"

A silvery half-moon shone in the dark, hazy sky. Slivers of black cloud floated in front of it. Shadows lengthened, then shifted over the gray beach.

They were walking slowly along the edge of the dunes. Below them, ocean waves rose, dark and threatening, then crashed noisily against the sand.

The wind ruffled through Ashley's hair. She

tugged at the sleeves of the white sweatshirt she wore over black spandex leggings.

"Ross, what's your problem?"

"I *saw* the way you were looking at him," he muttered, his voice barely carrying over the roar and crash of the tumbling waves.

"I was just being friendly," Ashley replied, having to hurry to keep up with Ross's long strides. "He seemed like an okay guy. We don't have to go play on his tennis court if you don't want to."

He scowled, but didn't reply. They walked on in silence for a while.

The beach house came into view. In high tide, its stilts disappeared, and the house seemed to float on the water.

"Ross, say something. I'm getting cold. I don't want to keep walking."

He stopped and turned to her, his expression unhappy. He had his black hair tied back in a ponytail. His soulful eyes again reminded Ashley of Matt Dillon.

"Ross — say something. *Please.*"

She could see the anger spread across his face, see the hurt glow in his dark, unblinking eyes.

And suddenly she realized she was afraid of him.

He took a step toward her, his mouth frozen in an angry scowl.

Her throat tightened with fear.

She had seen him angry before. She had seen him, out of control, shove his fist through a plate-glass window.

He had the same anger now. She could almost feel it radiating from him.

This is so silly, she thought.

He's all worked up about *nothing*.

But she felt the fear just the same.

The chilling fear that if he lost his temper, he might do *anything*.

She took a step back as he moved toward her.

What was he going to do?

8
Into the Beach House

"I thought we were going to spend a great summer together," Ross finally said, standing very close to her, so close that she could practically feel the tension and anger in his body.

Ashley breathed a silent sigh of relief. At least he was keeping it under control. He wasn't going to hurt her.

He never had.

Why had she suddenly felt so afraid of him?

Maybe *I'm* the one who's losing it, she thought.

"Yes. Well — " she started.

"It was supposed to be just you and me this summer. But first you let Denny carry you into the water — "

"*Let* him?!" Ashley cried. "I didn't have much choice, did I? He came at me like a charging bull. And I didn't exactly see you come running to my rescue!"

Ross ignored her impassioned defense.

"Will you get serious?" Ashley cried. "You don't really believe I'm interested in Denny, do you?"

" — And then you start coming on to that wimpy rich kid," Ross continued, avoiding her eyes. "In front of everyone."

Now he's totally gone bananas, Ashley thought bitterly. She hated this jealousy of his, this possessiveness. It really made her furious. And afraid.

But it was also nice to know that Ross cared so much about her.

Only why did he have to be so insecure?

She *liked* to flirt with guys. It was fun.

Harmless fun.

Why couldn't Ross just lighten up once in a while?

They had discussed this before, and he'd promised that he'd try. But here they were discussing it again.

Oh, well. Ashley knew there was one quick way to end the discussion.

She reached up and grabbed his shoulders. And pulled him to her. And kissed him. A long, passionate kiss.

She didn't pull her face away until they were both breathless.

She stared into his eyes. His expression had softened. He had stopped scowling at her.

Works every time, she thought.

And kissed him again. Longer this time.

"Now are you going to shape up?" she asked playfully.

He shrugged and smiled.

She shivered. "Ooh, it's so cold. I'm totally frozen."

"I have an idea," he whispered. He gestured toward the beach house just up ahead.

Ashley hadn't realized they had walked that far. They were standing a few yards from the deck that surrounded the old house. It loomed over them, a black shadow against the starless, purple night sky.

"Let's go in and warm up," Ross said, tugging at her hand, pulling her toward the wooden stairs that led up to the deck from the dunes.

"Go in? How can we?" She pulled back.

"The door's probably open. No one has ever lived here, remember? Come on, Ashley. It's bound to be warmer in there than it is out here."

She looked up at the dark windows and shivered.

"Come on," he urged, pulling her hand. We'll pretend the house is ours."

She laughed. "Who would *want* it?" But she relented and followed him up the creaking wooden steps and onto the deck.

"Careful," he warned, whispering for some reason, and pointing down toward his bare feet. "Some of the deck boards are rotting."

They made their way around to the glass door that faced the ocean. Below them, they could hear the rush of the ocean as it flowed under the house.

Is the deck swaying in the water? Ashley wondered, gripping Ross's hand tighter. Is the whole house swaying? Or is it just my imagination?

"Ross — we really shouldn't do this," she whispered. She pressed her face to the glass door and peered inside.

Blackness. It was too dark to see anything.

"There won't be any electricity or anything," she said, backing up a step.

"So? It'll be fun," he insisted. "Our own private place." He squeezed her hand.

Then he gripped the door handle with both hands and tugged.

The glass door slid open easily, silently.

"Told you it'd be unlocked. Come on." He disappeared into the house.

"But, Ross — " Ashley called in. "We don't have a flashlight or anything." She cautiously took a step forward, then another, feeling herself swallowed up by the darkness of the house.

"BOO!"

She gasped and nearly fell back into the open doorway.

Ross loomed at her side, laughing. "Gotcha," he said in her ear, holding her shoulders.

"That was mean," Ashley said, shoving him away.

It was surprisingly warm inside. Ross slid the door shut. As Ashley's eyes began to adjust to the darkness, she began to make out the forms of the few pieces of furniture in the room.

It was all old-fashioned looking. Very fifties. A vinyl and wrought-iron couch. A low, canvas chair. A chrome floor lamp.

She made her way across the room, the wooden

floorboards creaking, the rush of water below, and tried the lamp.

Nothing.

"You're not afraid to be alone with me in the dark, are you?" Ross teased, stepping up behind her, leaning against her, slipping his arms around her waist.

"I'm afraid to be *anywhere* with you!" she joked. She lowered her hands and covered his. "Look at this place. It's all furnished and everything. Ready for someone to move in. But no one ever has."

"*We* have," Ross insisted, and pulled her down onto the vinyl couch.

He kissed her, wrapping his muscular arms around her, holding her tightly. "Feeling warmer?"

"A lot," she whispered. And kissed him again.

She pulled away with a start when she heard the clatter from the hallway.

They both listened.

The bedrooms must be back there, she figured.

And then she heard the clump of shoes against the floor.

And whispered voices.

"Ross — " Ashley whispered, grabbing his hand. "There's someone else in here!"

9
Murders

Ross leaned over Ashley and reached up to the lamp. He clicked it twice before he remembered there was no electricity.

The footsteps from the back hallway grew louder.

They both jumped to their feet.

A pale rectangle of moonlight spread on the floor in front of them. The ocean waves splashed noisily below the floor.

"Who's there?" Ashley called, her tight voice revealing her fear.

The footsteps stopped.

"Who's there?" she repeated, leaning against Ross.

She heard loud whispering. Then two figures appeared, moving slowly side by side, stopping just past the hall door.

"Who is it?" a girl called. A familiar voice.

"Hey — " The voice of her companion was also familiar.

"Lucy?" Ashley cried.

Kip and Lucy moved forward to greet Ashley and Ross. All four began talking excitedly at once, laughing with relief.

"How did you find us?" Lucy asked.

"We weren't exactly looking for you," Ross said dryly.

"We discovered the house was open a few nights ago," Lucy said. "It's really awesome, isn't it?"

"It was our own private place till you two barged in," Kip said unhappily. He walked to the glass door and stared out at the ocean.

"Well, we didn't know — " Ashley started to explain to him.

"It's like being on a boat," Lucy said happily. "The house even sways a little, like a boat. I just *love* it!"

"It's a little . . . creepy," Ashley said, peering into the dark kitchen.

"I don't think so. I think it's romantic," Lucy gushed.

"Me, too," Ross said, putting an arm around Ashley's shoulder.

Kip continued to stare silently out the door. Ashley figured he was really angry that she and Ross had barged in on them like this. He's so hostile and unfriendly, she decided. Why does Lucy like him so much? "I wonder why no one lives here," she said.

"Maybe it's because of the murders," Kip declared without turning around.

"Huh? Murders?"

"There are a lot of stories," Kip said mysteriously. He finally turned back and joined them in front of the couch. "Really gross stories. About murders."

As Kip said this, Ashley saw his eyes light up, his face come alive.

"Murders? Here? In this house?" Lucy asked.

"Yeah," Kip said. "You don't live here, so you don't know the stories. But everyone in Dunehampton knows. About the murders, I mean."

"Who was murdered?" Ashley asked, crossing her arms over her chest as if for protection.

"Teenagers," was Kip's curt reply.

The whole idea of murders in this house really pumps him up, Ashley thought, studying Kip's glowing eyes and his amused expression.

"Teenagers were killed here. In and around the house."

"When?" Ross asked.

"A long time ago. Sometime in the fifties. Just after the house was built." The amused smile spread across Kip's face. The stud in his ear sparkled as he stepped into the rectangle of light.

He narrowed his eyes. "They never caught whoever did it. Never solved the mystery." He stepped back into the darkness. "And no one has lived here since." He snickered, looking from face to face.

"That's really gross," Lucy said, shaking her head.

"Ross, let's get out of here," Ashley urged, reaching for his hand. She suddenly felt thoroughly chilled again.

Ross laughed. "You're frightened because of some silly story that happened over thirty years ago?"

"It's not a story. It's true," Kip said defensively.

"The idea of kids being killed right here — it just creeps me out, that's all," Ashley said, starting toward the door.

"Hey, come on, not so fast," Ross called to her. He turned to Kip. "Tell us more about it. More details."

"No!" Ashley insisted heatedly. "I really don't like it here, Ross. I'm leaving." She slid open the door. The roar of the ocean swept into the room like an angry cry. "Bye, guys," Ashley called, stepping out.

"Later," Ross said, running after her.

As he turned to slide the door closed, he saw Kip put his arm around Lucy and lead her to the couch.

He's a weird guy, Ross thought.

Wonder why he thought those murders were so funny? . . .

Ashley waited for him on the steps. "It's late," she said, yawning. "All this fresh air makes me sleepy."

"Why do you think Kip is so weird?" Ross asked as they headed over the dunes toward the road that led to their rented houses.

"He's just got a problem because he's a townie and we're not, and he thinks we all look down on townies."

"Well, we do, don't we?" Ross joked.

She laughed, pleased that his mood had improved so much. As they walked, holding hands, they talked about Lucy and Kip and the beach house.

The half-moon was high in the sky. A few stars had poked out from the clouds. The beach was deserted. In the dark ocean, sea gulls sat on the purple water, riding the rolling waves as they slept.

Ross's parents' house, a small, white clapboard bungalow, was first along the narrow, winding road. They stopped at the walk. "I'll walk you home, then come back," Ross offered.

Ashley shook her head. "No need. You know my house is just over that hill. Go to sleep. I'll call you in the morning."

Before he could protest, she kissed him quickly, missing his mouth and bumping his chin, then turned and began jogging over the hill to her house.

The road was lined on both sides with tall, grassy reeds, tilting in the wind, brushing against each other, whispering and bending.

Ashley made her way over the low, sloping hill, the reeds leaning over the road as if reaching for her. As her house came into view, she slowed to a walk.

And someone leapt out of the tall reeds to her right and grabbed her from behind.

10
Disappeared

With an anguished cry, Ashley struggled to free herself. But her attacker held her around the waist in an unbreakable grip.

She flailed out her arms and tried to kick.

He laughed and spun her around to face him.

"Denny!" she cried, her voice hoarse from her terror. "Denny — you *animal!*"

He leered at her, bringing his beefy, perspiring face close to hers. "Did I scare you?"

Furiously she swung her hand in an attempt to slap him. But he caught her hand inches from his face and held it.

"Hey, I was just goofing," he said, sounding hurt.

"I'm going to call the police. I really am," Ashley insisted. "Let *go* of my hand, Denny."

Slowly, he released her hand. She rubbed her aching wrist. Denny was stronger than even he realized.

"You could have given me a heart attack," Ashley said, her heart finally starting to resume its normal rhythm.

"I looked for you at the clambake on the beach," he said, still leering at her. He reached up a big gorilla hand and scratched the top of his head through his long, black hair.

"Ross and I didn't go," Ashley said coldly. "Who invited *you* to the clambake?"

"Nobody," he said, with some sadness. "I just crashed."

"Are you going to let me go home or what?" she snapped angrily, still rubbing her wrist. "You've done your bad deed for the night."

He pouted his lips in an exaggerated expression of hurt. "Boo-hoo. It's still early, you know."

"Well, why don't you go step on people's sand-castles or something?" Ashley said wearily, giving him a wave of dismissal with one hand.

"I already did that," he joked. A grin spread across his broad face. "I know you're hot for me," he said.

She laughed scornfully. "Denny, you've been drinking, right?"

"Admit it, Ashley," he leaned toward her menacingly.

"Yeah, I'm hot for you, Denny. Like I'm hot to have my body ripped apart by sharks."

He thought about this for a moment, eyeing her unsteadily, letting her sarcasm sink in. Then he shoved his hands into the pockets of his denim cutoffs and frowned. "Give me a break," he muttered. "I'm sorry I scared you. Really."

"Apology accepted," she said flatly.

"It's just my dumb sense of humor, you know. How about coming for a walk with me? On the beach. A short walk."

"How about not?" Ashley replied.

His eyes flared angrily for a brief moment, then quickly cooled. "I'm serious," he said softly.

"You're not serious — you're *grim*," Ashley cracked.

He glared at her, started to say something, then stopped. "Okay, Ash. See ya, kid," he muttered. He turned away and began walking up the hill, slapping at the tall reeds along the roadside as he walked.

Ashley sighed wearily. She stood watching Denny until he disappeared over the hill.

How long had she known him?

Since second grade, at least. She had never liked him all that much. Or disliked him. He had always been around. Just one of the gang.

But, now, for the first time, she realized she was frightened of him.

He's so big, she thought, turning up the flagstone walk to her house. I don't think he even realizes how strong he is.

And he seems to have so much pent-up anger. He pretends to be playful, to be goofing, kidding around. But just below the surface, he's really kind of mean.

Mean enough to hurt someone if he didn't get his way?

Ashley yawned. She was too sleepy to think about Denny now.

Besides, he was just a pest.

He didn't really mean any harm.

Ashley slept late the next morning, arising about ten-thirty. Her parents, she learned from a note on the refrigerator, had left early for the golf course.

All they care about is golf, she thought, shaking her head.

I don't know why they drag us to the beach every summer. They don't swim. They don't like to sunbathe.

Just golf, golf, golf.

She downed a quick bowl of Wheaties, threw some stuff into her beach bag, checked the batteries on her Walkman, and headed to the beach.

She was wearing her favorite new two-piece bathing suit. Very glitzy and sexy, and an amazing shade of red. It fit her fabulously, even though it looked like something Madonna might wear, and she was eager to show off.

It was a Saturday, so the beach was already crowded. She searched for her friends, wandering back and forth, stepping around blankets and beach umbrellas. No one around.

A major disappointment. I should've saved this suit till later, she thought wistfully.

She settled close to the water, spreading out her red and white Coke beach blanket. The sun kept disappearing behind high clouds, casting the crowded beach in shadow. When it emerged, it became hot and sticky. There was barely a breeze, even so close to the ocean.

Using her beach bag as a pillow, she settled back and lifted a paperback novel to her lap. She wasn't really in the mood to read, but decided she couldn't just lie there by herself, looking lonely and idle.

A few minutes later, the sun out full force again, she saw Brad walking by the shore. He was walking slowly, laughing and talking with a tall, redheaded girl, very pretty, very skinny, in a skimpy black bikini.

Ashley waved to Brad, but he didn't seem to see her.

She sat up and started to call to him, then decided not to. She felt a pang of jealousy. She realized she resented the tall redhead.

I'd like to walk on the beach with you, Brad, Ashley thought.

You're so cute.

And so rich.

Then, as if he had read her thoughts, Ross came into view.

He was several beach umbrellas down, walking slowly, stopping every few yards, his eyes surveying the crowd.

Ashley realized he must be searching for her, so

she stood up and waved. "Ross! Hey — Ross!"

He spotted her after a few seconds and came running over.

He didn't smile the way he usually did when they met.

She could see immediately that his expression was troubled.

"Hey, what's the matter?" she asked.

He mopped perspiration from his forehead with the back of his arm. She saw that he was breathing hard.

"Hi, Ashley. I — uh — "

"Ross, what's wrong?" she demanded, feeling her throat tighten in dread.

"I guess you haven't heard," he said, awkwardly standing very close to her, unable to decide what to do with his hands.

"Heard? Heard *what*?" Ashley asked impatiently.

"It's . . . Lucy and Kip," Ross said, his chin trembling. "They didn't come home last night. They've both disappeared."

PART THREE

Summer of 1956

11
Who's in the Beach House?

In Amy's dream, the blue-green water was calm at first and smooth as glass. But as she swam, farther and farther from the shore, tall waves began to toss and tumble around her.

The beach became a thin, brown line in the far distance, but she kept swimming. Face in the water. Now up for a gasping breath. Face in the water.

Stroke. Stroke. Stroke.

Her arms ached with each pull. Her legs ached, but she continued her rhythmic kicking.

Face in the water. Noisy, gasping breath.

Stroke. Stroke. Stroke.

Until even the brown line of shore disappeared from the horizon, and she was surrounded by the blue-green water, frothing white as the waves fell around her.

Surrounded by the waves, which became moving mountains, looming over her, then crashing noisily, sweeping her up in their rolling white foam.

Face in the water. Now out. Deep breath and hold it.

Stroke. Stroke. Stroke.

Until her chest felt about to burst.

And the tall waves lifted her up so that she couldn't swim any farther.

Lifted her up and held her. Held her high so that she could see the dark triangles gliding through the water, gliding so quickly, so effortlessly. While she struggled to free herself from the tall wave. While she struggled to get away.

The dark triangles riding so high in the water. Ignoring the seething waves.

"Let me go!" Amy cried.

But the wave held her high.

And the sharks closed in.

Stroke. Stroke. Stroke.

She kept moving her arms, thrashing her legs, even though the waves wouldn't let her swim.

Stroke. Stroke.

She wasn't going anywhere. And the sharks — so many sharks — so many hungry sharks — were gliding so easily, like arrows floating to their target.

Their teeth were shiny, white like pearls. Their enormous mouths opened like bottomless wells.

All together, they tore at her skin, pulling off chunks of flesh as the water darkened. Pulling at her with those gleaming white teeth, tearing away her skin as if it were paper.

And again she woke up screaming.

Again she opened her eyes to find herself bathed

in sweat, the bedclothes tangled about her bare
legs. The tiny bedroom stifling. No air to breathe.

Stroke. Stroke. Stroke.

Awake, the dream followed her, stayed with her,
kept its frightening rhythm.

Face in the water. Breathe. Breathe.

I can't breathe, she thought, sitting straight up
in bed, her chest heaving. The room tossed about
like an ocean wave.

Stroke. Stroke.

She shut her eyes tight, waited for the rolling
waters to recede, for the rhythm to fade.

How many nights will I have this dream? Amy
wondered.

Her heart pounding, feeling exhausted, drained,
as if she had swum for miles, she pulled herself to
her feet, made her way dizzily to the open window,
and peered up at a pale half-moon in the purple sky.

How many nights?

She had had the dream every night since Maria
and Buddy had disappeared. Every night.

"What am I going to do?" she asked the moon.
"What am I going to do?"

"What am I going to do?" Amy asked, picking up
a white pebble from the sand, holding it up close to
examine it, then tossing it into the ocean.

"Hey, the dreams will stop after a while," Ronnie
replied. But he didn't sound so sure.

High clouds covered the midmorning sun. The
air carried a chill off the water. Black storm clouds

on the horizon were moving quickly toward the shore.

The darkness suited Amy's mood. She adjusted the pink-and-yellow flower-patterned scarf she had tied over her tight curls. She was wearing the same tan Bermuda shorts she had worn the day before, and one of her father's old, long-sleeved white shirts, with the sleeves rolled halfway up.

She hadn't paid much attention to what she put on that morning. She really didn't care. She hadn't been able to stop thinking about Maria. Awake or asleep.

"It's going to storm," Ronnie said, shielding his eyes with one hand as he studied the horizon. Two dark ships appeared far out in the ocean, moving so slowly that they appeared to be standing still.

"I don't care," Amy said glumly. "Let it rain. I don't care if it rains for the entire summer."

"I keep thinking about Maria, too," Ronnie said, hunching down as he walked, his hands shoved into the pockets of his tennis shorts. His leather sandals slapped noisily against the hard, wet sand. "And Buddy. Buddy was such a good swimmer. I just don't understand — "

"Maybe they were attacked by sharks," Amy said, swatting at a fly on her leg. "It's the only thing I can think of. Maybe that's why I keep having that dream. Maybe — "

"I don't think we'll ever know," Ronnie said softly, putting a hand on Amy's trembling shoulder. "It's been days, and there's been no sign of them."

"That's what puzzles me," Amy said, reaching up to put her hand over his. "Where are Buddy's parents? Why haven't they contacted the police? Why hasn't anyone heard from them? Where *are* they? Don't they even *care* that their son has drowned?"

"Whoa," Ronnie said, raising a finger to his lips. "Slow down, Amy. Slow down. Take a deep breath."

She obediently took a deep breath.

"I can't help it, Ronnie. I'm just so upset!" She could feel the hot tears welling in her eyes. She wiped them away and glanced down the beach to the beach house, jutting out to the water on its fragile-looking stilts.

"It's a mystery," Ronnie agreed, running a hand back through his blond flattop as he turned to follow her gaze. "Someone should have been asking about Buddy. *Someone*."

Thunder rumbled in the distance.

"What a *horrible* summer," Amy said, shaking her head.

They started walking, but stopped when they heard someone calling their names. Spinning around, Amy was surprised to see Stuart running toward them, waving.

"Hey — glad I found you." He stopped, putting his hands on his hips, and waited to catch his breath. His black hair was slicked down. Even the gusting storm wind off the ocean couldn't blow it out of shape. He was wearing a short-sleeved sportshirt of wide brown and yellow stripes hanging over baggy Levi's that looked stiff and new.

"Stuart, what's shaking?" Ronnie asked.

"I just came to say good-bye," he replied.

"Huh? You're leaving?" Amy reacted with surprise. She had seen Stuart once since Maria's death. He had been on his way to a barbecue with a bunch of kids. He had waved and smiled at her.

"My family is going home. My dad has to go back to the salt mines. So . . ." He shrugged.

"That's too bad," Ronnie said, shaking his head.

"What are you going to do the rest of the summer?" Amy asked, turning her eyes to the darkening sky above.

"Well, my uncle owns a drive-in back home. I'll probably work there till school starts," Stuart replied, kicking up clumps of sand with his Keds.

"You'll be a carhop?" Ronnie joked. "Do you know how to skate?"

"Yeah, I skate pretty good," Stuart bragged. "I could probably be in the Roller Derby. But I don't look so hot in the short skirts. I'll probably be manning the French fry grease pits."

"Well, good luck," Amy said.

"I'm just taking my last walk on the beach," Stuart said unhappily. "You know. Collecting some shells." His voice broke. "It's not really a summer I want to remember." He gave them a wave and headed down the beach.

Amy watched him as he walked past the beach house, stopping occasionally to pick up a shell. A short while later, he disappeared around a curve in the beach.

"Hey, look. There's a hot dog truck up on the road," Ronnie said, pointing. "I'm starving all of a sudden. Want one?"

"No. But I'll watch you eat yours," Amy said agreeably, thinking about Stuart, how funny he was, how much fun he had been — until Maria and Buddy disappeared.

Maria and Buddy.

They were gone. And everything was different now.

Everything.

They walked quickly over the grassy dune to the road.

The hot dog vendor was sitting on a folding chair inside the hot dog truck, reading the morning newspaper. He finished what he was reading, then looked up, surprised to see customers.

"You see this ship that got sunk?" he asked, holding up the front page of the paper. A photograph showed an enormous ocean liner tilted on its side. "The *Andrea Doria*," he told them. "You imagine that? A ship that big? As big as the Titanic, I'll bet. Filled with rich people. It got hit and it's sinking. You see it on TV?"

"We don't have a television here," Ronnie told him.

The man grunted, wiping his mustache with one hand. "You're gonna miss Martin and Lewis on Sunday," he said.

"Yeah. I guess." Ronnie ordered a hot dog.

Amy stood with her arms crossed, watching Ronnie gobble it down. He put mustard, relish, ketchup, and sauerkraut on it. "Some breakfast," she muttered, feeling queasy.

"Want a bite?" He shoved it into her face.

"Ugh. You're not funny, Ronnie."

A short while later, they were back on the beach. A few hardy swimmers were in the water. A group of teenagers were hanging out in front of a tall, grassy dune. An elderly couple was walking a panting German shepherd along the water. Otherwise, the beach was empty.

"Hey, Mouse, want to go into town or something?" Ronnie suggested.

Instead of replying, Amy grabbed his arm.

"What's the matter?" he asked, startled by the fearful look on her face.

"Ronnie — look." She pointed to the beach house.

"Huh? What?" he asked, bewildered.

A wave of dread swept over Amy. Her breath caught in her throat.

"Amy, what is it?" Ronnie demanded.

"The beach house," she managed to say. "Look, Ronnie. There's someone in there."

12
Murder

A jagged streak of bright white lightning slanted over the ocean. A few seconds later, thunder rolled in like the tide.

Holding Ronnie's hand, Amy took a few cautious steps toward the beach house. "Did you see it? I saw a face in the window. *There*. See? There it is again."

"Yeah. I see," Ronnie said, picking up the pace to lead the way. "There's someone in there, all right."

"I'm . . . frightened," Amy admitted. "I mean — " She gasped and let go of Ronnie's hand as someone came out through the sliding-glass door and walked around the deck. "It's *Buddy*!" Amy exclaimed in a high-pitched squeak of a voice that revealed her shock.

"Whoa. I don't *believe* it!" Ronnie cried.

They stood frozen in place on the sand as Buddy

spotted them and came running across the beach, waving and calling. "Hey, guys! Guys!"

Another streak of jagged lightning burst high in the clouds, followed by the low rumble of thunder.

"Buddy — you're okay!" Amy cried. "We thought — "

"What happened? Where've you been?" Ronnie asked, slapping Buddy on the back.

"Hi," Buddy said shyly, pushing back his dark hair.

And then Amy and Ronnie both noticed the blood on the front of Buddy's white T-shirt. Still red. Still wet.

"Oh. Yeah." Buddy quickly realized what they were staring at. "I just cut myself." He held up a bandaged finger. "Making a sandwich. Do you believe how clumsy I am? I can't even slice bread."

"Buddy, where've you been?" Amy demanded, forcing her eyes away from the fresh bloodstain on the shirt. "We all thought you were . . . you know. Dead."

"I'm sorry," Buddy said, shifting his weight uncomfortably. "I went to my cousin's in Rockford. I mean, my mom took me there. I know I should've told you or something. But I was pretty messed up. I mean, after Maria died. I — "

"The police have been looking for you," Amy interrupted, studying his brown eyes, looking for the sadness there.

"I called them from my cousin's," Buddy said,

avoiding her hard stare. He started to walk. They followed beside him. "It . . . it was real hard to talk about it. But I told them everything. I mean, everything I knew. Which wasn't much."

"We were real worried," Ronnie said, patting Buddy's shoulder. "I mean, we felt *terrible*. No one told us you were alive."

"Really?" Buddy's face filled with surprise. "Someone should have told you. I called the police right away. I mean, as soon as I could talk without . . . as soon as I could talk."

"Well, what happened, Buddy?" Amy asked, stepping in front of him, forcing him to stop and face her. "What happened to Maria? Did she drown? When you two went swimming, did she — "

"We didn't," Buddy said, holding up a hand to stop her questions.

"You didn't go swimming?" Amy couldn't keep the shock from her voice.

Buddy looked away and cleared his throat. "It's still hard to talk about this, you know?"

"I'm sorry," Amy told him. "But we've all been so upset, so crazy. Every night, I dream that — "

"Maria went swimming, but I didn't," Buddy explained. "After you left, Amy, she and I tested the water. Maria wanted to swim. But I thought the undertow was too strong. It was pulling like crazy. I'm a real good swimmer, but I was afraid of it. So I decided not to go in."

He picked up a flat, gray pebble and heaved it

high in the air, his eyes following it as it landed back on the beach.

"And Maria?" Amy asked impatiently.

"She wanted to swim. I told her no. The water was too rough, too unpredictable. She called me a chicken. We sort of had an argument." His cheeks reddened. "You know how I get sometimes. I don't like to be called names."

"Was it a bad argument?" Amy asked.

Buddy shook his head. "No. It was short. I just said I wasn't going to swim, and she said she was going in without me. I said, fine, do whatever you want. I didn't really mean it, but I was angry. So I said good-bye and went into the house."

He stooped to pick up another stone, a smooth white oval. He swallowed hard a few times, then raised his eyes to Amy. "That was the last time I saw her."

Amy glanced at Ronnie to see if he believed Buddy's story. Ronnie's features were set in a grim frown. Then she turned back to Buddy, who was rolling the smooth rock around in his hand. "You really think she went swimming by herself?"

"Yeah. I think so. Out of stubbornness, probably." He heaved the stone to the ground. A loud sigh escaped his lips. "The next thing I knew, the police were all over the beach. When I heard they were searching for Maria, I realized what had happened. That she had . . . drowned."

He stooped down again and, unable to find a

stone, picked up a handful of sand. "I felt so guilty.
I guess I went a little crazy then," he said softly,
watching the sand as it sifted through his fingers.
"At least that's what my mom said. She said I wasn't
making any sense at all, just jabbering like a crazy
person. So she got me out of here and drove me to
my cousin's. It took me a couple of days before
. . . before I could *think* straight."

"I *still* can't think straight," Amy muttered.

Ronnie put a hand tenderly on her shoulder.

"I wasn't going to come back," Buddy said. "But
I decided you can't run away from things."

"Yeah, I guess," Ronnie said softly.

The sky grew even blacker, turning the rolling
ocean waters a dark olive shade. The wind picked
up, gusting and dipping around them, causing small
cyclones of sand to rise up off the beach.

"I didn't know Maria long," Buddy said, staring
at the water. "But I really cared about her."

Amy shivered. She buttoned the top button
of her dad's white shirt. "It's really getting
cold."

"Want to come in and warm up?" Buddy gestured
to the beach house. "I could make some hot chocolate or coffee."

"No. No thanks," Amy replied, glancing at Ronnie. "I want to get home. Thanks anyway, Buddy."

"I'm sure glad you're okay," Ronnie said, giving
Buddy another friendly slap on the shoulder.

"Yeah. Right. Thanks," Buddy replied. "Catch

you later." He turned and jogged back to the beach house.

Amy and Ronnie watched him disappear inside, the glass door sliding shut behind him. Then Amy looked up at Ronnie, her expression thoughtful, troubled. "Do you believe him?"

"Believe what? That he was at his cousin's? Yeah, I guess," Ronnie replied, rubbing his chin. "We *know* he got out of here in a hurry. When the police searched the beach house, it was empty."

"But do you believe the part about Maria deciding to go swimming by herself?"

"Well . . ." Ronnie shrugged.

"That doesn't sound like Maria at all," Amy said heatedly. "She was always very enthusiastic, always ready to do things. But she wasn't foolhardy or reckless."

"Yeah. You're right," Ronnie agreed. "But why would Buddy make up a lie? I mean — " He stopped, staring toward the shore.

Amy immediately saw what had caught his eye.

Something was huddled on the beach, just out of the swirling water.

Not something. Some*one*.

Someone lying facedown in the sand.

Running against the strong wind off the water, they arrived together. At first, they didn't recognize the boy, lying with his arms and legs sprawled across the sand, his face buried.

And then Amy cried, "Stuart!"

Puddles of dark blood had clotted on the back of

Stuart's head. His scalp had been smashed open, a slice of white skull showing through. Blood had soaked into his shirt and onto the sand around his head.

A few feet from his battered body lay a thick, driftwood log, bloodied at one end.

"He's been murdered," Ronnie said, holding Amy tightly, his hands suddenly as cold as death.

13
It's So Easy

Buddy pressed his forehead against the cool pane of the window as he stared out at the busy scene on the beach. Dark-uniformed policemen had formed a circle around the body down near the water. Other policemen spread over the beach and dunes, searching for clues.

A radio reporter stood outside the circle of policemen, trying to get his equipment to work. The local newspaper had sent two young reporters and a photographer to get the story.

Such a commotion, Buddy thought, unable to keep a satisfied smile from spreading across his face. The cool glass felt so good against his feverish forehead.

Such excitement.

He was excited, too, he had to admit.

Murder was so exciting.

And so easy.

All those movies and TV shows made it look hard, risky. TV murderers always had such remorse.

No one ever said how easy it is to kill someone.

Or how exciting.

He glanced up at the clearing sky. The storm had been a disappointment. A lot of noise and light, but little rain. It had passed over the beach in a matter of minutes, barely dampening the sand.

Barely washing away the blood.

The police had scurried to cover Stuart with a canvas tarp. But there was hardly any reason to bother, Buddy thought.

Now he watched them huddle around the tarp, talking among themselves, the fat photographer snapping away.

"Let's see you put me down now, Stuart," Buddy said aloud, pushing himself away from the window and starting to pace back and forth through the sparsely furnished living room. "Go ahead. Let's see you make fun of me now."

Stuart thought he was such a riot, Buddy told himself bitterly, pacing rapidly now, clasping his hands in front of him. He enjoyed giving me a hard time, making me look ridiculous.

They all did.

Well, Stuart had to pay.

Maria had to pay.

They'll *all* pay.

Sure, I'm an outsider, Buddy thought bitterly. Sure, I'm different from them. Maybe I don't belong in their crowd.

But they had no reason to laugh at me. To *lie* to me.

No one likes to be laughed at.

He stopped at the window and glanced down toward the shore. No one had moved.

No one's laughing now, Buddy thought happily.

An entire beach, and no one's laughing.

Off to the side, several yards from the circle of policemen, he saw Amy and Ronnie being questioned by two grim-faced policemen.

What's the matter, guys? Not laughing? Not spending your day laughing at Buddy for a change?

It was hard to decide which of them to kill first. He only knew that they both had to die.

And it was so easy. So *easy*.

Especially when you knew you could get away with it.

Humming "Earth Angel," a song he had just heard on the radio, Buddy changed into the clean T-shirt he had brought with him. He carefully packed the bloodied T-shirt into his backpack and hid the backpack in the big bedroom closet.

Then he hurried out to join Amy and Ronnie, fixing a shocked and horrified expression on his face as he ran.

High, white clouds still covered the sun, but the air had grown hot and humid. People clustered along the beach, gathering in small groups to talk and gossip about what had happened. Back near the dunes, a volleyball game was in progress, providing the only shouts and laughter that could be heard.

"I don't believe it," Buddy said to Amy and Ronnie. "Are there any suspects?"

Ronnie shook his head. Amy, her face pale and frightened, didn't look up.

"Any clues or anything?" Buddy asked, his face filled with concern.

"That's the murder weapon. Over there," Ronnie said, pointing to the driftwood log on the sand. The photographer was snapping shot after shot of it from every angle.

"Looks pretty heavy," Buddy said, staring at it.

"It's like a bad dream," Amy said to no one in particular. "First Maria. Now Stuart."

"Who are *you*?" a voice demanded.

Buddy turned to see one of the policemen who had been questioning Amy and Ronnie standing inches behind him. The police officer was wearing black uniform Bermuda shorts and a loose-fitting black, short-sleeved shirt with a silver badge pinned over the pocket. He had a slender, pale face dotted with pimples, topped with a close-cropped blond crewcut. His eyes were tiny, gray, and intense.

Buddy told the officer his name. "My mom and I are staying at the beach house." He pointed.

"Where's your mom?" the policeman asked curtly, his tiny eyes locked on Buddy's.

"In town, I think. She isn't home."

"You knew Stuart Miller?" The policeman's eyes continued to accuse Buddy.

Buddy stared right back at him. "I just met him about a week ago. I guess you'd say we were kind of friends."

"Did you see him this morning?"

Buddy shook his head. "No."

A team of white-uniformed medics had arrived and were struggling to load Stuart's body onto a canvas stretcher. As they tried to lift the stretcher, one side dipped, and the body rolled off, giving everyone a view of Stuart's bashed-in skull.

"Did you see anything at all from the beach house?" the policeman asked, keeping his voice low and professional.

"No," Buddy told him. "I just got back a few minutes ago. I was away."

Amy jerked her head up, suddenly remembering something about Buddy. The bloody shirt. The bloodstain that was splattered over the front of it.

"I was at my cousin's in Rockford. I haven't even unpacked yet," Buddy was telling the policeman.

But you unpacked a clean shirt, Amy thought, staring hard at Buddy.

Could all that blood have really come from a cut finger?

She studied his face as he answered the policeman's questions. But it revealed nothing to her.

You have no reason to suspect Buddy, she scolded herself. Buddy is as upset as you are.

He's just another teenager. He isn't a murderer.

Staring at him, Amy suddenly saw a different picture of him. She suddenly saw him stranded in

the water, calling frantically to them. And she saw
Ronnie and Stuart running across the beach, waving
Buddy's swim trunks.

Once again, Amy saw the distressed look on Buddy's face. She saw him floundering about, trying to
keep afloat on the incoming waves, shouting to
them, begging them for his trunks.

It was all so funny.

It was all so much fun.

Hard to believe it was only about a week ago.

Funny how the mind jumps around, Amy
thought. When there's a tragedy, when something
truly horrifying happens, the mind wants to leap
away to happier times, to brighter pictures.

She pictured poor, frantic Buddy, bobbing
around helplessly, stranded in the ocean and, without realizing it, started to laugh.

"What's so funny?" Buddy asked sternly, cutting
into her thoughts.

"Nothing," Amy replied quickly — and felt a
stab of fear.

Buddy had the strangest, angriest expression on
his face.

14
Running From Buddy

"Rotate! Rotate!"

The girl with short blonde hair, a dazzling emerald-green swimsuit, and a figure like Jayne Mansfield's, cupped her hands over her mouth as she shouted. The other team members obediently changed position.

"Your serve!" the girl called to Amy, heaving the volleyball at her.

Amy caught the ball against her chest. It nearly knocked her breath away. Why did that girl have to throw so hard? And why was she always yelling "Rotate!" at the top of her lungs?

"Serve it over the net, Mouse," Ronnie called to her from his position at the net.

"Very helpful advice," Amy replied, rolling her eyes.

Some kids laughed.

Amy didn't think it was funny. The net looked

so high. She held the ball up in her tiny palm and poised her other hand to hit it.

If only I were six inches taller, she thought, this game would be more fun.

Clouds drifted over the sun, immediately cooling the air. The forecast called for more rain. It had rained every single day this week.

Such a gloomy vacation.

"Serve it — don't study it!" a boy on the other team yelled. Also very helpful.

Amy slugged the ball with all her might. She cried out, watching it sail right into the net.

"Net ball!" the girl in the emerald swimsuit yelled.

A picture flashed into Amy's mind of serving the ball right into that girl's teeth.

"Do over!"

Ronnie retrieved the ball from the sand and tossed it back to Amy. "Over the net! Over the net!" he called.

"What's the score?" someone yelled.

"Hey look —" someone else shouted. Everyone turned to the water to see a boy water-skiing behind a roaring powerboat, very close to shore.

They clapped and cheered when the skier toppled over almost immediately, disappearing in a tall splash of white froth.

The sky darkened. Four sea gulls glided overhead, slender white Vs against the charcoal sky.

Amy positioned herself to serve again. She raised

the ball and tightened her other fist, preparing to
hit it.

The net loomed over her, ruffling slightly in the
quickening breeze.

Everyone is watching me, she thought, concentrating, staring at the ball, then raising her eyes to
the net.

Over. Over. Over. *Please* go over.

She hit it solidly. It rose higher this time, but
skimmed the net as it went over.

There were sighs and groans from her teammates. She glanced to the side to see Ronnie shaking
his head.

Hey, guys, it's only a game, Amy thought
bitterly.

"Your serve!" the girl in the emerald suit called
to the other side.

"Rotate! Rotate!" came the cry over there.

"What's the score?" a girl called.

"It's sixteen to three. A tie!" some joker replied.

"Look alive, gang!" the girl in the emerald suit
instructed, hands on her knees, eyes on the ball.

Who made *her* captain? Amy wondered.

Ronnie grinned at her. She stuck her tongue out
at him.

These kids sure take their volleyball seriously,
she thought, studying their intense expressions as
the serve flew over the net and everyone sprung
into action, jumping high, arms flying, hands
slapping.

The ball swooped in front of her. She dived toward it, bringing her hands up fast.

Success!

The ball sailed over the net and bounced on the sand.

Grinning happily, Amy picked herself up from the ground, brushing off her pink short-shorts.

"Good hit!" the girl in the emerald suit called, giving her a thumbs-up.

"Thanks!" Amy cried. "What's your name?"

"Amy," the girl called.

Amy's mouth dropped open in surprise. "Me, too!" she yelled.

"Hi, Amy," the girl said, laughing.

"Hi, Amy!"

This was fun. Amy and Ronnie didn't know these kids. None of them were from Ridgefield. But they seemed like a nice bunch of kids, all very enthusiastic and very athletic.

It's great to lose yourself in a game, to concentrate on having fun, Amy thought, watching the next server get into position.

But she couldn't help it. She couldn't concentrate entirely. She couldn't control her mind. She found her thoughts wandering to Maria.

She couldn't stop thinking about her.

Every time a girl with a long, dark ponytail walked by on the beach, Amy was ready to call, "Maria!"

Buddy also hovered in her thoughts.

The blood on his T-shirt.

The strange, angry expression on his face as he had stared at her that afternoon.

It had frightened her so much.

It still frightened her.

She had no reason to believe that Buddy was a liar. But his story about Maria wanting to swim in a dangerous undertow — swim all by herself, even though she wasn't a strong swimmer — it didn't make sense.

It didn't ring true.

Maria wouldn't have swum very far out by herself. She would've stayed close to shore.

And if she had stayed close to shore, if she had drowned close to shore, her body would have washed up on the beach by now.

Her body.

Ugh.

Amy couldn't stop these dreadful, frightening thoughts.

No matter how hard Amy tried to push her to the back of her mind, Maria was always there. Maria and Buddy.

The bloody T-shirt.

Stuart's battered, bloody head.

"Look out!" someone yelled.

The ball hit her on the shoulder, bounced up. She slapped at it, kept it alive. And the girl beside her slapped it over the net for a point.

Amy joined in the jubilant cheering by her teammates.

This is fun, she repeated to herself. I am entitled to have a little fun this summer.

She was sorry when the game ended. Twenty-one to fourteen.

"I think we were just warming up," Ronnie said, walking over to her, the front of his navy blue, sleeveless T-shirt darkened with a circle of sweat.

"I've got to practice my serve," Amy said, smiling.

"We'll get you a stool to stand on, Mouse."

"Har de har har," Amy said sarcastically, imitating the TV comedian Jackie Gleason. "That's rich. That's really rich! You're cruisin' for a bruisin', Ronnie."

He dropped to his knees to search through his beach bag. Pulling out his wristwatch, his eyes went wide with alarm. "Oh, my gosh! I promised my parents I'd come home early and help. They're having a big barbecue tonight. About twenty people."

Amy glanced up at the darkening sky. Black clouds were rolling rapidly over the beach. "Looks like it might be rained out," she said, buttoning her dad's white shirt she always used as a beach wrap.

"Oh, great," Ronnie muttered, rolling his eyes. "Twenty people crammed into our tiny cottage. Dad out barbecuing in the rain. Sounds like a great evening."

"Have fun," Amy said wistfully.

"I've got to run," Ronnie said, zipping up the beach bag and climbing to his feet. "You coming?"

"No. Think I'll stay and watch the clouds for a

bit," Amy said. "I love this kind of weather. So cool and wet. So dramatic."

He waved a quick good-bye and, carrying his sandals, ran full speed over the sand toward the road.

Amy watched him for a while, thinking of how he resembled a long, lanky giraffe when he ran. Then she turned back to the beach.

A few minutes before, it had been crowded with swimmers and sunbathers. But the threatening clouds had nearly emptied the beach. Carrying their beach chairs, umbrellas, coolers, and blankets, people were making their way over the low dunes to the road, eager to get home before the rains came.

Wrapping her arms around her chest against the chill air, Amy wandered down to the water. The cold, wet wind felt so refreshing blowing through her hair. Wine-colored waves washed noisily to shore. She walked in up to her ankles. The water felt surprisingly warm.

The beach was deserted now, except for two elderly fishermen far off at one end, standing patiently, poles in the water, and a cluster of teenaged boys up by the dunes, dressed mostly in blue denim, sneaking cigarettes, laughing boisterously.

Amy walked for a while, letting the warm, frothy water wash over her bare feet. She had finally decided to return home when, out of the corner of her eye, she saw someone running toward her at full speed.

She squinted against the glare, watching him

grow larger as he approached. Who would be running to her with such urgency?

"Buddy!" she cried his name aloud as his face came into clear view.

And felt the alarm race through her body.

Such heavy dread.

Buddy. Running after her.

Before she even realized what she was doing, Amy splashed out of the water and, her heart pounding, her dread weighing her down, began to run from him.

Her bare feet sank into the soft wet sand.

She felt as if she were running uphill.

She glanced back to see him pick up speed, his arms outstretched, his face bright red. He was shouting something, calling to her, but the roar of the wind drowned out all other sound.

She was running fast now, as fast as she could.

Trying to outrun the dread. Trying to outrun her sudden burst of fear.

But he was right behind her now.

She uttered a silent cry as his arms circled her waist and he tackled her to the sand.

15
Amy's Big Decision

Crying out in protest, Amy pulled out of his grasp and struggled to her feet.

To her surprise, Buddy remained on his stomach, laughing, reaching for her playfully. Her chest heaving, gasping to catch her breath, Amy stood tensely poised, trying to decide whether to stay or run.

His laughter made her hesitate.

"Amy, you're pretty fast!" he exclaimed, climbing to his knees.

Waiting for her heart to stop racing, she eyed him warily.

"Why'd you run?" he asked, not standing up. "Didn't you see that it was me?"

His dark hair, normally neatly brushed, was in disarray. The front of his T-shirt was covered with wet sand.

"I — I don't know," Amy replied, starting to feel a little calmer. "You scared me," she added.

Why *did* she run? she asked herself.

Why *was* she so filled with dread at the sight of him, so filled with *terror*?

"Sorry," he said, finally climbing to his feet, brushing himself off with both hands. He walked close to her, close enough that she could smell his sweat. He was more than a head taller than she, and so broad and muscular.

He was usually so awkward, so shy, that she'd never realized how powerfully built he was, how solid.

"I didn't mean to scare you," he said, his expression turning serious. "I was just running to catch up to you."

"I . . . I was just going home," she said, avoiding his dark eyes.

"I thought maybe we could talk or something," he said, disappointed.

"No. I think I have to go," Amy replied, realizing that they were the only ones on the beach. Even the two fishermen had disappeared from view.

"It's just that . . . well, I've been feeling really sad," Buddy said shyly, lowering his eyes to the sand.

"I'm sorry," Amy said. She fiddled nervously with the shirt flaps that came down below the legs of her short-shorts.

"I've been kind of lonely, I guess," Buddy continued. "I mean, I've had a lot of time to think. And I can't stop thinking about things. You know."

Amy eyed him silently, surprised at his honesty,

surprised that he felt close enough to her to confide in her like this.

"I've had such terrible dreams about Maria," he blurted out. He sighed, as if he were relieved that he'd managed to say it.

"Me, too," Amy said quietly.

"I wanted someone to talk to," Buddy said, turning his eyes to hers. "Someone who knew Maria."

Maybe I've misjudged him, Amy thought.

He seems so sad, so broken up.

He's being so honest with me. And here I've been, imagining such dreadful things about him. Accusing him of being a murderer.

The wind gusted, carried a sting. Black clouds hovered low.

None of us were fair to Buddy, Amy thought, studying him. He was an outsider, and we never really gave him a chance.

"I wondered . . ." he started. "Could we take a short walk, just to my house? We could talk on the way." He trained his eyes on her, pleading eyes, his expression hopeful.

"Well . . ." she glanced up at the lowering sky. "It's going to storm, I think."

"Just a short walk," he pleaded. "If it starts to rain, you can come inside and wait it out."

"Well . . ."

"Come on," he urged, a smile slowly forming on his handsome face. "I won't bite. Promise."

Amy gazed into his eyes, so dark and sad.

Then she glanced over his shoulder. In the near

distance, at the spot where the beach curved away, the beach house loomed darkly in the water. The incoming tide lapped at its fragile stilts.

Should I go with him? Amy wondered.

She realized that her heart was still racing. Her mouth felt as dry as sand.

Such uncertainty.

Should I go to the beach house with him?

He stood watching her, hands at his sides, patiently waiting for her to decide.

PART FOUR

This Summer

16
A Discovery
in the Beach House

"I keep thinking we'll run into Lucy and Kip," Ashley said, her eyes scanning the crowded beach.

It was a hot, humid day, the sun high in a hazy gray sky, no breeze at all, not even near the ocean. The waves were low and far apart, breaking right on the shore. Ashley noticed that the ocean was nearly as crowded as the beach, filled with people trying to cool off.

She and Ross made their way past tilted beach umbrellas and sleeping sunbathers and headed toward the water.

Nearby, two tall young black men in baggy Hammer pants were practicing a complicated dance step, their bare feet sinking into the sand, their boom box blaring.

"It's so noisy today," Ross complained.

"You're starting to sound like an old man," Ashley teased. She did an imitation of a grouchy old geezer: *"Turn that radio down! Are you deaf or something?"*

He frowned. "I don't sound like that," he protested, giving her shoulder a playful shove, nearly sending her sprawling into two young women sunbathing on a blanket with their halter tops off.

"If it's too loud, you're too old!" Ashley declared. She cried out suddenly, grabbed his arm, then quickly released it.

"Sorry," she said, shutting her eyes for a moment. "I thought I saw Lucy. This keeps happening to me." She reopened them and pointed. "That girl over there. Doesn't she look just like her?"

Ross tried to follow her gaze. "Sorry. I don't see her."

"She just sat down," Ashley said. "Never mind."

They walked on a little farther, the cry of children's voices in their ears. A boy of ten or eleven, running with his yellow boogie board in his hands, ran right into Ross.

"Whoa!" Ross staggered backward.

"Sorry!" the boy called, and kept right on running.

"Spring a leak!" Ross shouted after him.

Ashley laughed. "Boogie boards can't spring leaks, you dork."

"I *know* that," Ross said edgily, his eyes on a tall, extremely well-built girl in a chartreuse string bikini.

After the girl disappeared behind a beach umbrella, he turned back to Ashley. "I keep thinking

I see Kip and Lucy, too," he said quietly. "I mean, they've got to be somewhere — right?"

"Yeah," Ashley agreed, taking his arm. "Yuck. You're sweaty."

"What do you expect? It's really hot, isn't it?" he said defensively. He glanced up to the sky as a large, dark cloud rolled over the sun, sending a wide shadow rolling over the beach. "Maybe it'll rain and cool things off."

"Two people can't just disappear into thin air," Ashley said, sighing, lost in her own troubled thoughts.

"It's so weird," Ross agreed, shaking his head. "It's been days. No sign of them. Not a clue."

"The police tried to make Lucy's parents believe that she and Kip had run away together," Ashley said. "Do you believe that? I mean, Lucy wasn't that serious about Kip. I don't even think she liked him that much."

"I don't know," Ross said thoughtfully. "It's not nice to say. I mean, since he's missing and everything. But I didn't like him much, either. I thought he was a creep."

"Kip had such a chip on his shoulder," Ashley agreed. "He really thought we looked down on him just because he was a townie and had to have a summer job."

"I tried to be friendly to him," Ross said, readjusting his ponytail as they walked. "But he'd just turn away. You know. Turn his back and take a nap or something."

"And he had no sense of humor at all," Ashley added. "Joking around actually made him angry."

"I can't believe we're talking about Kip as if he's dead," Ross said, swallowing hard.

"Yeah. If Kip is dead, it means that Lucy . . ." Ashley didn't want to finish her sentence.

"I kept thinking maybe they were kidnapped," Ross said, staring out at the ocean, olive green under the darkening sky.

"But why would anyone kidnap *them*?" Ashley asked. "Lucy's dad is a travel agent, and her mom's a secretary. They don't have any money. Besides, if it was a kidnapping, the kidnappers would have called by now."

"Well, if it's not a kidnapping, what is it?" Ross cried heatedly. "Where *are* they?"

"Let's change the subject," Ashley said, resting a hand on his shoulder. "We've been over this again and again. It's not getting us anywhere. It's only making us feel worse."

"Yeah, I know," he replied glumly.

Ashley slipped off her blue and white rubber Nike flip-flops and, carrying them, went wading into the water. "Ooh — I thought it'd be warmer!"

Ross walked with her, staying up on dry sand.

"So are we going to Brad's or not?" Ashley asked, speaking reluctantly, not eager to bring up what she knew was a sore subject.

"We?" Ross asked sarcastically. "You mean your new boyfriend asked *me* to come along, too?"

"Stop it, Ross," Ashley scolded, holding her temper. "He's not my new boyfriend. Don't be a jerk. And you *know* he invited both of us — not just me — to come play tennis."

"Who needs him?" Ross said bitterly.

"I just think it'd be fun, that's all. Brad says his clay court is fabulous. And it's his. It's private. You've been complaining about having to wait every morning at the public courts."

"I know, but — "

"And you've been complaining about how terrible the courts are. The bad nets. The holes in the asphalt."

"I know," Ross said petulantly. He picked up a handful of sand and tossed it back down.

"Brad seems like a really nice guy," Ashley continued. "Aren't you at all curious about his house? I mean, you know the houses along Ocean Drive. They're enormous! They're not houses — they're estates! We could pretend we're fabulously wealthy for a day."

"You want to be fabulously wealthy with Brad," Ross accused. "Admit it. You don't want me tagging along."

"Aaaagh!" Ashley uttered an exasperated cry. "Don't start that, Ross! I'm warning you!" She kicked angrily at the water, trying to splash him.

"Yeah, yeah. We've been over all this before, too," Ross grumbled, dodging away from the spray of water, making a disgusted face.

"I guess we've been over *everything* before," Ashley said, feeling her anger rise, unable to hold it down any longer. "I guess maybe we've said it all. We're bored with each other, huh?"

"I didn't say that," he quickly insisted, his dark eyes lighting up. "You're just trying to pick a fight, Ashley, so you can go out with Brad with a clean conscience."

Ashley groaned angrily. She ran out of the water, eager to confront him. "I warned you — "

His eyes went wide with surprise, and he raised his hands in a sign of truce. "Okay, okay." His hands still raised, he tried to back away from her, but stumbled over a large crab shell and fell over backwards, landing jarringly hard on the sand.

Ashley couldn't help it. She wanted to stay angry. But he looked so ridiculous, she started to laugh.

"What's so funny?" he demanded, reddening, still sprawled in the sand.

"You looked like a big crab yourself," Ashley teased.

He scowled.

She knew he hated to be teased. But she *wanted* to make him angry. He deserved it.

"Better watch out," he said, his expression softening a little. "Crabs like to pinch."

She laughed and reached out to help him up. But he grabbed her hands and, with a hard tug, pulled her down on top of him.

"Ross, stop it!" she scolded, trying to free herself. "It's too crowded here. It — "

His arms had slipped around her waist, and he

was reaching his head up to kiss her. She decided not to resist. They kissed, long and hard.

"Get up!" he groaned as she pulled her face away from his. "You're *crushing* me!"

"Okay. Don't be insulting."

As she started to lift herself off him, the rain started, a sudden downpour, enormous raindrops pounding the beach, drumming the sand like thunder.

In seconds, the sound of the rain was drowned out by the shouts and squeals of swimmers and sunbathers, who were frantically gathering up their coolers, blankets, and equipment and making a mad dash for cover.

Ashley leapt to her feet and pulled Ross up. "It's freezing cold!" she shrieked as the large raindrops pelted her skin.

Ross laughed. "I told you the rain would cool things off!"

She grabbed his hand and began pulling him away from the ocean. "I'm freezing. We've got to find a place to — "

Her hair was already sopping wet, flattened against her head. Sheets of rain hammered down, making it hard to see.

"Where are you pulling me?" Ross shouted over the rain.

"I don't know. I'm just — " And then the beach house came into view.

Without even thinking about it, she began pulling him toward it. He saw it, too, and they both began

to run. The rain stung their shoulders. Shivering
from the cold, they made their way, running as fast
as they could, stumbling blindly toward the beach
house.

Ross reached it first, raced up onto the deck, and
ran around to the sliding-glass door in front, pulling
it open. A few seconds later they were huddled
together in the living room, soaked through and
through, staring out at the sheets of rain through
the glass door at the long stretch of beach, now all
shades of gray, completely deserted.

"I — I'm freezing," Ashley said through chattering teeth, wrapping her wet arms around her
bare skin. Her string bikini didn't provide much
warmth. "Lend me your T-shirt."

Ross was shivering, too. "Are you kidding? It's
totally soaked. It wouldn't warm you up."

"Maybe there are some towels in this house,"
Ashley suggested in desperation. "Or a robe or
something."

Ross hopped up and down, forcing some of the
water off. "In a deserted beach house that's been
empty for thirty years?"

She made a disgusted face. "It's worth a try.
Let's look."

Without waiting for him to reply, she headed for
the hallway. Rain drummed on the roof and spat-
tered the windows. The steady wash of the ocean
waves competed with the pounding of the rain.

There were no towels in the small bathroom.
Leaving a trail of water, she hurried into the first

bedroom. It was unfurnished except for a dresser and a wooden double bed with a bare mattress. Frantically, she pulled out the dresser drawers. Empty.

With an unhappy groan, she made her way to the closet and slid open the door. It was dark inside. She peered in. It appeared to be empty.

She stepped inside.

Wow, she thought. She stuck her head out and called to Ross. "Hey, Ross. Ross! Come look at this closet. It's enormous!"

"What?" he called, sounding very far away. He must still be in the living room, she realized. But she could barely hear him over the sound of the rain.

"Come see this closet!" she repeated, screaming from the closet doorway.

"No, thanks," she heard him call back to her. "I'm not real interested in closets. Did you find any towels?"

"No," she replied, discouraged.

It's so dark in here, she thought. This closet seems bigger than the bedroom!

Shivering, she started to make her way out when her foot touched something.

Something soft that clung to her foot.

Gasping for breath, Ashley kicked at it, but it wouldn't let go.

And then she started to scream.

17
Trouble for Ross

"Ashley — what? Where are you?"

Ross burst into the open closet, his voice filled with alarm. "Are you okay?"

"Yes. Sorry," she said, her voice still quavering. "There was something on the floor. I — I picked it up. It's — "

She put a hand on his chest and gave him a soft push, then followed him out of the dark closet.

In the gray light from the bedroom window she examined what she had found.

"It's just a scarf," Ross said.

Her eyes wide with surprise, Ashley didn't reply.

"Ashley, it's just a scarf," Ross repeated impatiently. "What's the big deal?"

"It's Lucy's," Ashley finally managed to say, still staring at it in horror. She ran the green, silky scarf through her trembling fingers. "It's the fancy silk scarf I gave Lucy for her last birthday."

"How did it get in the closet?" Ross asked.

Ashley stared at the scarf, then raised her eyes to his. "I don't know."

Behind the tall, perfectly trimmed hedges that shielded it from the road, Brad's summer house rose up like a castle. Three stories tall, it hovered over a wide, manicured lawn, an enormous pink-gray stone structure, rows of tall windows reflecting the sun, each window framed by white shutters.

Ashley pulled her parents' station wagon up the seemingly endless driveway, past a flower garden the size of a meadow, and parked in the circle in front of the four-car garage.

"Is this a house or a hotel?" Ross asked, wide-eyed as they made their way along the curving flagstone walk.

"Brad wasn't kidding when he said he was rich," Ashley said, admiring a delicate brass sculpture of a ballerina surrounded by a sea of bright orange and yellow tiger lilies.

"I can't believe just one family lives in this house," Ross said, shaking his head. "I mean, there are so many rooms — how do they find each other?"

"Which is the front door?" Ashley asked, swinging her tennis racket onto her shoulder. From their vantage point on the front walk, there appeared to be three different doors that could be the front door.

"Let's just get out of here," Ross said.

Ashley stared at him, trying to decide if he was serious. He was.

"We don't belong here," Ross said, tugging at

his short ponytail nervously. "We don't *like* tea and crumpets."

Ashley laughed. "We're here to play tennis, remember? Just because the house is kind of big doesn't mean they serve tea and cumpets."

"What *is* a crumpet, anyway?" Ross asked fretfully. "I don't even know what one is."

"Well, I'm not leaving just because you don't know what a crumpet is," Ashley insisted. "Did you bring a bathing suit? Brad has a pool, too."

"I know." Ross rolled his eyes. "Brad has everything."

"Don't start," Ashley warned. They stopped in front of the first door, freshly painted white like the shutters, a polished brass door knocker in the middle. "Let's try this door."

Ashley looked for a doorbell. Not finding one, she reached for the brass door knocker.

She had just started to pull it back when the door swung open. "Oh!" Ashley cried, startled.

A stern-faced servant in a starched white uniform stared out at them. She was a thin, middle-aged woman with dramatic, dark eyes ringed by dark circles. She had short, bushy hair that must have once been black but was now streaked with wide stripes of gray. "Won't you come in?" she asked coldly, motioning for them to enter.

Ashley stepped into the front entranceway. Despite the July heat, the servant's uniform was long-sleeved, and the starched white collar of her blouse came up high on her neck.

"Brad is expecting you," she said, staring at them with her dark eyes, looking them up and down as if inspecting for fleas.

At that moment, Brad entered the room, dressed in tennis whites, carrying a racket. He was followed by the tall red-haired girl Ashley had seen with him at the beach.

"Your guests have arrived," the servant announced. She turned and walked quickly from the room, her white, rubber-soled shoes squeaking across the parquet floor.

"Hi, how's it going?" Brad called cheerfully, twirling the tennis racket, his eyes on Ashley. "Don't pay any attention to Mary. She's a bit weird."

"She kept staring at us," Ashley whispered, not certain whether the servant was still in hearing range.

"Probably just nearsighted," Brad said. He gestured to the tall girl beside him. "Have you met my cousin Sharon? Sharon, this is Ashley and Ross."

She's his cousin, Ashley thought, finding herself somewhat relieved. Everyone said hello. Ross stepped forward awkwardly to shake hands with Sharon. "Nice little cottage you have here," he told Brad. He tried to make it sound light, but it came out sarcastic.

"It's a perfect day for tennis," Brad said, smiling at Ashley. "Let me see your racket." He took it from her, unzipped the cover, and examined it as he led them through the house. "Excellent. This is excellent. I used to have one like this."

Ashley tried to see the house as they followed the wide hallway to the back. There were so many rooms. She saw at least two sitting rooms, elegantly furnished in heavy-looking, country-style antiques. They passed an enormous library, and a dining room with an endless oak table, set for at least sixteen people, a centerpiece of purple and white orchids decorating the center.

Mary, the servant, stood stiffly in the kitchen as they passed. She held a large silver tray stacked high with white dinner plates. She stared at them, her expression rigid, standing in a rectangle of sunlight from the kitchen window, her white uniform appearing to shimmer in the light.

The back yard rolled smoothly like a green carpet. Beyond another garden stood the pool house. Beyond it stood the Olympic-sized pool. A long, two-story guest house stood to the far right, and just beyond that was the red clay tennis court. In the distance, the grass gave way to sand where the dunes began, leading to the ocean.

"Wow! The ocean in your back yard!" Ashley exclaimed, her eyes trying to take in everything.

"Yeah. At night, I can hear it up in my room. It's like having one of those wave-sound machines," Brad said.

Ashley was suddenly aware that Sharon hadn't said a word. She turned to see Sharon staring at her thoughtfully. Wonder what *her* problem is? Ashley thought uncomfortably. And then decided that maybe Sharon was just shy.

"Any sign of Kip and Lucy?" Brad asked suddenly, the smile fading as his expression turned serious. He pulled the cover off his tennis racket. "Have they been found?"

"No," Ashley replied quietly. "No word about them. The police think they ran off together, but I don't believe it."

"Why not?" Sharon asked, her first words since they'd met. She had a husky, deep voice, low and sexy.

"Lucy isn't the type," Ashley replied. "I've known her forever. She wouldn't just run away." She turned to Brad. "I found a scarf of Lucy's. In the beach house."

His eyes widened in surprise. "The beach house?"

"You know. The empty house at the end of the beach."

"How did it get *there*?" Brad asked, shielding his eyes from the bright afternoon sunlight.

"Well, she and Kip used to go there to make out," Ashley said. "I found the scarf on the floor of a bedroom closet."

"But there was no sign of violence?" Brad asked, his eyes burning into hers.

Ashley shook her head. "No sign of anything. Just the scarf on the closet floor."

"Weird," Sharon said.

Brad didn't say anything. "Let's play doubles,"

he suggested, changing the subject. "Ashley and I will play you two."

Ashley saw a brief look of objection form on Ross's face, but he didn't say anything. Carrying his racket in both hands, he followed Sharon across the smooth court.

"Let's warm up a bit first," Ross said, adjusting his sunglasses as he positioned himself near the net. "I'm not used to a soft court like this."

"You'll like it," Sharon assured him. "It's a whole different sport." She arched her long body as she served, and the ball sailed easily over the net.

They warmed up, hitting the ball easily back and forth. To Ashley's surprise, Brad wasn't a very good tennis player. He moved awkwardly, uncertainly, and his swing was unpredictable, often wild.

Despite his lack of athletic prowess, she found herself drawn to him. He was really nice looking and seemed easygoing and modest, comfortable with being so rich, but not the least bit stuck-up because of it.

As they played, she could feel Brad's eyes on her. Whenever she turned to him, he flashed her his warmest smile.

He likes me, too, she realized.

In his shy way, he's coming on to me.

They played a complete set, pausing only when Mary brought out a tray of lemonade and iced tea. By the time they had finished — with Sharon and Ross winning the last two games and the set — the sun was lowering itself behind the house.

"How about a swim?" Brad asked Ashley, handing her a white towel to wipe the perspiration off her forehead.

"Well . . ." Ashley turned her eyes to Ross. He was glaring at her angrily.

He's obviously picked up the vibes between Brad and me, Ashley thought with dread.

Brad *had* been pretty obvious about it, talking only to Ashley, staring at her, smiling at her all afternoon.

Please, Ross, thought Ashley, staring at him meaningfully. Please don't lose your temper. Please don't make a fool of yourself. Please don't embarrass me in front of Brad and Sharon.

"I'd love to come back and swim sometime," Ashley told Brad. "But it's getting late."

"Okay. How about tomorrow?" Brad asked with obvious eagerness.

Ashley could see the annoyance spreading on Ross's face.

I'm so tired of his constant jealousy, of his stupid possessiveness, Ashley thought. I'm sick of it. Sick. "That would be great," she told Brad, avoiding Ross's eyes.

"One thing I wanted to show you," Brad said, putting the tennis racket back in Ashley's hand. "About your follow-through. I noticed this while we were playing."

He stepped behind her and put his arms around her, grabbing her wrists. "Now, I noticed when you swing . . ."

It was obvious to Ashley that Brad just wanted to put his arms around her. It was a clumsy trick, she thought.

But sweet.

Ross must not have agreed. Ashley looked up to see him heave his racket angrily to the ground. "Bye, Ashley," he muttered through gritted teeth.

"Hey, Ross — " Ashley started.

But Ross took off, jogging angrily toward the house.

"Hey!" Mary cried out. The servant was on her way to collect the drink tray, and Ross nearly barreled right into her. Her face turned scarlet as she dodged out of the way.

Ross called, "Sorry," and kept running.

"Ross, come back!" Ashley pulled out of Brad's grip and took a few steps toward Ross. "Come on, Ross! Brad was just showing me — "

Ross disappeared around the side of the house.

"Oh, let him go," Ashley said, exasperated.

"Hey, what's his problem?" Brad said, putting a hand on her shoulder. "I didn't mean anything."

Ashley sighed, staring at the house. "He's impossible. Really."

"What a short fuse," Sharon said, helping Mary pick up the heavy silver tray.

"Let him go," Ashley repeated.

This was the last straw. Ross had no right to storm off like that — and no right to embarrass her in front of Brad and Sharon.

No right at all.

I've had it with him, she told herself. And this time, I mean it.

She smiled at Brad. "How about that swim?"

She didn't hear from Ross that night.

The next afternoon, an afternoon of high clouds in a hazy, yellow sky, she was shopping in town, digging through the pile of bathing suits on the sale table at the Dunehampton Shop. She didn't see anything she liked. Everything had been picked over this late in the season.

Stepping out of the small shop, she decided to look in the bookstore across the street for something for her brothers. She was about to cross the narrow street when a hand grabbed her shoulder.

"Ross!"

His features were taut, his eyes locked onto hers. "I want to talk to you."

"No!" she cried, and pulled free. She started to cross, but the street was filled with cars, moving quickly.

"Come back!" he ordered.

The sidewalk was crowded. It wasn't much of a beach day, so everyone had jammed into town to stroll and window-shop.

"Go away, Ross. I mean it," Ashley said coldly.

"Ashley, I want to apologize," he said, reaching for her arm again.

"Ross, I'm sorry," she said heatedly, embar-

rassed that people were watching them, eaves-
dropping on them as they waited to cross the street.
"I really don't want to hear it."

"But I want to *apologize*," he insisted, his voice
tightening in a whine. Others started to cross, but
he held her back.

"Go away, Ross," she said in a low voice, trying
to keep calm.

"But, Ashley — "

Suddenly, a large figure loomed in front of them.
"Let go of her, man," Denny said. He raised both
of his big hands and shoved Ross into the curb.

"Whoa — " Ross shouted, reddening with anger.

"The girl doesn't want to talk to you, man,"
Denny said menacingly, glancing at Ashley, then
giving Ross another hard shove.

"Don't touch me, man," Ross cried angrily, slapping at Denny's arms, lashing out with both hands.
Despite his anger, his face filled with fear. Denny
was bigger. And stronger. And meaner.

"I warned you," Denny flared angrily.

"Denny — stop! Please!" Ashley screamed.
"Denny — what are you going to *do*?"

18
A Word From the Dead

"Back off!" Ross yelled to Denny. "I mean it — back off!"

Behind Ashley, people were shouting in alarm. Ashley covered her ears with both hands. "Denny, *please!*" she screamed.

She tried to grab Denny's shoulder and hold him back. But he was so big, and moving so quickly now, she bounced right off him.

She regained her balance and turned her eyes back to the street in time to see Denny drive his fist into Ross's stomach.

To Ashley's horror, it all seemed to go into slow motion. She saw Ross's eyes bulge with surprise. Then his mouth burst open in a hideous groan. Denny's fist pulled back. Denny leaned away.

Ross's hands flailed in the air helplessly. His eyes rolled up in his head.

Another groan, this one silent.

And Ross toppled to his knees. His head went

down, and he dropped onto all fours and began to
retch onto the curb.

Loud, excited voices surrounded Ashley, grew
louder, even though her hands still sheltered her
ears.

And then two black-uniformed town police officers came hurtling across the street.

"Later," Denny said to her, a strange, pleased
smile on his face. And he darted into the crowd of
onlookers and disappeared.

This isn't happening, Ashley thought, staring
down at the retching figure on his hands and knees
in the street.

This can't be happening.

The two policemen were trying to pull Ross to
his feet, each one lifting a shoulder. Ross was
breathing a little steadier now, one hand still holding his stomach.

Without even realizing that she was fleeing, Ashley backed into the crowd. She turned and saw
Denny making his way down the block, swinging
both of his powerful arms as he hurried away.

Denny's dangerous, Ashley decided. I used to
think he was just a big clown.

But he's dangerous.

And he seems to have a thing about me.

A wave of fear swept over her. She pushed her
way through the crowd and headed for home.

That night when she was getting ready for bed,
Ross called. Ashley chased her brother from the

room and sat down on the edge of her bed, holding the cordless phone, trying to decide how to talk to him.

She felt bad about that afternoon.

But she had made up her mind about Ross.

All afternoon, she had walked by herself on the beach. Starting at the low, grassy dunes, she had walked to the beach house and back, staring out at the rolling, tossing water, staring at the sea gulls soaring and diving, riding on the surface, so calm and untroubled.

All afternoon she had thought about Ross.

And she had decided that she couldn't go out with him again.

Ross thought he owned her. He really did.

And, she decided, he had no right to think that way.

She knew that Ross wouldn't give up, wouldn't stop pestering her.

But she had decided not to accept his apology. Not to forgive him again. Not to go out with him anymore.

Now, all she had to do was tell him.

Her heart racing, she cleared her throat and raised the phone to her face. "How are you feeling?" she asked.

"Better," he replied. "I'm still a little sore. That Denny is an animal."

"Yeah. I know," she said without warmth.

"What are you doing?" he asked.

"Talking to you," she replied.

"Listen, this afternoon — " he started.

"This afternoon, I meant what I said," Ashley told him, interrupting and talking rapidly.

"Huh? What's that supposed to mean?" His tone grew angry.

"It means I won't accept any apology from you."

"And what's that supposed to mean?"

"It means I'm not going out with you again."

"But, Ashley — "

"Good-bye, Ross. Have a good summer, okay?"

She hated the way she sounded, so cold, so heartless and uncaring.

But he had asked for it. He had promised at the beginning of the summer that he wouldn't be a jealous idiot.

"You didn't keep your promise, Ross," she said, her voice breaking.

She stifled a sob that wanted to burst from her chest.

She *did* care about him, after all.

"Hey, I promise it won't happen again. I just lost my temper. You know. I won't — "

"Bye, Ross."

She forced herself to click off the phone.

Then she dropped the phone to her lap and sat staring at it for a long moment, waiting for her heart to stop racing, waiting for her breathing to return to normal.

Finally, she picked up the phone and was about to set it down on her bed table when it rang. Startled, she nearly dropped it.

This is Ross again, she thought angrily.

He's so stubborn.

Why can't he believe that I mean it this time, that I really mean it?

"Hello?"

The voice in her ear wasn't Ross's.

It was husky, dry, a throaty whisper.

"Is this Ashley?"

"Yes?" Who can this be? Who do I know with this strange hoarse voice?

"Stay away from Brad."

"Huh?" Ashley cried. "I can't hear you very well. Can you speak up a little? Who *is* this?"

"Stay away from Brad," the husky voice repeated in its raspy whisper. *"Or you will die."*

"Huh? This is a joke, right?"

Ashley wanted to believe it was a joke, but the voice was so serious, so strange, so grating in her ear.

A chill of fear streaked down her back. She realized she was gripping the phone so tight, her hand hurt.

"Ross — you're not funny," she said angrily. "This is really childish."

"It isn't childish. It is true," the voice rasped. *"I am already dead. You will be dead, too."*

Ashley suddenly believed she recognized the voice. "Sharon? Sharon — is it you?"

Silence.

"Sharon — why are you doing this? I thought you were Brad's cousin. I thought — "

"I am not Sharon. I am dead. And I am warning you. Only one warning. Stay away from Brad. Or you will be dead — like me."

The line went silent.

Ashley clicked off the phone and dropped it onto the bed table.

She realized she was trembling all over.

That voice, she thought. That ghastly voice.

So empty. So completely empty and dry.

It really sounded *dead*.

19
A Secret

Ashley leaned on Brad's shoulder as they stepped out of the movie theater, their eyes adjusting to the brightness of the street lights. "I thought it was funny," she insisted.

"I know," Brad replied, rolling his eyes. "You were the only one laughing." He stopped to study the Coming Attractions posters on the theater wall.

"I didn't embarrass you, did I?" Ashley asked. "I can't help it. Chevy Chase just makes me laugh."

"You sure thought it was hilarious when he fell off the ladder," Brad said, shaking his head. "It wasn't even him. It was a stuntman."

"So what?" she declared. "It was funny."

The old movie theater, a squat brick building that recently had been turned into a six-plex, stood at the edge of town. Beyond its brightly lit marquee, the street was dark. Nearly all the shops and restaurants had closed for the night. A few couples drifted slowly up and down Main Street, peering

into shop windows, enjoying the cool night air,
which carried the smell of the ocean.

"Want to walk for a bit?" Brad asked.

"Sure," she said, smiling.

They stepped out from under the marquee and
crossed the street. It was their third date, Ashley
realized, and she was beginning to feel comfortable
with Brad.

It hadn't been easy at first. She had found him
to be surprisingly shy. And it was nearly impossible
to get him to laugh, or even smile much.

But, she discovered, he was very intelligent, and
he had an intensity, a seriousness about things that
she admired.

"What are you thinking about?" he asked.

"Chevy Chase," she replied, and burst out
laughing.

"Are you going to be laughing like that all night?"
he asked.

"Probably."

"Look at those dogs." He pointed.

Two mangy houndlike dogs were trotting along
the sidewalk side by side, looking like two human
window-shoppers out for a stroll.

"They think it's their town," Brad said dryly.
"They think it's all been put here to amuse them."

Ashley laughed. The dogs stopped together to
gaze into a shop window. Then they resumed their
walk. She watched them jog around the corner by
the local savings bank and disappear. As she stared
at the corner, she realized that someone was stand-

ing there, hidden in the shadows against the bank building.

He was there, staring back at her, watching her in the safety of the darkness.

And then he slipped away into the shadows and was gone.

Ross, she realized.

I saw you, Ross.

How stupid. How childish.

Was he following her on her dates? Spying on her?

All week Ashley had had a feeling that someone was watching her. A prickly feeling on the back of her neck when she walked in town, when she was sunbathing on the beach, when she went to meet Brad.

But every time she had turned around, had tried to discover who it was, no one had been there. She had dismissed the feeling, chalking it up to creeping paranoia.

But she wasn't going crazy. There *had* been someone spying on her.

Ross.

The big baby.

She felt like shouting out to him, calling his name, embarrassing him.

But the street was empty now. Ross had slipped away.

Is he going to follow me around *forever*? she wondered, feeling her anger grow.

And then she wondered: Did Ross make that

frightening call to me, warning me to stay away
from Brad? Or did he get someone to make the call
for him?

If he's childish enough to follow me around on
my dates, he's childish enough to have made that
call, she reasoned.

What a dumb practical joke.

Did Ross really think it would work? That it
would keep me from going out with Brad?

If anything, the call had made Ashley more eager
to go out with Brad.

So stupid, she thought. Such a stupid prank.

But the call had been on her mind ever since.
Again and again, she had heard the husky, dry
voice. The voice of the dead. Threatening her.
Warning her.

So stupid.

Several times she had started to tell Brad about
it. But each time she decided not to.

It would only trouble him, she decided. Only
make him feel bad. Make him angry.

The voice had never called again. Ashley had
decided to forget the whole thing. But that was
easier said than done.

Every time the phone rang, she remembered the
call, heard the eerie voice, and became angry and
frightened all over again.

But now I really can forget it, Ashley thought,
squeezing Brad's hand as they crossed the dark
street. Seeing Ross lurking there against the bank

wall, spying on her from the shadows, she realized that he *had* to be the caller.

It was so pitiful. Such a pitiful, desperate attempt to try to get her not to go out with Brad.

Having solved the mystery of the call, she could dismiss it from her mind.

With these thoughts stirring in her head, she walked, holding hands with Brad. Before she realized it, they had walked to the beach, empty and silent, the color of pearl under a bright full moon.

"Are you okay?" Brad asked suddenly, his expression concerned. "You're so quiet tonight."

"No, I'm fine," she protested. "I — I thought I saw someone back in town."

"Someone? Who?" He turned to face her, to stare into her eyes as if searching for the answers to his questions.

"Ross," she told him. "I think he's been following me or something."

"That's kind of sad," Brad said sympathetically. "Don't you think?"

Ashley nodded. "Yeah. And stupid."

"Have you talked to him since . . . since . . .?"

"No," Ashley replied, turning her eyes to the water. "I haven't talked to him in days. I really don't want to."

Black waves rose up and crashed along the shore. It was such a clear night, Ashley realized. There were a million stars in the purple sky. She didn't want to think about Ross. She wanted to enjoy

being with Brad, enjoy the shadowy beauty of the
beach, the magical night sky, so bright, so vast.

Suddenly, Brad pulled her face to his and kissed
her.

Pleased, she closed her eyes and kissed him back.

When she pulled her face away, he clung to her,
pulled her face back up to his, and kissed her again.

He's never done this before, Ashley thought,
kissing him with her eyes wide open this time.

He seems so . . . needy.

She had to give a hard tug to break away.

He looked disappointed. His dark eyes caught
the light of the full moon and filled with sudden
excitement. "I want to . . . show you something,"
Brad said breathlessly.

Ashley took another step back to see him more
clearly. She had never seen him like this. What was
on his mind?

"It's something kind of special," he continued. "A
secret."

She stared back at him, trying to guess what he
was talking about. "A secret? What is it, Brad?"

He was breathing hard, nearly panting. "No one
else knows about it," he said mysteriously. "I've
never really trusted anyone. I mean, I've never
trusted anyone enough to show it to them, to share
it with them. But — "

"You're driving me bananas!" Ashley declared.
"What are you talking about?"

Caught up in his own excitement, he didn't seem
to hear her, didn't seem to recognize her impa-

tience. "Can I tell you something?" he asked, his eyes wide with eagerness, leaning toward her, bringing his face very close to hers, his hands shoved deep into the pockets of his faded denims.

"Yeah, sure," she replied, feeling uncomfortable.

Brad hesitated, then plunged in with what he had to say. "I've never had a girlfriend before. I mean, really. I'm sixteen and I've never had a girlfriend. I mean, you're the first girl I could really *relate* to. Other girls didn't understand. But you're different, Ashley. You really are."

Whoa! Ashley thought. This is getting too intense.

What is he going to do — propose?

Why is he telling me all this? And why is he breathing so hard?

What is he leading up to?

She casually let her eyes roam the beach. No one. No one in sight. "What do you want to show me?" she asked, her growing fear edging into her voice.

"Something very exciting I discovered," Brad answered. "In the beach house." He gestured toward the dark structure at the end of the beach.

"The beach house?" Ashley nearly gasped at the sound of the words. "You want to take me to the beach house?"

"Yeah," he said, grabbing both of her hands and starting to pull her, an eager, imploring smile on his face.

Ashley held back. "What's in the beach house?"

"Come on," he insisted. "I'll show you. It's my

secret. You won't be sorry. Really."

Sorry.

A wave of fear swept over her.

Won't be sorry.

She thought of Kip and Lucy in the beach house.

She thought of finding Lucy's green scarf on the closet floor.

She thought of Kip's stories about the beach house. Stories about murders that supposedly took place there more than thirty years ago.

"Come on," Brad insisted, tugging her hand. "Come *on*."

Reluctantly, she followed him, feeling her throat tighten with dread, feeling her legs grow heavy, and her heart start to pound.

And now they were standing just below the deck, staring up at the old house. The beach house, so dark, so empty, so cold.

Why did he want to bring her here?

What was Brad's secret?

PART FIVE

Summer of 1956

20
Real Gone

"I just feel so bad," Buddy said as they trudged over the sand toward the beach house. "You know, about Maria and Stuart. It's just so awful. Two people I knew." His voice cracked with emotion.

Amy put a sympathetic hand on his shoulder, and they walked on in silence. The evening sky darkened to the color of charcoal. A few drops of cold rain hit Amy's head.

It's really going to storm, Amy thought. I probably shouldn't have come with Buddy. But the poor guy just looked so forlorn.

She thought of Ronnie and the twenty people that were coming to his summer house for a barbecue. They're all going to end up indoors, Amy thought, as she felt more raindrops.

The beach house loomed in front of them. Oh, well, Amy thought. At least Buddy and I can go inside and keep dry. She wondered if there was a phone inside where she could call her parents and tell them where she was.

"Do you think about them all the time?" Buddy asked, his voice still choked with emotion.

"I think about Maria a lot," Amy admitted. "But, sometimes, you know what I do? I force myself to think about other things."

"You do?" Buddy seemed surprised.

"Yeah. I just shut Maria out of my mind. Otherwise, I think I'd go crazy from sadness," Amy said. "The summer is ruined. It's been the worst summer of my life," she continued. "But we have to go on, right? I mean, what choice do we have?"

"I guess," Buddy said thoughtfully, staring straight ahead as the beach house hovered over them.

"I keep thinking of that song Jane Froman sings on TV every week. 'When You Walk Through a Storm, Keep Your Head Up High.' I know it's corny — but it helps me. It really does."

"I don't watch much TV," Buddy said quietly.

A gust of wind splashed raindrops in their faces.

"Didn't you see Elvis Presley on TV last night?" Amy asked.

"Who?"

"Elvis Presley. He's a new rock-and-roll singer. He was on that show last night with the two band-leaders. You know — Tommy and Jimmy Dorsey. And when Elvis Presley came out, all the girls in the audience started to scream and carry on. Didn't you see it?"

"No," Buddy said glumly. "Elvis Presley? That's kind of a stupid name, isn't it? Is he any good?"

"He's *gone!*" Amy gushed. "He's really *gone!*"

Buddy chuckled, his dark eyes filled with amusement.

At least I'm cheering him up a little, Amy thought. She shivered. The rain started to come down steadily, pattering noisily against the sand.

"Buddy, can we go inside? We're going to get drenched." She pointed up to the house.

He shrugged. "I kind of like it. It's refreshing, don't you think?"

"I'd really like to go inside," Amy insisted. "I had the sniffles this morning. I really don't want to catch cold."

"Well . . ." He seemed very reluctant.

"If you're worried about your parents or something . . ." Amy said, glancing up at the house, which appeared dark and empty.

"My mom isn't here," Buddy said quickly. "She had to . . . go somewhere." He changed his mind. "Okay. Let's go in. I don't want you to catch cold."

She followed him up to the deck, then around to the sliding-glass door, where they entered, closing the door behind them. It was warm inside, but it took Amy a little while to stop shivering.

"My hair is soaked. I must look like Little Orphan Annie," she said, pushing at her tight curls.

"No, you don't," Buddy replied, smiling. "You look like Marilyn Monroe."

Amy laughed. "Yeah, sure."

Her arms crossed over her chest, she began walking around the living room, checking out the furnishings. "I love everything in here," she said, gesturing to the vinyl and wrought-iron couch. "It's all so modern."

"Yeah, I guess," Buddy replied, his expression still one of amusement.

"And, gosh, look at the TV!" Amy gushed. "Such a big screen. Is it a sixteen-inch screen? Do you get good reception here? We can only get one channel at our cottage. And I have to keep moving the rabbit ears to get it to come in good."

"I don't really know," Buddy said, his smile fading. He walked to the sliding-glass door and stared out at the rain.

He's getting restless, Amy thought. Maybe I'm chattering too much. Maybe I'm boring him. He wishes he hadn't brought me here.

Well, I'm just trying to cheer him up.

What am I supposed to do?

"Okay if I look around the rest of the house?" she asked, heading toward the hall. "I just love exploring other people's houses."

He didn't reply, so she took herself on a short tour. To her surprise, the rest of the house was barely furnished. In fact, it didn't appear as if anyone had lived here at all.

"Hey, Buddy, this closet is enormous!" she called from the bedroom closet. "I can't even see the back of it! Buddy!"

A hand grabbed her shoulder roughly.

"Buddy?"

With startling force, he jerked her out of the closet.

"Hey —" she cried in surprise.

"Better stay out of there," he warned sternly, staring intensely into her eyes.

"Oh. Okay," Amy said, rubbing her shoulder as she backed out of the room. "Sorry. I really do think this house is neat."

"Yeah. Neat," he muttered, following right behind her as she made her way back to the living room.

She peered out through the glass door. The sky was as black as night, but the rain had slowed to a drizzle. Beneath the house, the crashing waves sent up a steady roar.

"It's like being on a boat," Amy said, turning and leaning her back against the door. "The house is just so neat."

"Yeah, you're neat, too," Buddy said, his expression turning sour.

Amy forced a giggle. "Now you're making fun of me, Buddy. Why are you making fun of me?"

"No, I mean it," he said, moving toward her, his hands on his hips, his eyes narrowed, locked on hers. "You're neat, Amy. You're gone. You're really *gone*."

A cold chill ran down Amy's back.

Something was wrong.

Something was wrong with Buddy. With the look on his face. With the way he was talking to her.

She didn't like this. He was scaring her now. He was deliberately *trying* to scare her.

"I'm going home now, Buddy," she said, staring back at him. "My parents will be worried. They expect me for dinner."

"But you're gone," Buddy said. "You're real gone, Amy."

"Buddy, please —" Still facing him, her hand grabbed for the door handle.

"Ronnie's gone," Buddy said, taking another step closer, still squinting at her, his face set, expressionless, cold as metal. "Ronnie's gone — and now you're gone."

"Ronnie's gone?" she stammered. "What do you mean?"

"Ronnie's gone," Buddy repeated. "He didn't make it home for his barbecue. He's gone. And now it's your turn."

As Buddy moved closer, Amy gasped and struggled to open the door. It wouldn't budge.

Without thinking, she pushed away from it, darted past Buddy, and into the kitchen.

"All gone," Buddy said, his eyes glassy now, like a store mannequin's, his expression just as wooden. "All gone, Amy."

I'm cornered here, Amy realized in her panic. I can't get away.

21
Amy Tricks Buddy

"Buddy — what's the matter? What are you going to do?" Amy cried, backing against the kitchen counter. Her eyes searched desperately for something she could use as a weapon — *anything* — but the kitchen was completely bare.

He stood in the entranceway to the kitchen, blocking any path of escape. His eyes were narrowed, studying her, enjoying her panic.

"You hurt my feelings," he said softly.

"Huh?" She groped for words, but her mind was suddenly blank, as if her fear had erased everything.

Think, think, think, she told herself.

Think of a way out of this. Think of a way to calm him down.

Calm him down?

He seemed perfectly calm, Amy realized to her horror.

She was the one about to shriek at the top of her

327

R.L. STINE

lungs. Buddy stood staring at her calmly from the doorway, speaking so quietly, she had to strain to hear.

"You shouldn't have made fun of me," he said. He raised a hand, examined a finger, and began picking at a hangnail, concentrating intently on the operation.

"But, Buddy, we were just joking," Amy blurted out in a voice she didn't recognize. "No one meant any harm."

"*You humiliated me!*" he screamed, losing his temper. Forgetting the hangnail, he balled both hands into fists. "Everyone made fun of me. Everyone. Why, Amy? Why'd you do it?"

Amy didn't reply. She gaped at him, openmouthed.

"Maria made fun of me, too," Buddy said. "And she lied to me. So now she's gone."

"Did you . . . did you kill Maria?" Amy finally managed to stammer, feeling cold all over, cold and trembly.

"Of course," Buddy said, frowning.

"And Stuart?"

He nodded. "And Ronnie. Why did you do it, Amy? Why did you have to make fun of me?"

"Oh, no," Amy moaned, and grabbed the countertop to keep from sinking to her knees.

She felt so weak, too weak to stand. Too weak to face Buddy.

"I'm waiting for an answer," he said sharply.

"Buddy —" She was panting so hard, it was

nearly impossible to choke out any words. "Buddy, people play jokes on people. It isn't serious. It doesn't mean anything."

He stared at her coldly and didn't reply.

"Why did you kill them, Buddy? Because of some stupid practical jokes? Because of a little fun? Why did you kill them?"

"Because it's so easy," Buddy said, a strange, lopsided smile forming on his face. "So easy."

"That's why?"

"And because it really doesn't matter," he added with a sneer.

"Huh? Doesn't matter?"

He's crazy, she realized.

He's a crazy murderer.

It doesn't matter what I say. I won't be able to reason with him.

He killed all my friends. Killed them because of some jokes.

And now he's going to kill me.

Again, her eyes darted around the kitchen in search of something to use against him. But there wasn't even a potholder. Not a spoon. The counter was bare, as were the shelves by the window.

The window.

Could she pull it open and yell for help?

Probably.

She could yell for help until she was blue in the face.

But no one could hear her over the rush of the ocean, the roar of the wind.

No one was within miles, anyway.

Calling for help was out.

I've got to keep him talking, she thought. Got to keep him talking till I think of a way to escape.

"What do you mean it doesn't matter?" she asked, locking her eyes on his, trying to determine if he really was going to come after her. "How can you kill people — people you know — and say it doesn't matter?"

"It doesn't matter," Buddy said slowly, as if talking to a three-year-old, "because I don't live here anyway."

"Huh? You mean you don't live in this beach house?"

He shook his head and snickered quietly. It seemed to strike him as funny. "No one lives in this beach house," he said mysteriously.

How am I going to get out? Amy asked herself, trying to think clearly, trying to clear the fog of panic so that she could make a plan.

Think, think, *think*.

Buddy took a step into the kitchen, his fists balled tightly at his sides.

"If you don't live here, where do you live?" Amy asked.

Keep stalling. Keep him talking.

It's your only chance.

Oh, Amy, you were so stupid, she scolded herself. You were right at the door. You were so close to escape.

Why did you run to the kitchen?

Why did you run to a room where there's no way out?

"Where do you really live?" she repeated, her voice high-pitched, revealing her terror.

He didn't reply.

Keep talking, Buddy, she pleaded silently. *Please* keep talking.

"No, really," she insisted. "Tell me. If you don't live here, where do you live?"

"No one lives here," Buddy said in a flat, frightening tone. "Everyone dies here."

He took another step toward her.

He was halfway into the room.

I have to try to trick him, Amy thought. I don't have much time.

She could only think of the oldest trick in the book.

Suddenly, she raised her eyes above Buddy's shoulder, gazed into the other room, and cried out in surprise.

"Ronnie! You're still alive! You're okay!"

Stunned, Buddy spun around to look.

And in that moment, Amy pushed herself away from the counter and made a run for the door.

22
Race for Freedom

Amy shoved Buddy hard as she ran past him.

He cried out, more in surprise than in pain.

She stumbled by him, arms outstretched toward the door.

He hesitated for only a second, then moved after her.

Reaching the glass door, she pulled the handle with both hands.

She was breathing so hard, her chest ached.

She could feel the blood pulsing in her temples.

The door resisted. She tugged again, harder, and it slid open.

And she was out on the deck, slippery from the rain.

I'm out of there! I'm *out!* she told herself happily.

But there was no time to celebrate. He was right behind her. She heard his sneakers clump across the wooden deck as she leapt down the stairs and onto the sand. And kept running.

Where was he?

Right behind? Gaining on her?

Her chest about to explode with pain, her legs so heavy, so heavy, she had to force them to take every step. She glanced back.

Saw him pick up the long-handled shovel from against the side of the house.

Saw him carry it in one hand as he came running after her, his eyes wild with fury, his mouth open in a silent scream.

"Help me! Somebody — please help me!"

Her words, shouted at the top of her lungs, seemed to fly right back to her, blown back by the wind.

She ran over the wet sand, her sandals kicking up clumps as they moved.

He was getting closer.

Keep going, keep going!

"Help! Please — somebody!"

But the beach was deserted. No one. Not even a sea gull to watch their desperate race. To hear her cries.

Over the sand, cold, wet sand crunching under her sandals. The ocean crashed to her right. The empty dunes rolled to her left.

No one. No one around.

The rain started again.

And he was gaining. She could hear his breathing, loud, rhythmic groans. She could hear his sneakers thudding over the sand.

Her chest was about to burst.

She knew it would burst. It hurt so much.

Everything hurt.

Keep going, keep going!

There's got to be someone. Someone walking on the beach.

Someone who can stop him.

Someone who can save her from him.

His groans grew louder, closer.

She was panting now, too. Panting and crying.

And the wind tossed the cold rain into her face.

She leaned into it, squinting against the rain.

He was so close behind now.

Closer. Closer.

She cried out, a wordless shriek, as she fell. Stumbled forward and landed hard on her elbows and knees.

She looked up to see him raise the shovel with both hands.

With a fierce groan, he swung the heavy metal blade at her head.

23
It Really Doesn't Matter

When Amy opened her eyes from the darkness, blacker and deeper than any darkness she had ever seen, the pain lingered.

The back of her head throbbed. The vibrating, ringing pain ran down the back of her neck, all the way down her back. So much pain, she closed her eyes again.

The feel of the water brought her back.

The cold shock of it.

Her eyes went wide when she realized she was waist deep in the ocean.

The green water leapt at her, pushed her, crept up on her, then pulled back only to leap again.

It was only when she tried to swim that she realized her hands were tied. She twisted around to discover they were tied with a heavy rope, tied to a wooden post of some sort.

She tried to cry out, but the water leapt again, and she swallowed a mouthful. Choking and coughing, she struggled to catch her breath, spitting away the briny taste.

The pain lingered, her head ringing like the inside of a bell. But she was wide awake now. Awake and alert.

And she knew where she was.

She knew she was under the beach house, her hands tied tightly behind her, tied to one of the stilts.

And she knew the tide was coming in. The waves were leaping higher. The water was up over her waist.

She saw it all so clearly now. But the pain wouldn't allow her to think. The ringing pain wouldn't allow her to try to make a plan.

She started to scream, an animal howl, high-pitched and frightened, that barely carried over the steady rush of the water.

Tossing her head back out of the thrashing waves, she howled like a frightened animal. Like an animal caught in a trap.

She stopped howling when she saw Buddy standing in the water, the water halfway up the legs of his jeans. Buddy, hands on his knees, by the side of the house, peering in at her.

Watching her fear.

Watching her pain.

Smiling.

She stopped screaming and stared back at him, struggling to loosen the ropes that held her in place.

"No one can hear you," Buddy said calmly, casually, as if commenting on the weather.

"Let me go!" Amy pleaded.

The pain at the back of her head made her wince and cry out. What was the warm trickle down the back of her neck? Was it blood?

"No one can save you now," Buddy said matter-of-factly. He took a step closer, the water creeping up to the knees of his jeans.

"Let me *go*! Please, Buddy!"

"You left me in the ocean," Buddy said, ignoring her shrill, terrified cry. "All of you. You left me in the ocean. You took my swim trunks and left me there."

"But, Buddy —"

"And then you walked away. You just walked away."

Shaking his head, he turned and started toward the sand.

"No — Buddy! Come back! Come back!" Amy begged.

He kept walking, his back to her now, his back to the rising, leaping waves.

"Buddy — stop! Where are you going?"

He stopped and turned back to her. "I'm walking away, Amy. I'm walking away, just like you did."

"No — Buddy! You can't! You can't leave me here! Buddy — please! You *can't*!"

He leaned under the house, one hand on the wooden stilt.

He's coming back, she thought.

He's going to save me now.

He isn't going to let me drown. He only wanted to frighten me.

"Don't worry, Amy," he said quietly, so quietly, she had to strain to hear him over the rushing water.

Don't worry, she thought. He's going to save me now.

He's going to untie me.

He isn't going to leave me here.

"Don't worry," he repeated. "The tide's coming in really fast. It'll be over your head in a few minutes. You won't suffer long."

He turned away again.

She could see only his legs. The wet denim jeans clinging to his legs. The white sneakers splashing to shore.

And then she couldn't see him at all.

And the water had risen to her shoulders.

"See you later, alligator," she heard him call from somewhere behind her. "You're a real gone chick. But now I've got to go home."

Buddy climbed the deck steps quickly and let himself into the house. He slid the glass door shut, closing out the sound of Amy's last terrified screams.

PART SIX

This Summer

24
Brad Gets Serious

Ashley stopped at the deck steps and looked up at the old beach house, a black shadow against the violet sky.

I don't want to go in there with Brad, she decided, feeling a shiver of fear descend her back.

Oil-dark waves washed under the house, lapping against the wooden stilts. The wind off the ocean was strong and heavy with the smell of fish.

"Come on. I'm dying to show you this," Brad insisted, tugging her hand, trying to pull her up the stairs.

The house shifted suddenly, creaking loudly, as if warning her to stay away.

"Brad, it's so late —" she started, trying to pull away.

"Come on, Ashley. I *have* to show this to you."

"My parents will be really pushed out of shape," she said. "I've got to get home."

His face fell into a disappointed pout.

"Tell me what's inside," she said quickly. *"Tell* me the secret. You can show it to me some other time."

His unhappy expression didn't change. He turned his eyes to the dark, tossing waves.

"No. I have to show you," he said in a low voice. He sat down on the top step, the old wood creaking under his weight. He patted the spot beside him, motioning for her to join him.

"Brad, it's getting cold," Ashley protested.

But she couldn't bear the unhappy pout on his face. Obediently, she sat down beside him on the step.

"I really want to share this secret with you," Brad said, staring at the ocean. "I would never share it with anyone else."

Ashley shifted uncomfortably on the hard step. From somewhere, the pungent smell of gasoline invaded her nostrils.

"Brad, you shouldn't get too serious," she warned.

He turned to her, his eyes revealing confusion.

"About me, I mean," Ashley said, tugging awkwardly at a strand of her blonde hair. "You shouldn't get too serious. I mean, we've only gone out a few times."

"Hey, I *am* serious," he replied. "I'm very serious, Ashley." He slid his arm around her waist. "I'm always serious," he said. "Haven't you noticed that about me?"

"Why do I smell gasoline?" Ashley asked in a

not very subtle attempt to change the subject.

Brad shrugged. "Maybe there were some pow-
erboats in the water around here. Some jet skis or
something."

"Brad, could we —?" Cold and uncomfortable,
troubled by Brad's insistence on taking her into the
beach house, Ashley really wanted to start for
home.

"I want to tell you something about me," Brad
said, his arm still protectively around her waist.
"Maybe it'll help you understand me a little."

"Well . . ." She realized he was ignoring her
discomfort.

His mind seemed to be somewhere else, lost in
his own thoughts. His eyes narrowed, focused on
the distance, as if he were seeing something there,
something that only he could see.

"The men in my family have always been ex-
plorers," he began, still staring straight ahead. "In
one way or another, that is. My great-grandfather
really *was* an explorer. He sailed to Africa when he
was in his late forties. He went up the Amazon,
photographing different tribes. Some of his photos
are in a museum in Washington, D.C."

"Wow," Ashley said appreciatively. "How do you
know all this?"

"My father told my brother and me about it,"
Brad said. He raked a hand back through his dark
hair, then continued. "My grandfather was an explorer, too. A different kind of explorer. He owned
a textile mill. He did his exploring right in the mill.

He explored new kinds of fabrics. Artificial fabrics."

"You mean like rayon and nylon?" Ashley asked. She had once done a home ec report on polyesters and other artificial materials.

"Yeah," Brad nodded. "That's how my granddad made his fortune. He became the rayon king of the world." He chuckled. "You see our big, fancy summer house, our tennis court, and swimming pool? The Jaguars and Mercedes in the drive? That's all because of my granddad. That's all because of rayon."

Why is he telling me all this? Ashley wondered, shifting her weight again on the uncomfortable step.

Something dark fluttered near. She saw a shadow dart low over the beach. A bat?

"Did you see that?" she asked, her voice a whisper.

"I guess you could call my father an explorer, too," Brad continued, so caught up in remembering his story that he didn't hear her.

Or didn't choose to hear her.

"A few years after my brother Johnny was born, my dad left us. Just didn't come home one day. I guess you could say he was exploring other lifestyles or something." He snickered. Bitter laughter. "We saw him from time to time. And he made sure we had more money than any twenty families would ever need. But he was too busy *exploring* to spend any time with us."

"That's terrible," Ashley said sympathetically.

"Yeah," Brad agreed, with even more bitterness.

"I haven't met Johnny," Ashley said, still wondering where this story was leading, why Brad was telling it to her.

Was it part of the secret he wanted to share?

"You won't meet Johnny," Brad said flatly, all expression fading from his face. He closed his eyes for a brief moment, then stared intently at Ashley.

"I think Johnny may have been the biggest explorer of all of us," he told her. "He was always desperate to explore everything he saw. *Everything.* I always had trouble keeping up with Johnny. I was the older brother. Two years older. But I couldn't keep up with him. I really couldn't.

"I was older, but I was the one who always tagged along, always followed Johnny."

He stopped for a moment. Ashley realized he was breathing heavily, excitedly.

She started to say something. But he continued his story.

"Johnny was always the most fun-loving kid. I was always the serious one. He was a real joker. He just loved to goof on people. But the main thing that was special about Johnny was his curiosity."

"He had a scientific mind?" Ashley asked.

"No. He just had this incredible curiosity. Like a true explorer. I mean, show Johnny a door, and he *had* to know what was behind it. Show him an *open* door, and he'd be through it in a flash.

"He was curious about everything," Brad continued, his voice breaking. He cleared his throat and continued. "Johnny was always taking things

apart just to see how they worked. Things like radios and TVs, and our piano. He drove my mother
bananas. He really did. But he just had to know
what was behind things.

"I tried to be like him," Brad said with growing
sadness. "I tried. But I just wasn't Johnny. I wor-
shipped the kid. I admit it. And then when he
died —"

He stopped abruptly.

Ashley didn't know what to say. Was he waiting
for her to react?

She had already guessed that Johnny was dead
from the way Brad was talking about him in the
past tense.

"How did he die?" she asked finally.

"It wasn't my fault," Brad replied, the light fading in his eyes. "It wasn't my fault, but I blamed
myself. For a long, long time. I still blame myself,
I guess." He sighed, then continued, speaking more
slowly, more carefully. "I was supposed to watch
him. But I just couldn't keep up with him. No one
could. They were building a new house, an enormous new house in the cul-de-sac down from our
house. Johnny couldn't resist new houses. He loved
to explore them, to climb around in them while they
were empty, while they were still going up.

"By the time I realized he had gone into the new
house, by the time I got there and went inside, he
was dead." Brad's eyes burned into Ashley's. He
stared at her as if trying to make sure she believed
him, trying to make sure she accepted his story.

"I didn't even hear him scream. He must have screamed. He fell from the second floor to the basement. The floor wasn't finished. He fell straight down and broke his neck on the concrete basement floor."

Brad was breathing hard now, his chest heaving. He turned his face away.

They sat in silence for a long while.

"I've tried to be like Johnny," Brad said finally, very softly, still avoiding Ashley's eyes. "I tried to be an explorer like Johnny. But I'm not Johnny. I know it. I can't be Johnny. I'm too serious. I don't have his mind, his energy, his *anything*. And ever since Johnny died, I just take everything too hard. Everything."

"You can't blame yourself," Ashley said, cringing from the hollowness of her words, but not knowing what else to say. "It was an accident, that's all. A terrible accident."

"Then at the start of the summer, *I* decided to go exploring," Brad said, not seeming to hear her. "I saw this old beach house here at the edge of the beach. Empty all these years. It must have been built nearly forty years ago. People told me that no one has ever lived in it."

"That's the same story I heard," Ashley said, turning to look up at the dark windows on the side of the house, staring back at her like bug eyes.

"So I decided to do some exploring," Brad said. "Just like Johnny would have done. Early one morning, I came here. There was no one on the beach.

Just a few early morning joggers. It was early June. Still cold in the morning. Anyway, I came up here. I went inside the house. And I did some exploring."

He stood up suddenly, grabbed her hands, and pulled her to her feet.

"Come on. I have to show you what I found."

His eyes glowed at her excitedly. An eager smile spread across his face.

"I found something incredible in there," he said.

Still Ashley resisted.

I really don't want to go in there, she thought, thinking of Kip and Lucy.

Thinking of how dark and frightening the old house looked.

I really don't want to go in.

But then she saw something stir back in the low dunes.

Someone was in the tall grass, crouched there.

She saw just a shadow, a quick movement. And she knew someone was there.

Ross, she knew.

Ross. Still spying on me. That childish idiot.

She could feel her anger grow inside her chest.

Okay, Ross. You want to spy on me? she thought. I'll give you something to spy on.

She took Brad's arm. "Okay," she whispered. "Let's go inside. Show me this amazing secret."

Brad smiled and led the way. "You won't believe it," he said excitedly.

He slid open the glass door, and Ashley followed him into the darkness.

25
Brad's Secret

Ashley stopped in front of the door. "It's too dark, Brad. I can't see a thing."

She felt his hand on her shoulder. "Wait here. Don't move. I'll be right back."

She heard his footsteps cross the creaking floor as he disappeared into the darkness. A few seconds later, she saw a wavering cone of yellow light darting across the ceiling and over the wall, like Tinkerbell in *Peter Pan*.

"I hid this flashlight under the kitchen sink," Brad said, smiling as he returned to view. "It's pretty bright, huh? It's a halogen light."

He motioned for her to join him in the living room. "Look around," he said, speaking loudly to be heard over the rush of water beneath the house. "It's really awesome."

"All this old fifties-style furniture is pretty amazing," Ashley said, obediently glancing around the big front room, her eyes following the bright light of Brad's flashlight. "Even an old TV. Look how small the screens were back then."

"Sixteen inches," Brad said, training the beam of light on the old TV.

"But I've been in here before, remember?" Ashley reminded him.

"Yeah, I know," Brad replied, smiling.

"So what's the secret?" she asked impatiently.

I don't like it in this house, she thought, moving her eyes along the shadowy furniture. I don't like the way the house sways, the way you can hear the ocean under the floor. It's like you're on an old boat, traveling *nowhere*.

"I'll show you the secret," Brad said, startling her by stepping up right beside her. "But first I want to tell you how much I like you."

"Thanks," Ashley said, flustered. Then she quickly added, "I like you, too."

And before she could back away, Brad had his arms around her and was pressing his mouth against hers.

The flashlight clattered to the floor and rolled away.

Ashley gave in to his kiss. Then she began to kiss him back.

But after a while, his intensity began to frighten her.

She tried to pull her face away, tried to take a step back. But he pulled her closer, held her more tightly with surprising strength, and continued to kiss her.

Harder, harder.

Until it was no longer a kiss.

Until it felt hostile, angry, like an assault.

Ashley raised both hands to his chest, and pushed.

Still he wouldn't back away.

She pushed harder and arched her neck, turning her face away from him. "Brad — please — "

Breathing hard, his breath hot against her cheek, it took him a while to recover. "I care about you, Ashley," he said finally.

She stepped back, relieved that he had let go of her.

"The surprise," she reminded him. "Was *that* the surprise?"

He bent to pick up the flashlight. When he stood up, she saw the hurt expression on his face. "Don't you trust me?"

She forced a laugh, trying to lighten things up. "Brad — how long are you going to keep me in suspense? Please, bring out the surprise."

His expression remained set, almost grim. "I can't bring it out. You'll have to come see it."

"Okay," she said, unable to hide her impatience. "Lead the way. It's really getting late, you know. Where is it?"

He was holding the light at his waist, shining it up at his face. In the yellow light, he looked eerie, frightening, like a Halloween vampire. His eyes seemed to glow with unnatural excitement.

"It's in the bedroom," he told her. "Come with me."

"Whoa!" Ashley held back. "The bedroom?"

After that uncomfortably intense kiss, Ashley was reluctant to follow Brad into the bedroom. "No. I don't think so, Brad."

"Ashley — come *on!*" he cried, whining, his voice rising several octaves. "You *have* to see this! I've never shown it to anyone else."

"Let's come back tomorrow," she suggested, feeling more than a little frightened. "You know. In daylight."

"Ashley." He said her name disapprovingly, shaking his head, his eyes still aglow in the cone of light from the flashlight. "I'm not going to try anything. Really."

She hesitated, studying his face.

"Don't hurt my feelings," he said softly. "I've told you more about me tonight than I've ever told anyone. Please. I trusted you. Now you have to trust me."

"Okay," she said, too weary to resist any longer. "Okay. I'm coming."

She took a deep breath and followed him into the hallway, the circle of light darting across the wood floor as they walked.

He turned quickly into the first bedroom, tilting the light to the ceiling so that it reflected over the entire room.

"I've been here before," Ashley said, examining the room in the dim light. Nothing had changed since the last time she had been there.

The day she had discovered Lucy's scarf.

"This way," Brad said, pointing the light to the closet.

"Huh?"

Moving quickly, he slid open the closet door. He stepped inside. The light dimmed as he entered. It seemed to lose some of its brightness, the yellow light turning to gray.

"Come on. Get in," he called.

"Get in the closet?" Ashley took a few steps toward him, then hesitated.

"Yeah. Get in," he called impatiently. "Hurry."

She stood just beyond the closet door. The enormous closet. So dark, even with the flickering, diving light of the flashlight. So deep. So endless.

"Brad — come *on*. Why do I have to get in the closet?" she demanded.

"Just *do it!*" he snapped.

She peered in. The gray light seemed to fade before it reached the closet walls.

"Do it! Get in!"

"No," she told him. "I don't want to."

"Come in here — now!" he commanded in a sharp, angry shout.

He grabbed her hand roughly and pulled her inside.

26
Who's in the Closet?

Ashley found herself encircled by the eerie gray light, as if she had stepped into a cloud.

Once she was in the closet, Brad let go of her hand. He turned his back to her and took a few steps, appearing to fade into a gray mist.

"Brad — stop!" Ashley called, frightened, her voice strangled, muffled.

It was cold inside the closet, and damp. The air felt heavy as she breathed, and she found herself gulping mouthfuls of it.

"Follow me," Brad instructed from the shadows, his voice still sharp. It was a command, not a request.

"Brad, I don't want to," Ashley insisted, hanging back. "I don't like this."

"Don't like what?"

Even though he was only a few feet in front of her, she had to squint to see him among the shifting gray shadows.

"I can't see," she protested. "I can't see where I'm going. I can't see anything. Not even the closet walls."

"I told you this was incredible," Brad insisted. "Get away from the door. You *have* to follow me."

"Just wait a second, okay?" Ashley pleaded. "Why can't you explain to me what we're doing in here? Why do you have to be so mysterious? You're *frightening* me. Really!"

Suddenly he loomed in front of her, bursting from the gray. His features were drawn in a tight frown, his dark eyes flashing angrily.

He grabbed her shoulder. Hard. And tightened his fingers around her until the shoulder throbbed with pain.

"Stop acting like a frightened baby," he said, leaning close to her, spitting the words in her face.

"Let go," she cried, the pain forcing her to whimper.

He loosened his grip only a little.

"Let go of me, Brad. I mean it. I'm leaving now."

"No, you're not," he insisted, his expression cold, his words low and deliberate. "You've already come too far."

"Too far? What on earth are you *talking* about?" she shrieked.

"Follow me."

As he squeezed her shoulder, Ashley began to see colors, flashing oranges and yellows, faint at first, then growing brighter.

Brad let go of her shoulder, grabbed her hand

quickly, tightening his grip on her — and pulled her hard.

As he pulled, the flickering orange and yellow light grew closer, brighter.

What is going *on*? Ashley wondered.

Brad pulled her deeper into the closet.

Then, to her horror, Ashley felt a hand, another hand, a cold hand, a stranger's hand, grab her around the waist from behind.

27
A Surprise House Guest

Ashley screamed.

She sucked in a deep breath and screamed again.

The flickering orange and yellow light came from a kerosene torch. The flames dipped close, licked at her face.

"Whoa!" Brad cried out, startled, and dropped her hand.

The arm around her waist tightened and pulled her back.

Away from Brad.

Back. Back.

Ashley was too frightened to resist.

The flames danced just above her. The gray shadows seemed to pull away.

Back. Back. Following the flickering light.

And then she was out of the closet. Back in the bedroom.

The torch dipped and whispered, then floated back up.

Her chest heaving, her breath caught in her throat, Ashley turned to see who had pulled her from Brad, from the gray mist of the closet.

She stared into the bright flames.

The person holding the torch was hidden in the darkness behind it.

"Help! Oh, help me!" Ashley cried, too terrified to even realize that she was speaking aloud.

"Hey — " Brad's head poked out of the closet, his eyes wide with fury. "What's going on?" He emerged in the closet doorway, his fists balled tightly at his side, poised for a fight.

Ashley staggered backwards, away from the torch. She backed into the wall, braced herself against it, her hands to her face, and didn't move.

Brad squinted at the torch, the flickering orange and yellow light reflecting in his eyes, dancing across his angry face.

"You?" he cried, suddenly recognizing the person holding the torch. "What are *you* doing here?" His voice suddenly revealed more amazement than anger.

Ashley's eyes began to adjust to the new light.

A white uniform came into view. Then the torch illuminated dark hair, streaked with gray.

A woman's face. Staring unblinking at Brad.

"Mary — " Brad called to the family servant. "Mary — answer me! What are you doing here?"

The housekeeper didn't reply.

She didn't move. She didn't blink.

Then slowly, she lowered the torch, pointing it toward him.

He started to take a step out of the closet.

"Get back," she said, her voice tight but controlled.

"Mary, I'm afraid you don't belong here," Brad said, staring at her warily. Again, he took a tentative step toward her.

She moved quickly, lowering the torch, thrusting it forward, threatening him with it.

Brad cried out in surprise and ducked back.

"Don't come out, Buddy," she ordered Brad in the same even, controlled tone.

The torchlight caught the hatred in her eyes, dark, weary eyes.

"Don't come out, Buddy. You're never coming out again."

28
Scars

Ashley sank to her knees, staring at the angry confrontation between Brad and the servant.

"Stay back, Buddy. I'm warning you. I'll torch you without a second's hesitation," Mary said, gesturing with the fiery torch.

"Buddy? Why do you keep calling Brad *Buddy*?" Ashley managed to cry.

Mary kept her eyes on Brad. "Buddy is his nickname. Brad has always been called Buddy. Haven't you, *Buddy*?" She pronounced the name as if it were some kind of horrible curse.

Struggling to regain his composure, Brad propped his hands against the frame of the closet door and peered out at Mary. "No one has called me Buddy in years," he said, his voice trembling despite his struggle to appear calm. "How did you know that, Mary? Who *are* you, anyway?"

The question angered her. She cried out in dis-

gust and swung the torch in front of her, leaving a
smoky trail of color in the air.

"Who am I?" She glared at him.

Ashley noticed that she was wearing the same
unusually styled uniform, with the heavy, long
sleeves and the white blouse with the collar up to
her chin.

"Who *am* I, Buddy?" She twisted her features
in disgust.

I've got to get out of here, Ashley thought, turning her eyes to the doorway.

I don't know what's going on here.

But I can feel the hatred. It's as hot as the flame
on Mary's torch.

She's crazy with anger.

Crazy.

She could even *kill* Brad or Buddy or whatever
his name is.

I've got to get out of here, get help.

But Ashley didn't move. Her fear held her in
place. Her curiosity held her there, crouched on her
knees, against the bedroom wall.

Mary took a step toward the closet. Then another. She held the torch in front of her, drew it
under her chin. Her face seemed to enlarge. It
seemed to float, to hover in the smoky air, shadowy
and orange.

"Don't you recognize me, Buddy?" Mary asked,
her dark eyes surrounded by shifting shadows, glaring at Brad like snowman eyes, cold and dead.

"No!" he cried, his face revealing his fear. "Get back, Mary! Stay away from me!"

She took another step toward the closet, holding the torch at her waist.

"You really don't know who I am?"

"No!" Brad repeated. "I mean it, Mary. Stay away. Don't come any closer."

Ignoring his warning, she took another step. She was only a few feet from him now.

I've got to get out of here, Ashley thought.

I've got to get help.

She pulled herself to her feet. But she didn't move away from the wall.

She couldn't.

She had to see the scene played out.

Why was Brad so afraid of Mary? Why did Mary hate Brad so much?

"I'm warning you, Mary — " Brad cried, holding up both hands as if to shield himself from her.

She stared at him, ghostlike, her entire body appearing to flicker and bend with the torch flame.

"Take a good look at me, Buddy. Do you recognize me now?"

"No. No, I don't!" Brad screamed. "Get out! Get out of here!"

"Maybe this will help you remember me," she said, her eyes burning darkly into his.

With startling quickness, she reached her free hand up to the collar of her blouse. "Maybe this will help your memory."

The ripping sound made Ashley jump as Mary

tore open her blouse. Buttons clicked and rolled across the wooden floor.

Tearing violently at the sleeves, Mary pulled off the blouse and tossed it to the floor, revealing her bra.

And her scars.

Red and purple scars.

Some raised up, like welts. Some etched deeply into her skin.

The scars spread over her chest, across both shoulders, down her arms.

Ashley cried out and shut her eyes.

"Do you recognize me now?" Mary demanded of Brad.

Brad stared back at her, stared at the scars, at her disfigured body.

"Yes, it's me!" she declared triumphantly. "It's Maria! You killed me in 1956!"

29
Secret of the Beach House

The room grew silent, so silent that Ashley could hear the hiss of the torch, the lick of the flames.

She heard the slap of the waves against the stilts below. The hushed, steady roar of the sea wind.

We're sailing away, she thought, feeling the beach house sway. We're sailing away from this world, away from the real world.

"Brad, I don't understand!" Ashley called across the swaying room. "What is she *saying*?"

But Brad didn't seem to hear her. His eyes locked in disbelief on Maria. On her strangely victorious smile. On the scars that covered her body.

"You can't be," he uttered, his voice barely a whisper. "You can't be Maria. Maria was sixteen. You're old. You're — "

"I'm in my fifties, Buddy," Maria said, steadying the torch in front of her. "You're right. I'm old. Older than my years. Thanks to you."

"But — but — "

"I've had to wait a long time to pay you back,"
Maria said, her voice trembling with anger. "A long,
long time. But . . . I've been patient. And, now,
here I am."

"No!" he screamed. "You *can't* be!"

"What's the matter?" she asked, taunting him
with mock sympathy. "You're not glad to see me,
Buddy?"

"You're *dead*!" Buddy declared.

Ashley couldn't stand it any longer. "What is
going on?" she screamed. She pushed herself away
from the wall and made her way toward Maria. "Will
somebody explain to me what you're talking about?"

Maria turned, a startled look on her face, as if
seeing Ashley for the first time.

"Don't tell her anything!" Brad screamed, more
a plea than an order.

"I'll tell her *everything*," Maria said, her triumphant smile returning.

"Tell me *what*?" Ashley demanded.

"Buddy learned the secret of this beach house,"
Maria said in a low, confidential voice.

"The secret?" Ashley glanced at Buddy, whose
face reflected his horror and disbelief, then turned
her eyes back to Maria.

"Buddy learned why no one has ever lived here,
why no one ever will," Maria continued. "And now
you will learn the house's secret, too."

She paused, as if gathering strength to reveal

the secret. Brad made a sudden move toward her, but she forced him back by thrusting the torch flame at his chest.

"I told you, Buddy. You're not coming out of there," she warned.

He scowled. "You're crazy! Don't listen to her, Ashley."

"Please — tell me about this house," Ashley pleaded.

"The house is a way station," Maria explained. "It was built on a time warp."

"Huh?" Ashley cried out. "A *what*?"

"A time warp," Maria repeated patiently. "The house is a way station between today . . . and 1956. Buddy, or Brad, as you call him, went exploring inside this house a few months ago, and he discovered the secret."

"You mean you can travel back to 1956 from this house?" Ashley asked, trying to believe Maria's words.

"No — it's not true! *It's not true!*" Brad cried.

But his desperation told Ashley that it *was* true.

Maria nodded solemnly. "Yes. Buddy discovered that he could go back to 1956. You step into the closet. You walk and walk through a heavy gray fog. It seems as if you're walking forever. But when you finally emerge from the fog, you are back in 1956."

"You can go back to 1956 and then return?" Ashley asked. "You can go and come back just by walking?"

Maria shook her head. "No. Going back in time is easy, just a long gray walk. But moving forward in time is hard. Somehow Buddy learned how to move forward, how to get back to his own time." Deep sadness crept into her voice. "It took me all of my life to figure out how to get here, how to follow Buddy to the future, to his time."

"Ashley, you don't believe any of this, do you?" Brad called from the closet doorway. "It's crazy — right? She's crazy."

"I believe it," Ashley replied, her eyes trained on Maria. "She's telling me the truth."

"Thank you," Maria said softly.

Ashley gasped as she had a sudden realization. "Oh, no," she uttered. "I know what happened to Kip and Lucy."

"Kip and Lucy? The two kids who disappeared?" Maria asked. "Were they in this beach house?"

"Yes," Ashley said, swallowing hard. "They must have discovered the closet, gotten curious about it. They must have stepped in, exploring, and walked back to 1956."

"And then they couldn't find their way back," Maria said, continuing Ashley's thought. "It's so hard to get back."

"It's tricky, okay," Brad said, snickering. "Kip and Lucy are probably in their fifties by now. Lord knows where they are!" He chuckled. He seemed to find the idea very amusing.

"How awful," Ashley muttered, shaking her

head. She turned back to Maria. "Why do you hate
Brad so much?"

"Ashley — I can't believe you're swallowing this
baloney!" Brad cried, sounding frantic. "Can't you
see she's wacko?"

"Buddy came back to 1956," Maria said, ignoring
his protests. "He made friends with me and with
three of my friends. Amy, Ronnie, and Stuart. We
had fun for a while. But then something went
wrong. Buddy got insulted. He went out of his mind
or something. Something must have snapped. He
went out of control. And then . . . he killed us. One
by one."

"No!" Ashley cried, raising her hands to her face
in horror.

"It's not true!" Brad insisted. "Not true!"

"He killed us. Coldly. Cruelly," Maria continued,
her dark eyes fading with sadness. "Then he returned to the future. He escaped, free and clear.
Until now."

Ashley opened her mouth to say something, but
was interrupted.

With a loud, angry cry, Brad leapt from the
closet. Moving with startling speed, he dived at
Maria, his arms reaching out to grab the torch.

30
Flames

Maria, determined to have her revenge, didn't flinch or shrink back.

As Buddy leapt, she thrust the torch forward.

The flame sizzled against his shoulder.

His eyes reacted first, growing wide with shock and pain. And then he cried out, falling heavily to the floor with a *thud*. Grabbing his shoulder, his shirt smoking, he crawled back to the safety of the closet.

"I told you, Buddy," Maria said, breathing heavily, the torch poised in both hands, "you're never coming out of there. Never."

Brad, on his knees in the closet doorway, groaned, rubbing his shoulder. "I just wanted to be like Johnny," he wailed. "That's all I wanted. I wanted to explore like Johnny. So I walked through the closet. That's just what Johnny would have done. I went back there. I met you and your friends.

I was exploring. I was really doing it, just like Johnny."

He swallowed hard, waiting for his breathing to return to normal. "But you wouldn't let me be like Johnny. You had to tease me, make fun of me, torture me. You wouldn't give me a chance. You had to humiliate me. So . . . so . . ."

He was gulping air, struggling not to burst into loud sobs. "If Johnny had been there . . ." he started. He lowered his head.

There was a long silence in the room. Then Maria turned to Ashley. "I tried to warn you away from him," she said. "I tried to scare you away."

"It was *you* who called me?" Ashley cried.

Maria nodded. "I saw you with him at his house, playing tennis. I saw the way he looked at you. The same way he looked at me more than thirty years ago. I wanted to warn you about him."

"You said you were dead," Ashley remembered, chilled by the thought.

"I *am* dead," Maria replied softly, lowering her eyes. "At least, my heart is dead. Somehow my body has survived." She gestured to her scars. "What is left of it."

"What happened to you?" Ashley asked, staring at the disfigured flesh, the red and purple scars. "Did Buddy do that?"

"He might as well have," Maria replied bitterly. "He cut my arm and left me for the sharks. The sharks came. They did a good job. It hurt so much. Pain beyond pain. And so much blood. Such horror.

I dream about it every night. Every night."

She stopped, took a deep breath, then continued. "As he swam away, I started to drown. I was choking, swallowing water. The sharks wouldn't quit. I finally gave up trying to fight them. I went under for the second or third time. Suddenly I felt hands pulling me up, strong hands. Two fishermen pulled me into their small boat. They saved my life. I wished they'd let me drown."

She stared into the yellow flame. The memories had become too painful to speak. Turning back to Ashley, she began again in a low voice just above a whisper.

"The fishermen got me to a doctor. They notified my aunt, my poor, horrified aunt. I was rushed to a hospital. I don't know how long I was there. Months and months. More than a year. When I got out, I was so ugly. So ugly, so deformed. I didn't want anyone to see me. Ever again.

"I never contacted my old friends. I never saw any of them again. I wanted them to think I was dead. Because, inside, I was dead.

"My aunt and I moved to a new town. I lived with her until she died when I was twenty-five. I kept to myself. I had no friends. I was too ugly to have friends."

She glared at Buddy, who avoided her eyes. He stared past her to the door.

"How — how did you ever find Buddy?" Ashley asked, horrified and fascinated by the story at the same time.

"I paid a visit to the beach house," Maria told her, her eyes on Buddy. "I don't know why. I don't remember. I guess I thought I could ease the pain by walking the beach again, by facing the scene of my nightmare. I crept into the beach house. I was just standing inside, right here in this room, when suddenly I saw Buddy come out of the closet. From thin air. He didn't see me. But I saw him. And then I knew. I knew his secret. I knew the secret of the beach house. I knew how he escaped after killing everyone. The police never figured it out. But I did."

"And you followed Buddy to the future?" Ashley asked, glancing at him as he leaned against the closet door frame, eyeing them both angrily, rubbing his burned shoulder.

"It took me a long time to figure out how," Maria said. "Getting here isn't as easy as going back to 1956. But I was determined to follow Buddy. I was determined. And, finally, I did it. This past spring. But when I came through, I had aged nearly thirty years."

She sighed. "But I didn't care. I really didn't care. I was dead anyway. My life is over. But I came back to make sure your life is over, too, Buddy."

He sneered at her. "You're pitiful," he muttered. "I'm coming out of here now. I'm going home."

She raised the torch, a trail of flame streaking the air. "No, Buddy. I told you, you're never coming out." She pointed the flame at his chest. "Go back to 1956, Buddy. The police are waiting for you back there. Go back and receive the welcome you deserve."

"No way," Buddy scowled, tensing his entire body, preparing to leap out again.

"We still had the electric chair back then," Maria told him, a strange smile playing over her lips. "It's waiting for you. Go back — now. Back is the only direction you can go. Because I'm not letting you out."

"That stupid torch doesn't scare me," Buddy said, his face filled with contempt. "I killed you once, Maria. Do I have to do it again?"

"Do you smell gasoline?" Maria asked, not the least bit impressed by his threat. "Do you, Buddy?"

He didn't reply.

Ashley had smelled it outside. The pungent gasoline aroma was even stronger inside the house.

"I've doused the entire house with it," Maria told him. She lowered the torch, the flame licking at the floor. "Now we're all going to die — for real."

A wave of terror gripped Ashley. She edged toward the window.

Maria meant what she said.

She was going to set the house aflame and kill them all.

She had come through time, sacrificed her youth, sacrificed her entire life for this moment of revenge.

No. No. Please — no, Ashley thought, backing

away, her heart thudding in her chest.

"Don't be stupid. Give me the torch," Buddy said, reaching out a hand for it.

"Back!" Maria ordered. "Back into the closet. Go back, Buddy. They're waiting for you."

"Give me the torch. You're not going to do it," Buddy insisted, his hand outstretched.

Maria hesitated for a brief moment.

Then she cried out, "You want it? Here!"

And she leapt forward and thrust the torch against Buddy's chest. It took only a few seconds for his shirt to flame.

Buddy's eyes bulged in surprise, in horror. He opened his mouth in an angry howl and reared back like a frightened horse.

Maria watched, her face a blank, her eyes cold and hard, as the yellow-orange flames climbed Buddy's chest, danced over his shoulders. She watched him swat wildly, frantically, slapping at his shirt — until his hands and arms were also aflame.

Then, her face still a blank, still dead, Maria lowered the torch to a puddle of gasoline by the doorway.

With a deafening roar, the beach house exploded in flames, killing them all.

31
Ashes

I'm dead. I'm dead.

The words repeated in Ashley's head.

To her amazement, she was flying. Flying through the air.

So this is death, she thought.

Death is flying.

I'm dead and I will fly forever.

But she landed hard on the deck. Outside. The cold, salty air swirling around her. The ocean's roar in her ears.

Outside. I'm outside. On the deck.

And she realized that the explosion had blown her out the window, out of the house, free of the flames that roared louder than the ocean, that reached for her through the gaping hole where the window had been.

Dazed, she was on her feet now. She leapt off the deck, the orange flames howling up to the sky behind her, the entire beach house engulfed, lost behind a wall of fire.

And now she was running across the sand. Running blindly.

Running into Ross's open arms.

Ross?

He *had* followed her.

Ross was there.

Ross, good old Ross.

"Oh, Ross," she managed to say.

She heard the beach house crumple and fall in on itself as the flames triumphed.

Then everything went black, and she died again.

"You're okay," Ross was saying, his worried face hovering over her. "You're okay, Ashley. You just passed out."

A white-jacketed medic loomed beside Ross, a professional smile on his face. "You'll be okay. You've had a real shock."

She raised her head, saw the black-uniformed firemen. They seemed to be everywhere. "The beach house — " she said, choking on the words.

Ross raised a finger to his lips. "Sssh. Don't get up too fast. Take it easy."

"But the beach house — "

"It's gone," he told her. "Nothing left but ashes."

"And Buddy and Maria?" she asked, up on her elbows now, struggling to force away the dizziness.

"Who?"

"Brad and Mary?" she corrected herself.

"Is that who the woman was?" Ross asked, bewildered. "Mary, the maid from Brad's house?"

Ashley nodded. She pulled herself to a sitting position. Someone, she realized, had put a blanket under her to protect her from the wet sand. She took a deep breath. The air was filled with the sweet-sour aroma of burnt wood, as if someone had had a fireplace fire.

"The firemen found a woman's body, completely charred," Ross said. "That's all. No one else."

"No one else?"

Ross shook his head.

Ashley stared at the black ruins of the beach house. A pile of ashes. Firemen were still hosing water on it.

Where was Brad? she wondered.

She had seen him howling in agony, the bright flames crawling over his body.

Did he fall back into the closet? Did he escape back to 1956?

It wouldn't be much of an escape, she knew. Even if he had survived the flames, the electric chair would be waiting for him.

And now that the beach house was gone, there was no way for Brad to come back.

Brad. Buddy. Buddy. Brad.

She sighed, shaking her head. The cold air was beginning to revive her.

"Here come your parents," Ross said, pointing across the beach. "I had the firemen call them from their truck."

Ashley leapt to her feet, eager to see them.

"Ashley! Ashley — what happened?" her mother called.

"Well, it's sort of a long story," Ashley said.

"How do you feel?" Ross asked, turning onto Ocean Drive.

"Great. I feel great," Ashley replied, settling back in the passenger seat. "Especially since summer is just about over."

Ross was taking them for a long ride in his parents' station wagon. Ashley had said earlier that she just wanted to drive and drive and keep going and never look back. "Straight into the future," she had said.

And Ross, glad to be back with her, was eager to oblige.

"It's been such a long, terrible summer," he said thoughtfully, following the curves of the narrow road through the dunes.

"I don't want to talk about it," Ashley replied. "I really don't. Let's just keep going, okay? I just want to sit back and enjoy this night."

"Sounds excellent to me," he said agreeably, reaching over to squeeze her hand.

"And I have one other request," Ashley said, turning to face him.

"What that?"

"Please get this oldies station off the radio!"

Ross obediently changed the station, and they rode on through the rolling, silvery dunes.

ABOUT THE AUTHOR

R.L. STINE is the author of the *Fear Street, Nightmare Room, Give Yourself Goosebumps,* and the phenomenally successful *Goosebumps* series. His thrilling teen titles have sold more than 250 million copies internationally—enough to earn him a spot in the *Guinness Book of World Records*! Mr. Stine lives in New York City with his wife, Jane, and his son, Matt.